DEDICATION

This book is dedicated to those people who know there is a zombie apocalypse coming, and who are doing their best to prepare for it. The rest of you are just weird.

The Devil's Buffet

The Devil's Buffet

Nigel Martin

ISBN: 10 1496194632
ISBN-13: 978-1496194633

CONTENTS

ACKNOWLEDGMENTS

To my friends.

1 IASOBOTS

It was all over the news. A virtually unknown scientist had developed a breakthrough in the battle against the common cold. They said it might be refined into a cure against all viruses, and possibly many more diseases in time. The face of Dr John Hodson appeared on newspapers and TV screens everywhere one looked. Already people were talking about a Nobel Prize for medicine for him. Excited talk show hosts vied to get Hodson to come on their shows to talk about the 'Iasobot', a revolutionary nanobot named after Iaso the Greek Goddess of cures and healing. Preliminary details about how the vaccination worked gave a glimpse into the cutting edge world of nanorobotics, a field few other people knew much about. Basically Hodson had created living nanorobots on a microscopic scale which would be inserted into the body and which would hunt down the cold virus and kill it before it could infect the host cells. The nanorobots were about the size of a human cell, and could simply be injected into the body or suspended in a solution that would then be sprayed up the nose, and left to do their work. There were a lot of scare stories out there as well, some of them planted in the media by the multi-billion dollar cold and flu industry, who were beginning to panic as they considered what their lost revenue would be. There were endless debates on TV and radio about the merits of this new technology, and the age-old debate of progress versus going too far raged with all sorts of intellectuals and interested parties lining up on both sides. There was even a conspiracy theory going around on the internet that the Iasobots were part of an alien invasion plot.

There was so much speculation, misinformation, and downright untruths going around that the normally publicity-shy Hodson felt obliged to appear on a popular news program to answer questions about his work. He was a small, slim man in his sixties with grey hair going bald on top.

Presenter: Tell me Doctor, what makes you think you may have finally defeated one of mankind's oldest enemies, the common cold?

Hodson: The way the cold virus works is that, once inside the body it has to enter individual cells in order to do any damage. The medical technology I use attacks the virus before it has a chance to enter any host cells, thereby preventing it from reproducing or damaging the body's cell tissue. Up to now drugs companies sold products that merely attempted to treat the symptoms of the cold, with limited results. This is the first time we are doing something to tackle the virus before it does any damage, and pre-emptively destroy it down at the scale it operates at.

Presenter: How do these 'nanobobots' work? What are they?

Hodson: They are a biological microorganism created in a laboratory. They can be programmed genetically to do certain tasks, such as killing certain viruses, and the rest of the time they simply remain inactive in the body. They will be watchful sentinels that you won't even know are there.

Presenter: You say they are biological, that means they're alive, what do they live on?

Hodson: We're talking about a microscopic living robot here yes. They will get what little nourishment they require from the body itself, through osmosis. Like every other living thing they have a lifespan, and once that's up they die, but they can be programmed to reproduce just enough of themselves to maintain the desired population level we want in the body. Before you ask, the way they reproduce is by cell division, and this can be controlled.

Presenter: Are there any dangers from these robots, some people are saying they are in essence a microscopic Frankenstein? What if something goes wrong? How do you get them out of somebody if they start to turn on the patient?

Hodson: You will always get crazies and luddites who want us to go back to the stone-age and live in grass huts and do basket weaving. This technology is safe, certainly much safer than the risks. If you think how many people die each year from infectious viruses, this technology will save millions of lives and improve the quality of life for millions of others. We have conducted extensive trials and replicated every possible scenario that seems likely to happen, and the Iasobots performed flawlessly each time.

Presenter: Does that mean you used human guinea pigs for your trials?

Hodson: Yes we used humans for some of the last trials we conducted. You can only go so far with experiments in the laboratory and then you have to try things out for real. Once we were satisfied with the safety of our product we moved onto those human trials. After a publicity campaign we had many people come forward on a voluntary basis who wanted to try the new vaccine. They were all financially remunerated for their services to science.

Presenter: Doctor, you have not mentioned your estranged former partner, Doctor Alan Howal. Reports say he is deeply unhappy with this technology going mainstream just yet. In fact he wrote an article called 'Death from inside' for a medical journal saying it was inherently unsafe, as the trials were not extensive enough. He said some of the tissues used in experiments began to act strangely and had to be destroyed. Are these legitimate concerns?

Hodson: Myself and Doctor Howal worked together during the preliminary stages of this work, but we disagreed on the direction that the work should take. Yes there were problems at the early stages, but that happens with most experimental research work. Nothing works one hundred percent perfect right off the bat. Unfortunately Doctor Howal left my research team prematurely when he still had so much to offer. I acknowledge the expertise he brought to our work, but he left just when we were on the cusp of a breakthrough, and he did not get to see the finished product which we now have. The product he last saw us work on is not the same product that will soon be available to the public.

Presenter: When can we expect to see the vaccination going mainstream Doctor Hodson? I hear there has been quite a scramble among the drugs companies to get their hands on your creations.

Hodson: Firstly, let me say that the term 'vaccination' is one we use loosely here. The way a true vaccination works is by invoking an immune response in the host. That's not quite how the Iasobots work, but because most people have started calling them a vaccination, it's as good a term as any to use as it seems to make sense to people. Now, to answer your question; I am at an advanced stage in talks with a major drugs company right now, to thrash out a deal in relation to the patent of this drug. Once the legalities are concluded we should be able to have it available to the public in a few months' time. As you pointed out, we have received intense interest from all the major drugs companies, and that shows the level of confidence that they have in this technology. If anyone has any concerns that should go a long way towards reassuring them. Drugs companies don't gamble on risky technology, there's too much at stake.

Presenter: If the nanobots can kill the cold virus what does that mean for other viruses, and indeed bacterial and other diseases?

Hodson: Once we have rolled out the cold vaccinations it is my plan to tackle other types of disease. In time I suspect we will be able to adapt the nanobots to kill any harmful viruses or bacteria. It's simply a question of adapting and refining their programming. We are on the verge of amazing things in medical science. This will end a lot of human suffering.

Presenter: Well good luck and we on this programme will be monitoring the success of the Iasobots Doctor Hodson.

****

Meanwhile in a laboratory in the suburbs surrounded by a multitude of test tubes, cultures and a host of mysterious bottles and containers stood a small gray-haired, balding man in his sixties. Doctor Alan Howal stared at the TV in disbelief. He had just watched the interview with Doctor Hodson. "You fool, you fool" he cried "the nanobots are not ready yet but you have to go looking for the glory. I hope and pray you haven't just doomed us all John!" He wiped his hands on his rather worn lab coat and scurried back to look at his slides again.

****

A few days later Howal appeared on the same news programme as his former partner had. Since Hodson's appearance he had been inundated with requests for interviews, and he felt he needed an opportunity to answer all the questions that were being asked of him. He was also a grey-haired man in his sixties and walked with a slight limp from his arthritis. He wore a business suit that looked like he'd had it a lifetime, and had the air of a man with important things on his mind.

Presenter: Doctor Howal the medical world and indeed a lot of other people have been agog with the story of Doctor Hodson's nanobot breakthrough. This thing has the potential to change our way of life, if it does what it says on the can, that is! However, along with all the excitement surrounding these things, there have also been a few dissenting voices, yours being among them and I suppose that because of your reputation and the fact that you actually worked on the project, people want to know why you're so worried?

Howal: I'm worried for a couple of reasons. Firstly the experiments we worked on were inconclusive. Some of the tissue samples reacted strangely in the laboratory under certain circumstances. We needed to do more work to determine how the nanobots would function long term. However Doctor Hodson was in a hurry to get what he saw as a product to market that he was rushing things through and hoping for the best. That's why I felt I could no longer be a part of his team and I left the project.

Presenter: You say "reacted strangely." What does that mean?

Howal: Under certain circumstances, for example, when exposed to electromagnetic energy, we were not able to predict the behaviour of the nanobots, and they would attack the tissue rather than defend it. That for me was a major worry but Doctor Hodson said that such circumstances were artificial and highly unlikely to occur in nature. A medicine should not attack healthy body tissue under any circumstances, and rushing the vaccine out without further trials is quite frankly reckless.

Presenter: But the Iasobots passed all medical trials with flying colours? After you left they carried out human trials. After being vaccinated dozens of people were exposed to the cold virus, and they were impervious to it. This would suggest to me that the vaccine is a success. This remedy could do amazing things for sick people everywhere.

Howal: Yes, but the trials were conducted in perfect laboratory conditions. Things tend to behave differently in the outside world. I'm glad those people were cured but I think we need to wait and observe their progress before we rush this thing out en masse. This leads me to another concern; the Iasobots might be self-replicating, they may be able to reproduce in the body under certain conditions, whereby an over-ride of their programming occurs. If such a problem happens with their programming they could multiply to higher levels than we want, and we don't know what might happen then. If you can't predict what consequences such an occurrence might have I really think that should be a reason to pause, and check things out more thoroughly. In my experience though, when you lose control of a process the result is rarely a good one.

Presenter: How are they able to reproduce contrary to their programming? My understanding was that they did blood tests on the guinea pigs, or whatever you want to call them, and after some months they had the same number of the nanobots inside them?

Howal: Again, when exposed to certain types of radiation, the Iasobots tended to behave erratically. When we did follow up checks on some of the tissue samples there seemed to be more than we began with, but there was a suspicion that the samples had been contaminated so we weren't sure. I left before determining precisely what happened.

Presenter: What are the medical implications if what you're saying is true?

Howal: It's hard to predict what the end result might be, but if someone is treated with the Iasobots and they mutate under certain circumstances it could make the person sicker than they were to begin with. Remember these things are a type of life-form too and without proper trials over an adequate timeframe we don't know for sure how they might behave. They could start to act like a virus or even a parasite themselves. I believe we should wait until we have a way of shutting them down in a worst case scenario before ploughing ahead with the roll-out of the vaccine. At the very least we should be conducting trials on small groups of people over a longer period. This technology is so revolutionary that it requires more extensive testing over a longer period than is being proposed.

Presenter: Forgive me for asking but there rumours that you are acting out of jealousy for a former partner who has made medical history, that you are angry that you left the research team just before they struck gold. Is there any truth to this? Is this just scaremongering to settle a score?

Howal: No. I left because I could not ethically agree with the progress of the trials. My only regret is that maybe I could have had more influence if I had stayed. However there is a lot more of this story to be played out yet and I continue to work with nanobots because there is knowledge as yet unknown that we will need in the very near future.

Presenter: What is the nature of your present work?

Howal: At the moment I'm working on what you might call an 'off-switch'. If the nanobots turn from friend into foe I want to have a means to neutralise them without causing harm to the person who has them in their system.

Presenter: What sort of progress are you making with that project?

Howal: Progress is slow but steady. I'm learning more and more about these things all the time, but as you can imagine, it's a lot harder to get nanobots out of someone than it is to put them in. It's not a simple reversal of a process you're dealing with, it's an entirely new process altogether. Still, I'm getting there.

Presenter: Let's hope it all works out in the end. Good luck with your work. Thank you Doctor Howal.

****

In due course the Iasobots were patented and licenced and went mainstream as a convenient vaccination for the common cold. Millions of people worldwide signed up and got the jab or had the solution sprayed up their nose. It was relatively cheap for a lifetime of relief from the hassle and inconvenience of colds. It was so popular in some places that the drug company, Faldor Jones, had to take on more staff and increase production. Needless to say, the company's shares went through the roof. The news also came out that Doctor Hodson was working on adapting the

Iasobots so they could also target the Influenza Virus as well, and this report was greeted with acclaim.

Not everyone was enthused with the idea of inserting nanobots into their bodies, and they abstained from participating in any vaccination program. Their reasons were varied. Some thought it was too soon to try it and wanted to wait until they saw the long-term results. Some figured that if so many others were getting vaccinated then the chances of catching a cold were greatly diminished anyway and it saved them the cost. Still others had heard the rumours that had originated with Doctor Howal about strange things happening during the trials and they figured that it was better to give the new technology a wide berth. After all it was a bit of a risk to take for a minor ailment like the cold anyway……………….

2 THE CANOE TRIP

Brad, Doug, Tom and Scott were work mates and life-long friends. Their ages ranged from their mid-thirties to mid-forties. They were going through the last minute preparations for a canoeing and camping trip which they had been looking forward to all year. A whole week away from a civilisation that had gone stale and weary of itself and its empty pleasures and idiot playthings. Their normal lives were office jobs and the city, going to work every day like ants in an ant army, but this was a chance to get away from all that into the mountains and the wilderness. Far away from the mundane pressures of ordinary life where each day blended into the next like a slow march to decay and death, every day a rehearsal for the last day. Far away from the rush and press of a humanity driven by goals that were not worth the effort and reasons that it had forgotten. A week of respite from the spirit-crushing world of policy and bureaucracy, paper processing and form-filling, religiously recording pointless information just for the sake of recording it. A life with few joys where many sought to numb the mind with alcohol or chemicals just to get from one day to the next, wondering what the point of it all was.

The four men were loading everything they would need for the trip into a truck and an SUV; two canoes, their tents, food, spare clothing, and all the miscellaneous items associated with a week in the wilderness.

Scott Lennon was the oldest and the informal leader of the group. He was of average height with a stocky build that spoke to his love of physical training. He had been an army man for years before his present role as a civil servant, and he never lost his love of exercise. He had a short beard and short brown hair, slightly greying around the edges. He had a calm, even temperament and liked to think things through before jumping into anything. He was a widower with two grown up kids, having tragically lost his wife to a drunk driver who had gotten off with a slap on the wrist from a weak judge, who believed his lame story that he was rushing to a pharmacy to get medicine for a sick child on the night in question. Scott never mentioned the sorrow and bitterness he carried within him, and never mentioned his anger with God, who had allowed a wonderful person to be taken from him and the kids, in the prime of her life. Indeed he cursed the same god who had given her to him in the first place. There was a pain he carried in his heart for which there was no earthly cure that he knew of. He lived alone, and planned to buy a small farm when he retired. He was a loyal friend though, and could be replied on in times of trouble with a mixture of knowledge, clear thinking and pragmatism.

Tom O'Hara was a slim, fair-haired happy-go-lucky kind of guy in his mid-thirties. He was famous for his wit and humour. He was athletic and a keen outdoors man. He had brought along his dogs 'Scout' and 'Keeper', a mixed breed brother and sister he had gotten from a shelter. They were looking forward to the trip as well, running everywhere wagging their tails and getting under everybody's feet. They knew they were going to the mountains where there would be lots of trails and interesting smells, and they were displaying the kind of excitement and anticipation that only dogs and small children can show. Tom was married to Caroline and had four young children. Before his present role Tom had been an explosive expert for a mining company for a few years. One day the company discovered that dynamite had been going missing for quite a while and suspicion fell on Tom. Someone had left evidence at the scene in order to frame him, and avert attention from themselves. Although he was able to prove his innocence, and they couldn't fire him, it became untenable to continue to work under a cloud of suspicion, and he left. Sometime later he got a tip-off from a friend as to the names of the persons who had actually done the stealing, other ex-employees of that company. They were a couple of anarchists who were planning a terrorist attack on a government building. When Tom informed the police they refused to take his story seriously, just saying he had a grudge against the company, so they did nothing. Taking matters into his own hands Tom had raided the anarchist's hideout one night, and taken possession of the dynamite himself. After his treatment by the company and the police, he never told anyone, but simply hid it in a safe place and forgot about it.

Brad McGrillan was a tall heavyset man with black hair. He was married with three young children between the ages of eight and twelve. His wife Christine was a schoolteacher, and was best friends with Tom's wife Caroline. Brad had been a mechanic in the navy before he retired from service and started working at a desk job. He still restored vintage cars, but that was a hobby for when his mind needed to rest. He also was a keen archer, and made his own bows. He found the activity both interesting and relaxing as a pastime, and he sometimes made bows for his friends as gifts. They said Brad McGrillan was a hard man to get to know and that was true. He was fiercely loyal to his family and few friends, but he tended to shut others out by and large. He had helped a lot of people in the past, but had been betrayed once too often and now he had a rather cynical view of the world. When dealing with strangers his generous, helpful nature was reined in, and all they saw was a stand-offish man of few words.

Doug Gilmore was wiry and tough looking. He had short red hair and a ready smile. He had been a paramedic for years before he got tired of shiftwork and started doing a nine to five in an office. Doug was recently divorced and lived alone with his memories and a collection of motorbikes, company he was happy enough with. One day he planned to marry again, if he met the right person, and he was optimistic that he would. He held firmly to the belief that there is someone for everyone, if only they would search hard enough. Doug had fallen foul of the law and done some time once. Some neighbours had taken advantage of his grandmother and defrauded her out of her life savings, while he had been overseas. When Doug had come home and tried to deal with things peacefully, they made false allegations against him and accused him of assault. It was all lies but he had no witnesses and was convicted. He got a suspended sentence, upheld on appeal. Figuring that he had a lot less to lose now, Doug went along one night with a can of gasoline and torched their house. The fraudsters were lucky to get away with their lives, but unfortunately for Doug a police patrol happened to be passing just as he was making his getaway. He got three years for his trouble, but was quietly released after nine months due to prison overcrowding. The experience left him bitter and a lot more dangerous. There was a war going on in his head which he secretly fought every day. He had been punished by a failed judicial system that had refused to help him in the first place. The stress of it all had killed his grandmother, but the grief he now carried served to keep the desire for vengeance alive in his heart.

****

"Did anyone remember to bring spare propane canisters?" Scott asked, as he double-checked the straps that held a canoe onto the roof of his SUV. "We can do most of our cooking over the fire in the evenings, but they're handy to have for quick stops along the river. I like a cup of tea when I stop to break".

"Yes I did" Tom answered, stuffing an extra sleeping bag into his backpack, "You can never have enough propane! I got a pretty good deal in that new sports place in town. They have a lot of good stuff and they're not too expensive either. We have enough propane for a few weeks, if we got stranded up there or just decided not to go back to work!"

"Well done" said Scott, "There's a good reason we invite you on these trips!"

"Thanks" Tom grinned. "By the way I saw you packing your pump action there. Are you intending to shoot something?"

"No not really" Scott answered, "But my cousin was up here two weeks ago and there were bear tracks all over the place. I'm bringing it just in case of an emergency. I don't intend being dinner for a hungry bear. Those things can smell food miles away, but the old pump action would soon scare them off. Added to that there are cougars and wolves up were we're going as well".

Doug threw another bag into the back of the pick-up truck. "I brought my rifle as well, an old army surplus 7.62 mil'. I haven't had it out in ages, and I figured that I might do some target shooting once we got away from civilisation. It's always good to keep your shooting skills up to date!"

The others laughed. Brad had brought his bow and some arrows, intending to do some target practice himself. It was a new one he had recently made and he couldn't wait to try it out properly.

"So I'm the only one who forgot to bring some kind of weapon" said Tom, "I thought we were going canoeing and hiking, not killing things!"

"Don't worry, you'll be fine" Scott laughed; "Here, this an axe I brought for you!"

He tossed an axe he had gotten especially for the trip, to Tom who caught it deftly, and swung it about, pretending to strike down imaginary enemies, and they all laughed.

"Hey did anyone see the news about some scientist guy who has invented a cure for the cold?" Brad asked.

"Yes, I saw it on the news, some kind of microscopic robot things you inhale up your nose, sounds crazy" said Tom.

"They're something called 'Nanobots', living microscopic mechanisms that can be inserted into the body which will theoretically perform certain tasks or functions. I'm not fully sure of the science behind them, but that's it in a nutshell," Doug said, looking thoughtful. "I didn't bother with it, I like to wait to see how these things pan out, has anyone else gotten the vaccination?"

Everyone answered in the negative. No-one had had time with all the preparations for the camping trip.

"I'm going to give it a miss, as I think it's too early to plough ahead with a relatively untested treatment" Tom said warily, "And I would advise the same for you guys."

"What could go wrong with something like that?" asked Scott. "Could they all go crazy and eat your brain?"

Everyone laughed.

"That's exactly the point; it's too early to say exactly what could go wrong. I just get the feeling they rushed this thing onto the market a little prematurely. There's a lot of money at stake, and there were several companies all racing to be the one to produce something like this." Doug was again thoughtful. "In fact I've advised all my family and my other friends to hold off for a while, to see how it goes. I've heard rumours that there were problems in developing these things that they didn't satisfactorily resolve, but who knows."

"In that case, I'm going to tell the wife to wait a while" said Brad, "She was talking about getting the whole family vaccinated before the kids go back to school." He took out his cell phone and made a quick call home. Scott and Tom made a couple of similar calls to loved ones. Doug was a man whose expertise and judgement they trusted implicitly.

The four friends then loaded the last of their belongings into the truck and the SUV, and they headed for the mountains. With just one quick fuel stop on the way they would reach their destination in about three hours and their vacation had officially started.

3 ECLIPSE ENTERPRISES

Billy Magee studied the blueprints laid on the table before him. He was excited by what he saw. Billy was CEO of Eclipse Enterprises Ltd, a technical company that designed and built electronic systems, mainly for the military and other specific clients. Lately they had diversified into biological weapons, and were in the embryonic stages of creating a marriage between technology and biology. The company had recently assembled a team of scientists for a certain project which they had codenamed 'Ghost Hand'. Eclipse Enterprises were studying the potential military applications for nanobots, and also counter-measures should any of their client's enemies get hold of them. Ghost Hand was a project concerned with neutralizing dangerous nanobots that an enemy might introduce into the general population en masse through a delivery system such as the water supply. Billy looked back up at the assembled boffins. It always pleased him that he had been able to assemble such a great team of experts around him. They all excelled in their chosen fields and were loyal to the company and its ethos. He planned to extend this team even further in the near future. His current scientists were brilliant at what they did but he knew there was genius to be had as well. That was something which you could not put a price on. All it needed was the right opportunity to get this genius working for him.

Magee grew up in a small town where he never really fitted in. He was the only child of a single mother, who told him his dad had died in the war. He stopped believing this around the age of fifteen but he never confronted her with this news. He knew she had her own burdens to bear and he did not want to hurt her further. He learned to depend on his own resources from an early age and when his mother died of a stroke when he was seventeen, he found himself alone in the world. He left home and joined the army, where he found a replacement family of sorts. He excelled at being a soldier and served a number of tours overseas with distinction. Lean and wiry he was naturally athletic, fearless, and a born leader. He knew how to make people want to follow him, rather than forcing them. He was charismatic when he wanted to be, but utterly ruthless too when it was required. He liked to think of himself as a visionary and a pioneer, and he resented the political interference which he felt constrained the ability of the armed forces to operate effectively. He was fond of saying that the only people who could defeat them were their own politicians sitting around on the hill with their endless talking and dithering. He left the army after a few years and considered setting up his own contracting company, but then he realised that the real money was in supplying equipment to the army, especially hi-tech innovative stuff that no-one else had. He knew from experience that the Generals loved having the latest this or that and it made them feel superior to their enemies, and that they were willing to pay a lot of money for these little toys. That's when he set up Eclipse Enterprises, ostensibly a company that supplied leading-edge equipment to technical and medical organisations, but that was a sideline to its main business of researching, designing and developing hi-tech solutions for the hi-tech wars that the army expected to have to fight over the coming years. Magee recruited the best employees he could find, and he was prepared to reward them for their talents. Under his guiding hand Eclipse Enterprises had gone from strength to strength and was even listed on the stock exchange, even though most people thought it specialised in medical equipment.

Eclipse Enterprises was ploughing huge resources into its own nanobot program going on the assumption that there might be only one winner in such a race, and no-one knew how much progress anyone else was making. Having seen the obvious destructive capabilities of such a technology they were trying to develop nanobots that could be used as weapons against enemy personnel. Therefore it was a smart move to assume that, if they were engaged in this activity, then their client's enemies would also be racing to develop the weapons potential of this new science. Sometime in the near future, the country's enemies would have access to nanorobotic weapons. Needless to say, there were huge profits to be made in designing and producing a defense against these weapons. Magee had watched with intense interest the fanfare over the development of the Iasobots and he knew that if a small, underfunded team could produce such stunning results then other, more resourced, organisations would not be far behind. For every sword there must be a shield. That's when Eclipse Enterprises decided to run a program for developing defenses against nanobots alongside its other operations. They were looking for any weaknesses or vulnerabilities that the nanobots might be susceptible to. So far in their research radiation seemed like the best way to kill rogue nanobots.

"Let me just clarify this, to see if I've got it right; What you're saying is that you can build a machine that would be able to transmit an electromagnetic wave or pulse that would kill the alien nanobots in the host person?"

"Yes" answered Professor Larry Irvine, scratching his nose.

"Using small amounts of radioactive material, the machine would use an electromagnetic wave to 'spray' the nuclear material at an infected person or area, killing the nanobots. It's a similar concept to the way we currently use radiation on cancerous tumors."

"Would that not also kill the person as well?" Magee asked.

"No, we have found that pulses of a certain wavelength and frequency will cause nanobots to breakdown and fail. They do this by a process known as ionisation, whereby the molecular bonds break triggering biochemical changes which they cannot survive. We would calibrate the device to only emit waves with these parameters so there is just enough to kill the nanobots, but not enough to kill the host person. Think of it like an x-ray machine, if used properly the risk can be minimised."

"I'm puzzled. How would it selectively kill the nanobots, but not the person's own cells?"

"We have found that nanobots don't have the same natural defenses against small doses of electromagnetism that the cells in your body have. We now know through extensive testing how to produce just the amount we need to disable the nanobots, but allow the host to survive. There may be minor health risks, but on the balance of things the risk is small enough to justify the cure. Think of it in the same way as getting a x-ray at the hospital," Irvine assured him.

"How big would this thing be? Most x-ray machines are too big to carry around; we need this device to be portable."

The Professor mused for a bit: "We figure that with enough high-grade radioactive material, we could make this thing a hand-held device, about the size of a large flashlight."

"That would be perfect!" Magee exclaimed, "The military would pay anything for an invention like that. In a few years' time nanobots are going to be everywhere, most doing good things, but some doing bad things. If terrorists ever got hold of some rogue nanobots they could create mayhem anywhere in the world they choose. Since we're the only company that will be making these things, we can clean up. Being the only game in town allows you to name your price and the customers will have to cough up……….no pun intended!"

His joke raised a chuckle around the room.

Magee looked down at the blueprints, all serious again; "How soon do you think you could knock a working prototype together? Bear in mind we need a device that will act quickly, and have a good range as well. There's no point in it working after you've been overrun by carriers of dangerous nanobots."

Irvine thought again briefly. "It would only take a matter of weeks to produce our prototype. We spent months on the design and we think we have ironed out any problems we had with earlier prototypes, dealing with the very issues you mentioned. Since the company was able to get hold of military spec radioactive material all we had to figure out was how to contain it in a small device, and then transmit it in a targeted way in the right quantity. Because of the great group of people we have here, the project has made rapid progress, and we feel we can produce a device that will kill or compromise nanobots within seconds at a range of about twenty yards."

"Excellent, once we get a working device that's a start. We can refine it as time goes by." Magee said.

"Well get to it, and send me regular updates on your progress. You will all get a bonus when the Ghost Hand is available for our customers."

****

Steven Grace pottered around in his garden and poked at his vegetables. This year he was doing carrots and potatoes. They were coming along nicely. Steven was a Chemist in his mid-forties, who worked at a local drugs manufacturer. He had never married, and as today was a Saturday, he was not at work. Steven had been raised a Roman Catholic, but had strayed from his faith in his twenties, when he went to college. That's when the conventional answers failed to answer his questions, so he decided that it was all made up by ancient kings to control the masses. Nothing had replaced his religion, and now he did not really believe in anything. Everything was just some kind of cosmic accident, and if it had never happened he told himself he would have been just as happy. Nothing seemed to fulfill him or give him a reason for continuing to exist. He drifted aimlessly on the tides of life, never finding any meaning and never finding anything to fill the empty hollow he felt inside. He often thought about killing himself and had suffered from depression in one form or another for most of his life. Probably the one thing that prevented him from doing this was the daughter he had. Erin had been the product of a brief fling he'd had ten years ago with a woman from work he didn't even like. The company had sent them all on a conference to another city, and put them up in a hotel. The speakers had been mind-numbingly boring with the result that most of the employees had gotten drunk at the bar the first night, in an effort to unwind after the day. He and Erin's mother had somehow found themselves together and in a lusty mood, so they had spent the night together. It had happened so unexpectedly that neither of them had protection, and she took no preventative measures the next day. She had never told him why, but when she had found out that she was pregnant, she decided to keep it. Getting together was out of the question, so she had been a single mother for a while, and then she had married a software engineer a few years later. Steven had found the guy polite enough, if not downright friendly, and he seemed to look after Erin ok, so there had been no real issues with that arrangement. So Steven stayed in this world more out of love for a single person and a sense of parental responsibility for a child he saw every other weekend than anything else. The suicide fantasy always remained just below the surface, and he knew that if the day ever came when no-one needed him anymore, then he would head to the mountains with a six-pack of beer and the shotgun, and then he would meet eternity at a time of his own choosing.

He had seen the news about the Iasobots on the news, and was immediately intrigued. Because he was always around lots of people, he was always getting lots of colds, and it was a pain each time. It involved taking sick leave a couple of times a year, as he worked in an area known as the 'clean room' and one could not work in that sensitive environment with a cold. He had heard the rumours that there might be issues with the vaccine, but he dismissed them; for every drug that there was, there were always conspiracy theorists claiming that it was bad for you, usually people who did not have the condition that required the medication themselves. He had decided to get the vaccine and be done with colds forever; on balance it made sense to him.

After he had finished in the garden, Steven drove across town to where the clinic was. He was surprised at the length of the queue, there were a lot more people into this than he'd expected, even at the high cost of getting it done. Presumably he was not the only person who had done a cost-value analysis, and figured out that it would be more than worth it long-term. He stood as the queue slowly shuffled forward, lost in random and meaningless thoughts about being other places and doing other things. It was a habit he'd always had his whole life, well as far back as he could remember. He had probably first picked it up in school, as a coping mechanism for dealing with long boring classes on summer days. He would gaze out the window and day-dream about adventures, where he was always the hero and always defeated the bad guys. It was fun and passed the time pleasantly, but without knowing it, he had become addicted to a world of fantasy that existed only in his head, and ever since it was been a crutch which he used to get through his mundane day-to-day life. His mind, unbidden, would feed him one gratifying dream after another, like a record on a continuous loop, and this could go on all day. As soon as one day-dream ended another would begin almost immediately, as his brain sought to insulate him from the drabness of reality. Ultimately it left him empty and frustrated and aware that he was always a day older and never any closer to achieving anything real except to count down the timer until the inevitable day when death brought the curtain down on the whole pantomime. He didn't however see any reason to stop this form of behaviour, and he assumed that most people were just like him, on a continuous action-repeat cycle of illusion. After all it was just harmless fun, and it kept him entertained when nothing else was happening.

Eventually it became his turn to go in, and he was waved through by a member of staff who greeted him with a pleasant smile and chatted a bit. A little surprised that she was so friendly after having had to deal with so many people, he found himself returning her smile with a big smile of his own and engaging in conversation. This was unlike him, as he usually kept to himself and preferred to keep interactions with strangers to a minimum, choosing to conduct any transaction as quickly as possible. He normally detested small-talk; he didn't think it was anyone's business how his day was going, and he didn't care how their day was going. On this occasion, he acted differently to the way he usually would, and chatted away with her. He gave her the form he had filled out earlier, and was somewhat surprised when she asked him for consent to do the vaccination. Surely the fact that he had showed up here, and queued for the last hour meant he wanted to get it done? He pondered the strange world we live in, but just assured her that, yes, he was giving consent. He didn't like the idea of the spray, even though she said that's how she'd had it done, opting instead for the needle. After all he was paying for this, so it was his choice. All it took was a few seconds, and he barely noticed the jab. Then she said that after eight to ten days he would be cold-free for life. Happy with the decision he had made, he walked back to his car with a spring in his step. He thought for a while how we were lucky nowadays; we could eliminate so many of the painful things that had plagued mankind for centuries. Then he went back to his dreaming and he sleepwalked his way through most of the rest of the day, his mind acting out his heroic scenarios for an audience of one, with itself being the creator and the observer of all the madness.

4 SOLAR STORM

Astronomers and astrophysicists had been talking excitedly about it for weeks – it was to be the solar storm of the century. Apparently they had been observing increasingly unusual activity on the surface of the sun, leading them to conclude that there was a build-up of epic proportions looming. All computer data and simulations suggested that there was an immense amount of pent up energy that was going to explode at any moment. When it happened it would send a solar flare hurtling through space at colossal speeds. If the Earth happened to be in the way of that flare, then it would be hit by a stream of highly-charged radiation, the likes of which had never been seen before. The effects would be uncertain. All ships and planes were on alert to be prepared to use alternative methods of navigation at short notice if necessary, and every organisation that used satellites were on high alert to prepare for the loss of their satellites in the event that a big solar flare hit the Earth. TV stations had warned their viewers that they might lose transmission, and people had taken to reading maps again, in the event that their gps could not be relied upon.

And then it happened; a coronal mass ejection from the sun spewed vast quantities of electromagnetic radiation and sent it hurtling straight toward the Earth. As predicted it arrived in two days. It knocked out satellites, interfering with TV and communications systems; it played havoc with electricity networks, leaving millions without power worldwide. It also did something else; it did something strange to the nanobots that were inside millions of people who had received them as a vaccination for the cold virus. It was not the right wavelength and frequency to destroy them. However it made them nanobots mutate so that they no longer behaved as they were supposed to. Instead of just blocking the cold virus from entering cells the Iasobots started blocking electrolytes like sodium, magnesium, chlorine and potassium from entering the brain cells of their hosts. This altered the conscious awareness of the victims. Then the Iasobots began to enter the brain cells themselves, in an altered state. They changed the programming of the brain cells, stripping away the parts that make us thinking, rational beings, leaving only a primitive remnant. The combined effect of this was to turn ordinary people into mindless zombies, with an insatiable thirst for human flesh. Unfortunately the only flesh they seemed to crave was that of uninfected persons. It was as if the infected people thought that they could make themselves better by ingesting the flesh of non-infected people.

Overnight it seemed as if humanity had started a civil war with itself, zombies against the uninfected. The emergency services quickly became overrun and shut down. The fact that half the fire, hospital and police personnel themselves became zombies, and turned on the others didn't help. Then nations called out their armies, the ones who weren't mindless, flesh-eating automatons, to try and take the situation under control. This helped a bit but not much. An army can only stretch so far, even the biggest armies, and when half the population is going crazy everywhere at once, the whole system breaks down. Then a lot of soldiers simply went home to protect their families, when they realised that the enemy was within and everywhere. Societies then turned into complete anarchy, where the law of the jungle prevailed. The weak were quickly overcome by the strong, as lawlessness, crime and looting took place on a grand scale. Currency as we know it became worthless but people began to trade with food, guns and other commodities. People banded together for protection against the marauding hordes of infected. Some barricaded themselves into their houses and bunkered down to wait out the storm. A lot of others fled the towns and cities, and sought refuge in the countryside, hoping to return once the zombies had been wiped out.

The zombies hunted the uninfected. They were not dead but they were not people anymore, reduced as they were to mindless killers. They attacked ordinary people on sight, tearing them apart and gorging on the flesh. With their minds taken over by the Iasobots they were not quick thinkers, and also their movements were slightly slower and clumsier than normal people, but what they lacked for in speed and dexterity they made up for in stamina and tenacity. Once in pursuit of someone they were relentless and fearless. They were not concerned for personal safety, nor did they avoid injury. They were a health and safety nightmare.

People said it was the Armageddon and the end of the world, and God's judgement on a fallen race.

****

Alan Howal got a panicked phone call on his landline:

"Alan, it's me, John…………"

"John" Howal said sadly, "I was expecting that you might call".

"I don't understand what's happening. The nanobots were working so well......................."

"There's no point going over that now, we need to focus on a solution before this situation gets any worse. By that I mean we have to stop this or civilisation will cease to exist. If the damage goes beyond a critical mass we won't be able to sustain the way of life we're used to and will go back to living in huts."

"What can we do?" Hodson asked despairingly.

"We have to put the old team back together and try and figure out a way to neutralise the Iasobots while there is still time to save some people. Is your laboratory still functioning?"

"There are a number of problems with that Alan. First of all half the team got the vaccination themselves, turned into zombies and ran amok trying to eat people. They were subsequently shot by a vigilante group called 'Zombie Watch' or something, formed to defend the area. Secondly my best assistants Tara Mahoney and Beverley Shenton are missing. They were working on implanting a kill-switch into the Iasobots, in case something went wrong. I don't know if they're alive or dead and I can't go to look. After you spoke on that current affairs programme on TV it started me thinking that perhaps you were correct in some of your thinking, and that we should develop some kind of antidote or shutdown mechanism in case something went wrong. We should have allowed her more time to develop the technology before we hastily put the vaccine on the market, but I thought that by releasing something like that would undermine confidence in the vaccine and less people would benefit from it. Thirdly, an angry mob burned down my lab, and I only got away from them by the skin of my teeth. Most of my files and my data were lost in the fire."

"That's not good John. We will have to use my lab so. You will have to come to me. I'm glad to hear that you took belated steps to create some kind of insurance policy in case things went wrong, it may prove critical in the end. Just make sure no-one follows you here. If we lose my lab we may lose mankind. Do you still remember the way?"

"Yes, I know the area well. I am holed up in a garage right now. I will wait until nightfall and make my way there. There are zombies all over the place. I will bring the two remaining assistants I have with me."

"Whose garage are you in, does anyone know you are there?"

"As we made our getaway, we crashed the car and had to ditch it. We were out of sight of our pursuers so we just ran to the first house where there was no vehicle outside, figuring that there was no owner about that we would have to explain things to. Entry was gained through the open garage door, which we locked and barricaded after ourselves. Then we waited for the heat to die down, so to speak. The occupiers did return a short time later, but that is not a matter we need discuss right now. As far as I am aware, no-one on earth knows we're here."

"Do you have any kind of weapons, if you get killed I don't know how much I can do on my own?"

"Yes, weapons are the one thing we have a surplus of" Hodson answered; "We luckily found our way into a house where there were several rifles and shotguns. We will travel on foot so we don't lead a horde of zombies to your door. It seems they're attracted to the sound of car engines and if they hear one they come running from all directions."

Howal thought for a moment; "While we're on the subject of zombies John, how come you aren't one right now? Why did you not take the Iasobots?"

"Honestly, I had a last minute thought that I should hold out, just in the event of a million-to-one chance that something did go wrong. I know it looks bad but I genuinely thought I was making a sacrifice not taking the vaccination, and leaving myself open to colds and flues. It was that interview you did on Modern News that made me hold back. I figured that, if something did go wrong, I'd be around to help fix it. I never imagined we'd be dealing with a world-wide zombie apocalypse though. Some of my assistants heard about my decision and followed suit." Hodson was referring to two others as well as Mahoney and Shenton.

"Ok, we have much to do. I will be waiting for you. I still have most of the data up until I left the team. I spent the last few months trying to come up with an antidote for the Iasobots in case something went wrong and I have already made some headway. I need some information from you in relation to the makeup of your final design though, and I think it's critical that we find Tara and Beverley, they are exceptional scientists and we need to know what they know. We should be able to pick up the pieces fairly quickly when you get here and see about finding a solution to this mess. Good luck John………"

****

John Hodson looked back at his assistants Belinda Porter and Blaine Maxwell once and nodded. As he had told Howal, just after they got to the garage and barricaded the door, the owners must have returned……….and also a whole lot of zombies. They had heard shooting and screaming and fighting. This went on for about fifteen minutes, then all they heard were grunts and the sounds of eating, and bones being thrown about. They had laid low in the garage for hours after the screaming upstairs had stopped. They had found food, water and the afore-mentioned guns there. Now it was time to face whatever was up there, and make the journey to Howal's laboratory at all costs. The owner of the house had been a bit of a gun collector, and each of them carried a rifle and a shotgun, ready for what lay ahead. They wanted to leave by the rear of the house, as they could hear activity on the front street, but that meant going through the house, and whatever was in it.

Hodson quietly removed the last item, a filing cabinet, which had been blocking the door, and picked up a bolt-action 30.06. He quietly opened the door and peered into the darkness beyond. There were no sounds from the house now, and no signs of activity besides themselves. Feeling somewhat relieved, he switched on a flashlight and looked down the hallway.

Hodson swore and Porter stifled a scream. They were greeted by a scene from hell, picked out by the light. There were several bodies in the hall, the bodies of zombies, full of gunshot wounds. There were also bones scattered about with the flesh ripped from them. There was blood everywhere. The house in the suburbs had been turned into a charnel house.

"God forgive us..........we did this......" muttered Blaine Maxwell.

"We weren't to know, how could anyone have predicted something like this happening?" Belinda Porter cried. "We did what we did to help people. We were creating medicine for Chrissakes."

"We can't dwell on this, we must push on. We have to prevent more carnage from happening. We don't have the luxury of stopping to mourn just yet" Hodson said grimly..

He picked his way gingerly down the hallway, gun at the ready. The others followed, trying not to slip on the congealing blood that lay pooled everywhere or step on bones. As they made their way along Porter drew their attention to the fact that the dead zombies had died from an assortment of wounds to different areas; "Looks like a normally fatal body shot will do the trick as well as a head shot," she noted "It's probably best to aim for the central body mass if you're not good with guns."

They made their way to the front window and peeked out into the street. The streetlights were not functioning but in the moonlight they could see the occasional zombie shuffling their way aimlessly about in the strange world of twilight they now observed. Porter shuddered;

"Oh my God, they're everywhere ! How long do you think they will be like that?"

"Hard to say" replied Hodson. "Since they're not actually dead, I suppose that with regular nutrition they could last quite a while, same as normal people. Whether their brains will degenerate further to the point where they die, or whether they will heal and recover, who knows, it's too early to tell. The body might start to recognise the rogue nanobots as foreign matter and begin to try and defend itself against them, and if it did, we don't know how effective it would be. How much the nanobots can adapt of change further is another unknown variable. It's all just a mess."

Porter shuddered again after hearing the bit about 'regular nutrition' and gripped her gun tight; "There's no way those 'things' are eating me! If they get a hold of me, you have my permission to end things quickly for me, as a final act of friendship."

"Let's hope it never comes to the point where we have to

shoot each other. Let's concentrate on getting to where Howal is. All we need is to be careful and a little bit of luck, and then we can start trying to find a remedy" Hodson replied tersely. He did not want to lose more friends and colleagues on top of the pain he already had to contend with.

Maxwell was scanning up and down the road, as much as the view from the front window would allow. There were too many zombies about to risk going out the front door. "Looks like it will have to be the back" he commented grimly. He gripped the loaded pump action closer, glad that he had found several buckshot shells for it. These were now in a bag slung by his side. Hodson's heart now felt like a stone, but he forced himself to think of the mission and not what he had done. "Let's go" he said quietly.

He led the way through the front room trying not to look at the bodies everywhere, down the hall towards the back. Just as they reached the utility room where the back door was, the three of them froze in their tracks and stopped breathing. The door of a walk-in closet on their left was opening slowly............

Three guns and the flashlight pointed at the door, ready to spew lead in a split-second.

"Who's there?" A voice asked from within the closet.

Relieved, the three scientists started breathing again, but they did not lower their guns. Just because the voice didn't belong to a zombie didn't mean that you dropped your guard.

"We're looking for a way out of here, come out slowly!" Hodson ordered. "Any wrong move will be your last."

A small man, aged about thirty slowly emerged from the closet, blinking as the light shone in his face.

"Well you're clearly not a zombie so what happened here?"

Hodson asked, remembering to whisper again.

"I'm Eddie Young, my friends own,……. or owned this house. We were at a place a few miles away, looking for our other friends, but they were not there, so we returned here. We parked our car a short distance away, hoping to sneak in on foot, but we ran right into a horde of zombies and they over-ran us before we could barricade the door. We were all armed and we shot and killed a lot of them but there were too many. They forced their way in here and began to overpower us. When the situation got hopeless I jumped into the closet. Luckily none of those things saw me, and I waited for it to go quiet. It was not an easy thing to listen to your friends being eaten alive………..George and Susan were my dearest companions in this life………" Now his voice turned to a sob and he did not continue.

Suddenly Hodson's attention was fixated on the man's left arm. He hadn't noticed until now but there was dried blood on Eddie's forearm. He shone the light at it. "Show me your arm!" he commanded.

Eddie pulled off a bloodied makeshift bandage and revealed a clear bite-mark on his arm.

The scientists gasped; "When did you get that?" Maxwell demanded.

"During the battle I was attempting to reload my pistol when one of them came at me. I could not retreat and when I raised my arm defensively the bastard bit me on the arm. I had to club it with the unloaded pistol to kill it."

"That's interesting" Hodson said; "You got bitten hours ago, but remain unchanged, do you feel anything besides the obvious pain of the wound, anything unusual?"

"No, I'm the same as normal, if you can call this normal" Eddie said sadly. "I don't think I'm about to turn into one of those things, if that's what you're thinking."

Hodson was excited now, and he felt a little of the weight lift off of himself; "Do you know what that means?" He asked the others; "It means that a bite from the zombies does not infect you with its Iasobots! It's not a contagious condition, given the nature of nanobots, if a bite doesn't do it nothing will. They must sync with the host DNA and that means if the bite itself is non-fatal, then you have a good chance of surviving, especially if you get some antibiotics to ward off any ordinary infection!"

"I cleaned the wound with vinegar, and then put some honey on it, because I found some honey in there and I heard somewhere it has anti-bacterial properties" said Eddie Young; "I'm not sure if that's true or not but that was the best I could do. Who are you by the way? What are you doing in here, and why did you not help us during the battle?"

"You must come with us, we are the scientists who unfortunately unleashed this plague on the world, and we are on a mission to find a cure. We sought shelter here to escape a pack of zombies and we didn't get involved because we're scientists, not soldiers. We wanted to help but we have a bigger mission that cannot fail, or what happened here is going to be just the tip of the iceberg as far as this country's concerned. This brings me back to you,.....you will be able to supply us with some of the rogue Iasobots we need to study, they will be in your system now, I'm certain of it. It saves us the tricky and dangerous task of capturing and somehow containing a zombie" Hodson said.

This news sank into Eddie Young's brain; this was the Icarus who had flown too close to the sun, and had brought half of humanity crashing down with him. He and his friends had hidden and done nothing while his friends were being butchered in their own house and they were the very ones who had brought this misfortune down on all their heads. Hatred and anger rose in his heart. "I recognise you now! Dear God you're the son-of-a-bitch that did this!"

"Look, I know what I did, and that's a burden for me to carry to the grave, but time is going by swiftly and we desperately need to get to Alan Howal's laboratory to work on a solution. There is no-one else on this planet who can stop this thing now but us. I know you're angry and upset, but I ask you to put aside your personal feelings and consider the fate of millions of others who are now relying on us to fix this mess. We need you Eddie, the Human race needs you, will you come with us?"

Young thought for a while. He had considered putting a bullet into Hodson with the silver 9mm pistol he had concealed in his jacket, but the mention of Howal's name made him pause. He fought to control his emotions and his desire for revenge. "Howal is here, and working on a cure? He knew this would happen! He's the reason me and my friends wouldn't go near those infernal nanobots. When we heard his warning we held off. God knows how many people he's saved."

"He's about three miles away, waiting for us as we speak. The Iasobots you now carry within you could prove critical to finding an antidote. We have no time to delay!"

Young paused. He decided that any revenge for his fallen friends would have to wait. First he would see if these damn egg-heads could come up with an antidote, and if they failed, then they would all die by his hand.

"Sure, I'll come..........." he said.

5 A GRIM REALISATION

Brad, Tom, Doug and Scott had been having a wonderful time on their Camping trip. The first day they had loaded everything onto the two canoes and had paddled for hours. The weather was glorious and they felt young and briefly free again. Tom had called home on his cell phone and his wife Caroline had warned him about the solar storm they were talking about on the news. He informed the others that there was a chance they would lose contact with the outside world if the storm knocked out all the satellites and electrical systems. This would only be a problem if someone got sick or injured and they needed urgent medical treatment. Otherwise the trip would carry on as planned, and they would explore the river and the mountains and pretend they did not have troubles or cares waiting for them at home.

Sure enough on the third day none of their cell phones had a signal, and they assumed that the promised solar storm had damaged the network. They wondered what other havoc it may have wrought, and pondered how dependent we all are on technology to survive nowadays. Apart from that they carried on down the river, two men and a dog in each boat, occasionally chatting but mainly lost in their own thoughts. There was just enough current to carry them gently along, without being too swift, so a lot of the time, all they had to do was to guide the boats along and relax. The weather was still glorious, with blue skies and a slight breeze at their backs, bearing the fresh smells of the wilderness and the occasional chirping of birds. Around them the mountains towered jagged and forbidding like the giant sentinels of some timeless secret. They were approaching a bridge over the river, which represented a milestone in their journey, and once past it, they would look for a place to pull in for a break.

Tom was in the front of the first boat, gently paddling and wondering what it would be like to never go back to his job. He found it hard to tear his mind away from it even though he had promised himself he would. "I'll tell you the problem with the job at the moment." he said, breaking the near-silence; "Too much political interference. Every time those idiot politicians have a meeting, they come up with some hair-brained scheme that never works. I wish they'd stop meddling and let us get on with things, or at least consult us. I have lots of great ideas about how we could improve things and no-one ever listens."

"I agree with you about that." Brad chuckled. There's too many meetings in general, and it's not just the politicians at it. The management are just as bad. They seem to have this mentality that you haven't achieved anything at the meeting unless you've added something to the job. Now, when I say 'added' I mean added another procedure, added more policy, more steps, more of anything and everything until it suddenly takes about ten stages to complete a task that you used to be able to do in two or three stages. All it does is to add to your workload and slow the whole thing down. I wish they'd have less meetings. It gets to the stage where everybody sits around trying to sound intelligent and that's when they come up with the bright ideas."

"That's exactly what I am talking about" Tom answered. "They seem to think they've achieved something by this continuous adding of steps to everything you do. Of course they dress it up as being essential, they have to justify it some way. I would like to know who has the job of taking things away from all the bureaucracy? Who's job is it to streamline things and try to make things more efficient? I've never seen such a person in any of the jobs I've had. You would imagine that every workplace would have such a person, but surprisingly it seems not."

"It's nobody's job" Scott laughed. "These people haven't realised that sometimes less is more, and that if they reduced the mindless bureaucracy and ass-covering, that the job would get done a lot more efficiently. It gradually makes the job more and more complicated and difficult to do, for no real benefit. It's not so bad if you've been in the job for a while and know the ropes, but for new people coming in it creates a vast amount of information and procedure that they have to learn. I'm glad they I will be out in a few years, as I shudder to think how much stuff you'll have to learn as time goes by if things keep going on like this. Of course there's no point in telling them that, they won't listen, although they pretend to. They know better than the people at the coal-face, who actually do the job!"

"Jeez, we're on holidays, can we leave talk of the job at home? You lot are starting to make me feel depressed!" Doug enquired. "We're never going to solve all the problems of the world or change anything. Just accept that there is no logic to a lot of the things we have to deal with, and most politicians are deeply insane, and they're going to keep on coming up with these bright ideas, then walking away to let someone else deal with the fall-out. Just try to do the best you can and don't let it get to you, otherwise you're letting it annoy you." He then went back to gently paddling and let the others carry on as they willed.

"That's true, to a point" Tom said. "But not everyone can tune out like that. I envy people who can, but it's not easy to see people interfering with the job who really know little or nothing about it, but make grandiose promises to all and sundry about all the great things they're gonna do, then walk away expecting us to make these promises come true."

"I've noticed that when some Minister makes a cock-up they just start switching people around" Brad said. "Sometimes it's like musical chairs with those guys. I sometimes wonder what will happen when every Minister has had some time in every department, will they just start all over again?"

The others laughed.

"Who the hell knows, probably." Tom chuckled. "They just keep trying everything they can think of and still they cannot make the job work better. Despite that they will always be afraid to consult those of us who do the actual job. It's like they're afraid to because they might start to feel that most of them are quite superfluous!"

"What gets my goat is the way they keep switching all the departments around" Scott added. "They'll try and cram two or more departments together, on the basis that that's the way it's done somewhere else, or that's the way it was done in the past, as if that was a criteria for anything. Then a few months or years later they realise that it's been a disaster and they separate them again. It seems to take them forever to realise that they've made a mistake but they never admit that. Because of all their interfering and adding to each role, they've made it impossible to amalgamate any two roles together. Every role is too complicated and too specialised for anyone to do more than one role, especially as you still only get paid for one. What they don't seem to realise is that, in these other places, the individual roles are way simpler and easier to manage, so they can do they type of thing. Here we have so much more issues to deal with and it can't be done."

"Maybe some of you guys should go into politics, and change the world?" Doug piped up.

They laughed.

"No, it's too late for that sort of thing. There would be too many battles to fight, and the system itself is insane, so achieving change would be nigh-on impossible. You'd be a lone voice crying out in the wilderness. We'll have to leave it to the next generation to get it right. Anyway, you have to be a narcissistic sociopath to go into politics" Tom said. "Maybe we'll just take your advice and learn to go with the flow, and just try to let the madness pass us by!"

Then he lapsed back into silence, as the others did, and returned to their own contemplation. He scanned the area around him, drinking in the majestic beauty and thinking that the mountains would still be there for eons after they and all their troubles were gone.

Suddenly he saw several people milling about where the river meandered near a road about half a mile up ahead. It looked like some vehicles had crashed.

"Hey, I think there's been a crash, we should go and see if they need help!" he called to the others. They now saw the commotion too and didn't hesitate to go and help.

They changed course and paddled harder, heading for a place where the shore gently sloped towards the river. They could beach the boats there and walk up to the road to offer their assistance. The distance from the river to the road here was about one hundred metres, most of it over gravel and loose stones, formed by millennia of erosion by the river. Doug tried to remember where they had stuck the first aid kit as he paddled along. He had a vague recollection of seeing it in his grey backpack. As they got closer something seemed strange to them. There were eight people on the road, all adults, but they seemed to be moving about in weird ways, shuffling about as if they had no destination or purpose in mind. There were three cars there, all bearing various degrees of damage, and the people moved about near them not really doing anything. As the boats got closer still it became apparent that something was badly wrong. Some of the people had blood dripping from fresh wounds, but none of the others were attempting to help them.

Then Tom's dogs, Scout and Keeper, began to bark and whine nervously. Surveying the entire scene Scott felt an uneasy feeling creep over him; "Something isn't right here" he cautioned the others. "Let's be on our guard."

When they got to the shore they pulled the boats up and started walking up towards the road. For some reason Scott felt the need to bring his paddle. Seeing this, the others also brought theirs. No-one asked why but there was an eerie feeling about everything that was difficult to explain.

Now that they had begun walking slowly towards the road, the people on the road turned to look their way. A collective howl rose in the air, unlike anything any of them had ever heard. It was the battle cry of the undead.

"Something's very badly wrong here" Doug muttered. "Why are they just watching us like that, and why is that guy with the broken leg just walking about?"

"I don't like this" agreed Brad. "I've never seen people behave like that before. I wonder if they're all in shock?"

"People who are in shock don't make noises like that, and why are they all coming towards us now?" asked Doug.

Indeed the group on the road had now begun to move with purpose for the first time, speeding up and heading straight towards them. They did not pick their way like people normally did, but walked straight over rocks and through bushes. It was then that Scott and friends first noticed the bones scattered around near the crash site. They were distinctly human bones and they had been picked almost clean.

"I think we should get back to the boats NOW!" Scott shouted as he turned and ran.

Without argument the other three followed him, sprinting as fast as the gravel underfoot would allow. A glance behind was enough to confirm that they were being chased by a pack of people afflicted by some strange condition that was unknown to them.

"Push the boats out as fast as you can and paddle like hell!" Brad shouted. "They're getting closer!"

The people were rushing ever nearer. Brad and Doug turned to face them, paddles at the ready, as Scott and Tom handled the boats. The first of the people got to them as the boats became waterborne again. The zombies tried to grab at them, but were beaten off with fearsome blows to the head from the paddles. Both were glad that they had the old-fashioned heavy wooden paddles, as they were stout enough to knock their assailants off their feet, causing others to trip over the ones in the water, where they trashed and flailed about in a determined effort to grab hold of someone.

"Get in the boats now!" Scott shouted. Brad and Doug ran for it, jumping in, and paddling like crazy. The zombies chased after them through the water, but were unable to match them for speed. The four friends paddled until their arms ached, then, checking to confirm that the zombies were far behind, they allowed the boats to drift close together.

"What the hell was all that about?" Doug spoke for them all. "Those people were acting like zombies that you see in the movies!"

"They were going to kill us, did you see all the bones on the road?" Tom panted breathlessly. "That's some kind of murder scene!"

"Lucky we brought these paddles and not the lightweight ones" said Doug, "I hit a couple of them as hard as I could and it was barely enough to stop them."

Scott was deep in thought; "As a medical man Doug, what would you say is going on here?"

"I don't know. It looks like something affected their minds as they were driving along, causing them to crash. Then they attacked and ate some other people, whether they were members of their own parties, or passers-by like ourselves, who knows. I think we can assume that those they attacked were uninfected like ourselves and that's why they were targeted. One thing is sure, there are zombies back on the road there, and we have to warn the authorities as soon as possible. Those people, whatever they are, need urgent medical attention, and others need to be warned about them. Who knows who might happen along and get attacked".

Tom was struck with a thought; "I bet I know what caused it, I bet it was that recent solar storm! I read something once that said that intense radiation can cause strange things to happen".

"If that's the case, how many other people are affected, and why aren't we zombies?" Doug pondered out loud. No-one could answer him. "Hopefully the ones we encountered back on the road were just a once-off freak incident and the authorities will deal with the matter quickly."

Scott was hit by a wave of fore-boding; "I've been watching the road since we had that problem, and I have not seen one single car go past. Doesn't that strike you as being unusual? There is something very badly wrong. We need to get back to civilisation right now and see what is happening and if this is an isolated event. There could be many more like them, for all we know. I'm afraid this canoe trip is over. We have to get back to our friends and families, they may need us."

"Just remember, we will have to proceed warily, there may be more zombies when we get back to town" Tom cautioned them. "We wouldn't be able to fight off significant numbers of them with a few paddles, so I suggest you guys load your guns Scott and Doug, and have them within easy access. I will keep the axe close by and Brad has his bow. If things are really bad we will just steal more guns somewhere."

With this cold realisation gripping their hearts, the friends decided to change their planned route and paddle up a tributary of the river that would bring them to the closest village to their present position. There they would make contact with the authorities, and ascertain what on earth was going on. A quick check of their phones revealed that none of them had a signal yet, so all that was left to do was to paddle urgently, each of them trying to come to terms with what they had just seen.

After two hours of paddling they came to a bend in the river, just before the place a village nestled in the mountains. It's residents were mainly members of the logging community. There were thick forested areas each side of the river, so they decided to conceal the canoes on one of the banks, and proceed with caution on foot until they could see what the lay of the land looked like. They watched and listened intently for any signs of trouble and then, seeing none, they dismounted quietly from the canoes. Taking their weapons they proceeded stealthily through the bush. After a while Scott motioned to his ears and shrugged his shoulders. They all knew what he meant; there were no sounds of cars or trucks or the usual bustle of activity that one would normally expect in the village. Indeed an eerie quietness pervaded the place, as if something that had been living was now dead and still. This was not a good portent and they carried on with even more caution than before. Finally they came over the crest of a hill and could see the village below. A scene of carnage greeted them; there were crashed cars and human remains everywhere and among them slouched more zombies, aimlessly trudging about. Brad had a scope on his rifle and they took turns using it to view the scene below. It wasn't an approved safety practice, but the circumstances were a matter of life and death and they had to use what was available to them. As on the road some miles back, they could see scatterings of human bones, blood and clothes where someone had fallen prey to the insatiable appetites of the undead. The dogs started to growl and whine, and Tom quickly hushed them, and retreated back into the woods. The rest followed to plan their next move.

"This is now starting to feel really bad." Tom said looking worried; "I have to get back to Caroline and my family. I have no way of knowing how they are."

"It looks like this zombie thing is more widespread than just one incident, what do you think Doug, is it maybe an area or even the whole county? How many people could this thing affect?" Scott wanted to know.

"Well, since we are unaffected we can assume that not everybody else is. Probably the survivors have fled or gone to ground somewhere. I saw the bodies of zombies down there as well as ordinary people, so it looks like someone was normal and that someone fought back. As to whether it could affect people over a larger area, it's hard to know until we get more information. The thing that's worrying me is that, if our theory about the solar storm holds water, then the affected area could be huge, this thing could even be global……………."

The others looked at him in stunned silence as the implications of this sunk in.

"Ok we have to come up with a plan, first thing I'd say is we need to get a vehicle, preferably even two." Brad was thinking of Christine and the children.

Scott thought for a moment, then suggested a plan; "Yes that's a good place to start, I propose we go, take two vehicles, and head for the city. While we're here we may as well look for food supplies and weapons. If this thing has been going on for a few days then the place is going to resemble a warzone, and normal food supplies will have been disrupted. Therefore we must plan ahead and stock up while we can. It is probably better to not split up as we don't know how many of those things are roaming about down there. We can provide cover for each other as we get what we need. If it gets too hot to handle we may have to retreat out of there on foot and run back to the canoes, but I'm seriously hoping it won't come to that. Our own vehicles are a long way away and up-river. Rowing back to them isn't really a viable option."

"Good thinking" said Tom, "Let's go for bigger vehicles too, pick-up trucks. If we have to ram some of those things off the road we want a bit more muscle behind us than a car, and it's probably safe to say there are lots of abandoned vehicles all over the place. The zombies won't mind us taking their vehicles, it's not like they will be needing them. Then we head for the city and collect our families. After that I suggest we head for the country, I know where there are some cabins deep in the woods where we can hide out. They belonged to a relation of mine who died recently so they will be empty. There's lots of fishing and hunting there as well, until this mess is over with."

"Good plan Tom. Ok so when we get vehicles we quickly identify a grocery store and load up fast. Then if we can, a gun store or sporting goods store, in fact now that I think about it, we'll hit one of those up first if we see it's closer. Keep your eyes peeled for large numbers of zombies, if there's just a few we can deal with them. I'm guessing that if this thing is fairly widespread, then there are going to be less zombies in a place with a small population like this than there will be in the city, so hopefully we won't need to execute a full scale retreat." Scott looked around for any reaction.

"I don't suppose there's anything in the law against killing zombies?" Brad wondered.

Doug thought for a bit; "It would depend on whether you would define them as being alive or not, so it's hard to say. There's no law against killing the dead but whether a court would see it that way is anyone's guess. Technically they are sick people so we won't gratuitously kill any but there's no law against self-defence if they're trying to attack us. Any successful attack by those things is going to be fatal as we have seen, so you can justify using lethal force to defend ourselves. Zombies don't do Common Assault. However all this may be a moot point as whether there's ever going to be any courts again as we know them is another story."

This answer made sense to everyone.

"Ok we move now, I want to be on the road before dark, as we don't know what's ahead of us." Scott lead the way, brandishing his pump action in front of him...............

****

Steven Grace was at work. Well his body was there, going through the usual motions. His mind was far away, lost in one of his favourite dreams. This was one where he rescued a number of children from a flood, risking his own life in the process. There were even some tourists who happened to be there, to record the event with their cameras, and this enabled his heroics to be beamed all over the world, so everyone could see how brave and how noble he was. Of course he became an instant hero, and they wanted to award him all sorts of medals and awards. The President himself would hold a ceremony and lavish praise on him and say how the age of chivalry was not dead, and the grateful parents were there, thanking him with tears in their eyes. He was accepting all the glory in his humble way, actually he would have preferred no fuss at all, but they had insisted. Such courage could not go unrewarded. At last the world realised what a great man he was. At last it showered him with the rewards he deserved, fame and fortune were his. This dream went on and on, as it usually did, making up for the empty reality he felt inside. When it finally ended, another dream took over as naturally as night follows day. In this one he was an important government minister, responsible for running the economy, and running the world the way he thought it should be run. Obviously things were a rousing success, and everybody was privileged and grateful to have him doing this and it was fixing all the stupid things everybody else had been doing up to the time of his appointment.

And so his day went on and on in much the same way as before, his mind feeding him the same old cycle of fantasy, like the drip-feeding of a comatose patient in a hospital. He knew it was nonsense, but he didn't see much point in stopping as long as nothing else important happened, and it was a pleasant way to spend the time. He didn't think it was doing any harm.

Something different would happen today though. Suddenly it felt like there was a storm going on in his head, and all his thoughts, memories and dreams were being washed away in that storm. He felt his mind begin to go blank. He began to forget who he was and what he was supposed to be doing. He looked at his chemicals and at his computer screen and lost all interest in them. A craving began to build inside him. He tried to fight it, but it was overwhelming and he was not able to resist it. He felt ever more lost and alone. He looked quickly around at his colleagues. No-one seemed to have noticed what was happening to him. Perhaps he was going mad? Perhaps his mind had finally decided to check out and he would wind up in an institution? Panic rose in him for a brief moment, but died again as he lost even that much thought, and then there was the emptiness and the fear growing. They grew and grew, swallowing his very soul into a black hole from which there was no escape. Then there was nothing left except for the emptiness and the fear. It was like how an astronaut might feel if his ship flew away for some reason, and left him floating alone in outer space, waiting to run out of air. Then he felt the hunger. It was the hunger of someone that is cut off from the rest of life. He became so hungry he could not bear it, he had to feed. He rose from his chair and looked around. He was barely aware that people were screaming and running away. Some of his work mates had also gotten the vaccine recently, and they had turned into zombies too. He saw them attack the others and begin to eat them. He knew by instinct who he must attack and feed on to get his soul back, and he grabbed for a screaming man who had worked beside him for years. The man was being attacked and surrounded by four or five of them, and they were eating him alive. They were oblivious killers now, and they had no choice but to try to make themselves whole again. This was how the zombie apocalypse started for Steven Grace, sitting on the floor with some others, covered in blood, feeding on a former friend like a pack of hyenas.

When Steven had gorged all he could, he slowly got to his feet. The hunger inside him was even stronger now and he knew he had to keep feeding. All the food he had just consumed had not satisfied him in the least, but he did not have the mental reasoning to know this. He was driven by mindless desires to fill the void at all costs so he made his was out through the building looking for food. The place was looking like an abattoir but he did not notice. The infected had turned on anyone who was too slow to flee or too weak to fight, and these had been the first casualties. Others had ran for their cars, and tried to get home or get to loved ones before the end of the world happened. He made his way to the street outside and his uncomprehending eyes watched a civilisation in collapse. People ran everywhere, being pursued by zombies. Two women saw him standing there covered in blood, screamed and ran away as fast as they could. On the road in front of him a car smashed into another and came to a smoking stop. Inside the two passengers had turned into zombies and they were attacking the injured driver and eating his flesh from his living body. He struggled and tried to escape, but they dragged him back inside the vehicle. He did not last much longer.

Steven saw a man stagger from the second car, bleeding from a head wound and too dazed to notice the zombies closing in on him from all directions. The injured man could not see Steven as he stalked over towards him with evil intent. The first thing the man knew was that he was being grabbed at and then bitten. He cried out in pain, and struck out in all directions, but he was hauled to the ground, overpowered by their weight of numbers, and their sheer wanton determination. Steven was physically full from his meal at his workplace but the hunger to feed the void made him want to go on gorging. When he could eat no more the food stayed in his mouth as he could not swallow it and other zombies fell on his victim and tore at the remains. Then Steven got up and wandered slowly without a destination through the city of the dead.

6 GHOST HAND

Professor Larry Irvine looked at his colleague Doctor James McCullough and shook his hand warmly;

I think we've done it James!" he enthused, "And judging by the chaos and turmoil in the world right now, not a moment too soon!"

The scientists were in the lab at the headquarters of Eclipse Enterprises. The place was a sprawling complex, heavily fortified with high walls and crawling with armed guards. The walls were originally there to keep corporate spies, thieves and other undesirables out, but they worked well for zombies too. They both stood back to admire their creation as it lay on the laboratory table in front of them. It was an electromagnetic pulse gun, designed to kill nanobots. As Billy Magee had wanted, they had christened it the 'Ghost Hand'. They did not know where he had gotten that name but he was fond of naming his creations with names only he knew the meaning of, and they assumed this was also the case with the Ghost Hand. When the solar storm had hit and people had started becoming zombies, the science team had redoubled their efforts and had worked day and night to produce the gun. It had performed marvellously in all their lab tests, killing nanobots they had stored from vaccine samples purchased from Hodson's original supplier. They had even added in a visible red beam to the device, to allow the user to get a better aim, and to know that the device was functioning properly. Now it was time to show the Boss. Irvine called him on the internal phone;

"Hello Mr Magee, we have the device ready for your inspection. Do you want to come down to the lab to have a look?"

"Well done Professor, but I'm down in basement level two. Why don't you bring the device down here, we have to do the ultimate test where I am."

"Ah, what do you mean, 'Ultimate test' Sir?"

"Success in the laboratory is one thing, we have to make sure that this thing actually works out in the real world, where the zombies are. Sometimes the real world is the best testing ground there is. Just get yourself down here and you will see what I mean."

Irvine looked worriedly at McCullough, who shrugged his shoulders in a resigned manner. They both knew they worked for an unscrupulous man who was willing to push the boundaries where others might hesitate, and they knew he was up to something, but they were in this venture and now had to go the whole way, wherever it might lead. With a little consternation they headed for the stairs.

Arriving in basement level two, they were somewhat surprised to see so many armed men there; Magee had beefed up security in the last few days, hiring all sorts of mercenaries to deal with the unexpected issues. These were mainly ex-forces types from a number of different countries, hired through Magee's numerous contacts in the world of arms dealing. These rough men stared at the scientists, with looks ranging from mild curiosity to barely concealed disdain. They usually solved their problems with a lot of explosions and gunfire, and instinctively distrusted anyone who did not do likewise. Magee came out of a restricted area to meet them.

"Well done gentlemen, well done!" he said, eyeing the device. "Now it is time for what we call the 'acid test'. If I am to sell the Ghost Hand to our customers, I must be able to verify its capability, otherwise it's just a toy gun with a light attached to it. Come forward gentlemen and I will show you............."

They followed him back into the restricted area and gasped at what they saw: there was a metal cage in there, and in the cage was a snarling zombie. It was a male, about twenty five years of age with a heavy build. It was dressed in a workman's high visibility coveralls, which now struck some of the witnesses as somewhat tragically ironic. It bared its teeth at the scientists and glared at them through bloodshot eyes maddened by the presence and its inability to get at them. It took them several seconds to regain their composure. Magee was watching them;

"This is what I was talking about gentlemen. Some of my men here, I call them the 'Ghost Team', went out on a capture mission and caught a bunch of these things that were clustered at the front gates like a bunch of zoo animals waiting for the zookeeper to throw them chunks of meat. We keep them down here, where we will study how effective our invention really is. If it works then we have less zombies and I imagine they'll be happy that we saved them. Clever don't you think?"

Conceding that he had a scientific point they both nodded. This was not the time for a debate on his dubious ethics. Then Magee turned to some of his men and ordered them to start filming proceedings from several different angles, with cameras that they had positioned strategically around the room.

"Ok Professor, the moment of truth is here, let's see what this thing can do!"

Irvine stepped forward, raised the pulse-gun and pointed it at the body of the zombie. He pulled the trigger and fired a three second cycle, the length of time the tests showed it required to work. The zombie glared and snarled away at them but after several moments nothing seemed to change. Everyone looked disappointed.

"Try aiming at the head" suggested McCullough "I have a theory that all the nanobots migrate to various critical areas in the brain, and remain there. We still don't understand why, but it may be their primitive way of trying to control the host organism."

Irvine tried again, this time aiming at the zombie's head.

They watched with bated breath and waited. Suddenly the zombie jolted slightly as if it had been given a mild electric shock. It looked confused and started blinking its eyes. Then it raised its hands to its head and started moaning softly. It looked like it was trying to speak. Then it lay down on the floor and looked like it was going to sleep.

"It works, it really works!" exclaimed Magee. "As long as you aim at the head that thing actually works! We're going to make a fortune off this thing! Now we have to make sure this fine fellow doesn't see us as dinner anymore. How long do you think we have to wait? Keep your guns ready men, in case this goes wrong.........."

They waited several minutes until it seemed nothing else dramatic was going to happen, then Magee ordered one of the men to step forward and open the door of the cage. His men aimed their guns at the creature lying there, but it did not stir. One of the mercenaries gingerly stepped into the cage. He was wearing body armour from head to toe, but he was still nervous, and wondering if the pay was still worth it. He ventured cautiously forward as everybody watched with bated breath. The man poked the creature with his rifle. Its eyes opened and it began to get up. The man jumped back, almost falling over in his haste to get away, but the creature just looked at him in a dazed manner. It slowly looked around. Then it simply said "Help me" in a slurred voice.

"Oh my God, it's coming back to normal!" McCullough gasped.

"Professor, what is happening now?" asked Magee excitedly.

"If the nanobots have been successfully killed, then the brain will slowly begin to regain its senses, almost like recovering from a brain injury or disease. Since this is our first candidate, I have no idea how long this will take, and it will no doubt vary from person to person. However right now I think we can say that this guy is regaining some of his humanity and is no longer a zombie. This is history in the making!"

"Study this one, and check to see if there are refinements that can be made to the Ghost Hand. Also feel free to experiment with the others we caught – there's no shortage of them. Restoring them is a service we will offer them free of charge, in exchange for their participation in all of this." Magee pointed to a cluster of stunned-looking people who had been observing from a short distance away.

"This is a team of medical experts assembled from around the world. They all have experience working with brain diseases and various neurological aberrations. I want you to work closely with them to see what it takes to nurse this one back to full health, if that is even possible. I have to speak with some people now that the phones are up and running again but I want to be updated on every single thing that happens, as it happens from now on."

With that he turned and strode away.

****

Scott advanced slowly through the woods, looking carefully around for signs of trouble. Without the usual rumble of traffic present he noted how easy it was to hear the slightest sound. Doug was in position next, his rifle at the ready. Then came Brad with his bow, an arrow ready in his hand. Tom took up the rear with the dogs, having warned them to keep quiet. He hoped they had understood. He held his axe at the ready, and pondered briefly the merriment with which he had first seized hold of it, what strangely seemed like an eternity ago.

A scraping sound up ahead caused them to freeze, and then they all dropped into a crouch, moving as one. Up ahead a short distance a zombie limped its way through the bushes, perhaps following some dimly held memory of its previous existence. It slowly turned its head towards them and sniffed the air. Then it paused, and turned straight to meet them. They hesitated; a shot from a gun would surely alert the attention of every zombie for miles, and still it was coming. Now it saw them and, with a growl it lurched straight for Scott. He was about to pull the trigger when an arrow came from behind him and ripped straight through its heart. It cried out in pain and made a futile attempt to pull the arrow from its chest only causing further damage, staggered a few feet, and then fell a mere foot from Scott. Brad had stood up at the last moment and quietly dispatched it from this life.

There didn't seem to be any more close by so the friends looked at it for a moment. It had been a man in his fifties. He had already taken a bullet to the right thigh sometime previously, hence the limping, another sign that there had been a battle in the village. His skin was a distinctive grey pallor, a clear way to identify zombies, but even more accentuated in this one because of blood loss from the bullet wound. The friends pondered how he had known they were hiding in the woods, perhaps the zombification process had given him a better sense of smell or hearing, or some other heightened sense?

"At least he's out of his misery, good shot Brad" said Doug approvingly. He studied the body carefully and, to the disquiet of the others, he did a quick physical examination, which included touching the extremities with his bare hands. He looked up at them and grinned at their disgust; "I used to be a Paramedic, remember, I've handled worse than this. I'm used to touching bodies" he said. "I find it interesting that his body is still warm all over. That means that he was still alive up to now, at least alive in some physical sense, and that his circulation was still functioning. Whatever makes them zombies seems to be mainly a condition of the brain rather than anything else. Some form of collective madness."

"That was a nice one Brad, you're handy with your bow. That could have caused us a whole lot of problems if we'd had to shoot the thing. Now let's get going again" said Scott.

They moved off slowly and even more cautiously than before, now that they were closer to the village. Scott saw a low wall and motioned them over to it. From there they took stock of their surroundings. The village consisted of a main street, where most of the stores were. It had the river on one side of it, and the residential area on the other side. Numerous vehicles littered the main street which was facing them. Some of the vehicles were crashed, some abandoned. There were bodies around too, zombies. They didn't seem to crave the flesh of their own dead for some reason, only the healthy people. Perhaps that would change as they ran out of prey, no-one knew. There was the gruesome sight of human bones scattered all over the place, as well as spent shell casings everywhere. When the villagers had overcome their initial shock at being attacked, they must have put up a desperate fight against their own friends and neighbours. That must have been a terrible experience for them.

There were about twelve zombies wandering about among the wreckage, the closest being about fifty yards away. Some of them bore the marks of the recent battle, various kinds of injuries, but they were still highly dangerous. The friends saw a grocery store only fifty yards away from their own location. Then they spotted a sign for sporting goods right down at the very end of the street, about three hundred and fifty yards away. As they watched the closest zombie move slowly away Tom had an idea;

"Just had what I think is a good idea folks. Some of those crashed pick-up trucks have only minor damage to them. I'm guessing that they still have the keys still in the ignition because they've just been left on the road rather than been parked up. All we have to do is to go down there and collect them!"

"That's smart thinking!" exclaimed Doug. "How about we sneak in the back of the grocery store, get supplies, then run to those two trucks over there by the water-front. Hopefully they have a lot of fuel on board, especially that blue one with the spare tank in the back, and then we make a run for the gun store. By then we will probably have attracted every zombie in the place, but I figure we only need a few minutes to grab a few guns and ammo and basically shoot our way out of there."

"Great plan!" said Scott excitedly. "I think that could work. Once we get moving in the trucks there's no point in sneaking about anymore, every zombie in town will know there's food on the move. We'll just blast our way through if it comes down to it. Let's go guys."

They crept along the low wall until they reached the end of it, still keeping out of sight. It only needed one zombie to glance up and spot them to wreak their plans, and they were too close to success to screw things up now. Then, after a last quick check that the coast was clear, they sprinted the fifty or so yards to the side of the grocery store. Then they slipped around the back. There were a couple of zombies further down the alley faced away from them, and they didn't see the four friends as they carefully crept in through an unlocked back door. Now they found themselves in the storeroom and had a look around. A bloodied supermarket uniform and scattered bones lay about. One of the store employees had provided a meal for ravenous zombies, possibly even their former colleagues turning on them. Whoever it had been, their shift had ended in a way they could hardly have expected when they clocked in that morning. The friends fanned out and did a quick check of the whole premises. Apart from more scattered human remains, all was quiet. Taking a shopping cart each they assigned a quarter of the store to everyone and then, rushing up and down the aisles as quickly and quietly as they could, took everything they thought they would need for hiding out in the woods. Canned goods, dried foods, utensils, clothes, what rudimentary medical supplies were there, more camping gear, tools, dog food, and miscellaneous other things. Then, when they had all they could carry, they went quietly to the front door to assess the situation.

Peering out they could see the zombies were still clustered down the other end of Main Street, and wondered what was keeping them there. Just then without warning a female zombie lurched in through the front doors and charged at Brad, baring her teeth with a growl. Brad recoiled backwards in surprise, trying to fend her off. Thinking fast Doug came round the side of her, and smashed in her head with a skillet frying pan he had picked up in house wares. She fell to the floor with a yelp, twitched a few times and then lay still, blood streaming from a huge wound in her skull, which had been bashed in by the heavy pan. Hearts racing, they looked in horror at the sight. Luckily there did not seem to be anymore zombies around. This one must have made her way up the street for some reason and had wandered in alone.

"I just killed someone's mother" Doug said sadly. "I wonder what led her in here, perhaps some vague memory of doing the family shopping?"

"Or what was once someone's mother" remarked Brad. "Who knows what brought her in here but thanks for the timely intervention."

"I'll have to get another pan, I suddenly don't like this one anymore" said Doug and he quickly hurried off, leaving them to contemplate the body in silence.

When he returned again, they scanned the street, decided who would go for which pick-up truck and prepared to run for it. Just then they heard a gunshot from not far away, followed by two in quick succession.

Scott turned to look at the others; "Crap!.......gunshots. Ok that changes everything."

"Those shots came from the end of the street, where the gun store is, no wonder the zombies are clustered there, there must be people in there and the zombies know it!" Tom exclaimed.

Realising that there was someone in trouble Scott came up with a quick plan; "Let's try and help them. We'll leave the stuff here and make our way down the alley at the back. We'll deal with whatever zombies we find there, then try and make contact with whoever is in the gun store. It's probably better not to go down Main Street cos there's more zombies and we don't want to get caught in the crossfire. We can worry about the stuff when we get back. Right now we're dealing with things as they happen so everyone just use your good judgement for whatever awaits."

They headed for the alley at a brisk pace and made for the gun store. Half way down they were met by the same two zombies they saw before. On seeing the men approach the zombies immediately tried to charge them. This time Scott and Doug simply shot them, as there was no need for quiet now. In fact they were hoping that the occupants of the store would hear them, preferably before the rest of the zombies decided to investigate. Then whoever was in there would know that there were more normal people outside. Running now, they arrived at the back door of the gun store. Unsurprisingly it was locked. There were no back windows so Tom pounded on the back door, and shouted out a greeting so that those inside would recognise that it was not just more zombies. They heard the sounds of bars and locks being undone, and after what seemed like an age the door opened to reveal a man in his seventies looking at them from behind a semi-automatic 30.06 rifle.

"Come in quick" he urged, then shot a zombie that had come around the corner drooling like a bloodhound and which tried to launch itself at them.

They hurried inside and he locked and barricaded the door. Without waiting for introductions he ran to the front as more shots rang out there. Following him, they observed a woman of similar age firing an under lever 30.30 rifle out through a crack in the front window. The man went to her assistance and were joined by Scott and Doug, as Brad and Tom went to the gun section to acquire firearms. Choosing a pump action shotgun each and grabbing all the boxes of shells they could carry they went to go to the front but there were no more positions from which to fire. Instead they had to run upstairs and commence firing from there. With six people laying down a barrage of lead there were zombies getting cut down everywhere. Eventually the zombies were beaten off and the elderly couple turned to look at their unexpected guests;

“Those were our friends and neighbours we just shot, I hope we will meet in the next life to forgive each other for this iniquity” the man said, with a deep sorrow. “I’m Josh Lawrence and this is my wife Ann. We own this store.”

The friends introduced themselves and gave a brief account of how they got there.

“Thanks for letting us in “ said Scott, “We would have been in a tight spot if you hadn’t”.

“No thank you for coming to help us, it’s like the devil is abroad in the world” said Ann. “It’s a terrible thing to have to shoot people you have known and loved for seventy odd years.”

“Can you tell us what the hell is going on, and how widespread is this madness?” Tom enquired.

“It started a couple of days ago” said Josh. “They think it had something to do with that solar storm. At least that’s what they said until the TV stopped working. Suddenly ordinary folks turned into them creatures, and started eating everyone around them. Some of the normal people fled, some fought, and some.........well you've seen what happens to the ones who get caught. Fortunately this place is built like a fortress, and we bunkered down here. We did not have time to flee, but we have regretted that deeply ever since. The zombies know we're here, and every now and then they try to storm the place. They haven't succeeded but we would like to get out of here because we don't know what's going to happen next. They say this plague is going on all over the world."

The friends looked at each other with utmost alarm as this information sunk in.

"Something like this could end civilisation as we know it if we're talking about a global pandemic. Humanity could be facing a mass extinction event. How many people turned into zombies, and do they know caused it" Doug asked.

Now Ann spoke again; "We still can get some information from the radio, roughly half the population of this country turned into the devil's army overnight. It's different in other places. There were rumors that it was the ones who took that infernal cold vaccination recently who turned into the creatures. We didn't bother with the vaccine ourselves because we were abroad on holidays, and never got a chance to when we returned."

A mixture of relief and horror went through them.

"That means our families weren't turned into the things!" Brad exclaimed. "We warned them about those nanobots. Oh my God, how fortunate was that, and at the last minute too!"

"That theory makes sense" said Doug, "In fact I should have thought of that. It means the numbers affected will vary wildly from place to place around the world, as some places didn't do a major roll-out of the vaccination like we did. This will have major geopolitical implications for years to come, and may even alter the global power-balance as we know it. Where that might lead is anyone's guess and it may not be a good thing from our point of view."

"What are your plans" asked Scott. "You said you wanted out of here? Do you have a destination in mind? We are more than willing to help you escape this place."

"We have a son and his family at a farmhouse miles out in the country and south-west from here, we want to go there until all his business is over" Ann replied. "Are you heading in that general direction?"

"That sounds a bit like our plan" said Scott, except we need to collect some medicine for some of our family members first. You can come with us when we go. We were down at the grocery store where we filled some shopping carts. Our plan was to run for some trucks that are left unattended on Main Street and make for the city. We should go back there now and you can get what you need. We will be heading south on the same road as you then and can be with you for much of the way."

"We leave the highway after fifty miles to take us to our destination. I do not envy you if you plan on going into the city, I can only imagine what kind of madhouse that place is" said Josh with a shudder. Take what guns and ammunition you need from here with our blessing. You will need them."

"Perfect" said Tom. "Now allow us to help you carry your belongings to your vehicle."

They took as many weapons as they could carry as well as ammunition and other kit and went out the back. Josh had a truck out there and they all piled in. There were no zombies around, but they did not delay in case more were on their way, attracted by the recent gunfire and the sound of the truck's engine.

They got back in the grocery store unhindered and once there they helped Josh and Ann fill shopping carts with goods, and then headed for the front again.

"Well this is take two" said Brad peering outside. "It looks clear. Let's go!"

They went as quickly as they could for two trucks that were in close proximity, pushing their carts before them. First they checked the vehicles for keys. The first one didn't have any keys in it, but the next two did, including the one with the spare fuel tank. Next they checked for the fuel levels. Luckily both trucks were nearly full; enough to get to their destinations. They loaded their goods in as fast as they could, just as more zombies arrived, attracted by the noise. Now all six of them opened fire, with volleys of lead, and dispatched the zombies before they could even get close. Then they took off out of there. Scott and Doug were in the lead vehicle, followed by Josh and Ann who were now both crying. They had just helped to shoot more friends of theirs, their only consolation being that they were now out of their misery. Tom and Brad took up the rear and they headed out. The friends felt deeply sorry for the elderly couple who had had to bear a terrible ordeal which was not of their own making. However, they had gotten away from that place and all in all they considered themselves fairly well prepared for what might lie ahead, but they had a long road to go yet.

7 LOOKING FOR A CURE

The zombie was hungry. He moved slowly and jerkily along a scene reminiscent of a warzone. It had several companions who loosely formed a hunting pack, bound by some primitive instinct that realised they had a better chance of finding and overpowering prey if they kept together. Their thoughts were not their old thoughts when they had been normal people. Now a fog had descended on their minds obscuring their old mental patterns about work and family and weekend shopping. All that remained was a desire to feed on human flesh, a desire that had initially been met with a plentiful supply in the first few chaotic days of the apocalypse. The zombification process had heightened their senses of smell and hearing, giving them the enhanced hunting abilities of a predatory animal. They could smell human flesh a mile away. Most humans had been easy prey as long as they were out in the open. Most people were not very fit and could not run very far, or fight for more than a few seconds, even when facing death. An adult zombie could eventually overpower most normal people, unless they were armed. When the electricity went off the stores closed, then the gas pumps stopped working. People started stealing from each other sometimes killing each other in the process. Gangs of looters were prowling from house to house in search of food and anything valuable. Sometimes they got killed by home defenders, sometimes the home defenders got killed. The zombies ate the dead. They weren't fussy when they got really hungry, and there was no availability of their preferred fresh meat. In fact they would readily eat someone who had been dead for days...........

Lately food had been getting scarcer. When the old, the sick the weak and the plain unlucky had been devoured, that left the strong clever ones and the strong clever ones all tended to have weapons and guns with which to fight back. The zombies began to cluster into groups, relying on sheer numbers to overwhelm their victims. They began to hunt more often at night, because that was when the prey were more likely to sleep, sniffing them out where they were holed up and breaking in to cause carnage. Some got really hungry and then they began to eat the other zombies who had been killed. After a while the rest followed suit. It was not their first choice of food, but it would have to do for the moment.

Suddenly the zombie stopped and sniffed the air; he had caught the delicious sent of human meat in the vicinity. He turned his head in an effort to locate the source. His senses told him roughly how many and that they were moving straight towards him. He uttered a low growl that caused the others to turn to him, recognising the signal that prey had been scented. They saw the direction he was facing and realised where the prey was. Soon they too could detect it. Initially zombies had simply charged straight at their prey when they found it, but retaining the basic ability to learn, recently some had adapted to become more like ambush predators. All the better for dealing with food that carried guns. The zombie moved in behind a still-smoldering truck and waited for the food to come to it. The rest of the pack took their cue and likewise found vehicles or scattered debris to conceal themselves behind. The tactic they were using had worked before, they would wait until the prey walked right into the middle of them, and then launch themselves at the food simultaneously, replying on surprise and force of numbers.

John Hodson crept along the alley clutching his rifle nervously. As the only one who knew the way to Howal's laboratory he found himself leading the group. He had never seen the city in complete darkness before, and combined with the carnage of the Armageddon, it all looked strangely alien to him. He had to keep reminding himself that he knew where he was. Blaine Maxwell followed behind, with Belinda Porter next to him. Trailing behind was their new acquaintance Eddie Young who was still uncertain if he was their friend or foe. They made their way through the urban wasteland moving quietly and without speaking. This wasteland had new rules and everything about it that assailed their senses was new and different and appalling. In the dim light they could see that the slippery things they sometimes stood on were human remains. Fires flickered here and there from burnt out buildings and cars, throwing shadows about that kept them guessing where the next zombie was going to spring from. The smells of rotting flesh and burning property filled their nostrils in a stomach-churning mixture. The normal sounds of their world had been replaced by the sounds of a strange and dangerous world of destruction. They were walking among the ruins of mankind. Whether this would be rebuilt depended a lot on them and what the next few days would bring. If they failed to reach Howal and find a cure, then all could be lost………….

Hodson was getting that uneasy feeling again; he quickly scanned the shadows. Was that something moving over there? No, it was a flickering shadow. What was that noise behind that fence? Just a can, blown by the wind. He felt vulnerable and exposed, like a man who knows there's a sniper watching him and he's got no place to take cover. The tension was beginning to get to him. He turned to speak to Maxwell just as they passed a group of abandoned vehicles:

"We can't get there quickly enough. My nerves are shatt......................"

Then the zombies struck. Leaping from the shadows in all directions, the group was caught off guard and disoriented. Screams of surprise and fear filled the rancid air. Shots rang out. A couple of zombies fell and one stumbled straight into Hodson. His shot had been too low, only catching the zombie in the leg, not enough to stop it. It grabbed his gun and began to wrestle it away from him. With a strength not present in a normal human it soon over-powered him and snatched it away. Frantically he stepped away and fumbled for the shotgun he had as a backup. Where the hell was the safety catch on this thing? Now there were two of the things on him, snapping at his face like wolves. He finally got the safety off and aimed. He shot the nearest one, missed the second and then had to use the gun like a club, lashing out wildly in every direction. He saw three of them on Maxwell, dragging him to the ground. He began to scream in agony as he took multiple bite wounds. Eddie Young shot a couple of them but more were now coming, attracted by the noise and the smell of humans. Porter had emptied her rifle into the lead zombie but in her panic and fear she was taking too long to reload. Seizing their chance the zombies closed in around her. Now there were too many on her as well, and she was taken to the ground too. She would never regain her feet. It was a blessing for her that she had fainted.

Young dropped the empty clip from the pistol and quickly rammed a full one home. Glancing about he saw a fresh wave of zombies approach. He looked at Hodson; "Run like hell, it's our only hope!" Then he put a bullet into Porter and the still screaming Maxwell to spare them any further pain, an act of mercy in the circumstances.

Hodson looked grimly at their fallen friends. Young was right, they would not win this battle, running now was the only option. They bolted down the street, leaving their friends where they lay, the main course for the zombie supper. Hodson reloaded as he went, and got off a couple of defiant parting shots at the pursuing zombies. He was glad their friends had no more worries in this life but there was a bitter pain in his heart. He was also awfully aware that he was gasping painfully for breath and still not getting enough oxygen to power his exhausted body. His energy was almost spent and he felt like he could not go on. He looked at Young;

"I can't.............I can't.........." he gasped.

"No you have to, you still have work to do, to fix this. You owe us!" Young shouted angrily at him.

Glancing behind he saw that they were still being followed. Desperately he looked around searching for options. There was a small blue car just up ahead, crashed into a wall. It wasn't too badly damaged and he quickly calculated that it was still drivable. It had better be.......

"C'mon!" he shouted urgently, pointing at the vehicle. Hodson had dropped the shotgun, barely able now to even walk. He had been a bit of an athlete in his younger days, and had even run a few marathons, but after years in the lab combined with the ravages of time he had gone to seed and looking at his flushed face, Young thought he might lose him. Young turned and fired at the two zombies who had nearly caught them, and then downed a third that came at them from the side. He didn't have many more bullets and realised that he would have to save the last two, if the worst happened. They were at the car now.

"Get in, get in!" he shouted. "Lock the damn doors!"

Mercifully the keys were still in the ignition, left by the previous owner. Unfortunately bits of what was left of the previous owner were still there as well. After the crash he had sustained a head wound and before he could recover his senses he had been rushed by a group of zombies, who had left quite a mess behind them. Throwing some bones into the back in disgust, Young turned the key as the zombies reached the car. They beat on the doors and windows as the engine turned and failed to start. Swearing, he tried again. This time it started, the sweetest sound they had ever heard. He threw it into reverse, knocking the zombies who failed to dodge them in time. Then he floored it and roared away down the street, the front bumper scraping on the ground as they went. Hodson was still gasping and wondering if he was going to have a heart attack, but his analytical abilities were returning to him. They were both aware that as soon as they had enough distance between them and their zombie attackers they would have to ditch the car or risk attracting more, and leading them straight to Howal.

"Down that street……" he panted the directions. Wearily he looked around him. He had to be certain of his bearings. Now he had no weapon and he knew he did not have the strength left to fight. If things went wrong at this point he was toast.

"Now turn here, and into here…………."

He scanned quickly, there were no zombies to be seen. He figured they were as close to the laboratory as he dared bring the car although he could have used a little more time to rest.. He signalled Young to pull in and he brought the car to a scraping halt. Hodson's breath had recovered slightly and he knew he had to give it one last push.

"Let's go, the lab is in that building over there!" He was pointing to a red brick building in between what looked like two office blocks. It had bars on the windows and video cameras on the outside. In times past when people still made things it must have been a small factory or a workshop of some kind, and it showed no outward signs of what was within. Howal was very secretive and discreet about his work and did nothing to draw attention to himself. Praying that no zombies were planning another ambush and praying that their sense of smell would not enable them to discover the laboratory Hodson and Young ran for it as best they could. As they arrived at the front door, it opened and Howal gestured urgently for them to enter. He had been waiting anxiously and had seen them approach with his security cameras. As they ran inside he closed the heavy door behind them and used several bars to secure it.

"Thank God for video cameras" he said. "Am I to assume that Porter and Maxwell didn't make it?"

Hodson nodded wearily. He was panting again and wondering how he had gotten so unfit.

"That's unfortunate. They were excellent scientists and good people. We will miss them both as friends and colleagues. We cannot afford to lose such great talent."

"Yes it's a big setback" Hodson rasped. He didn't want to dwell too much on recent memories. "This is Eddie Young. We met him at that house we were hiding in. He was bitten by a zombie several hours ago, and has experienced no discernable side-effects. I figure that he will be carrying the rogue nanobots in his system, which we can study to help us to find an antidote."

Howal was fascinated; "Yes I heard on the radio that bites

from zombies do not one a zombie make, numerous people have been bitten and have lived to tell the tale. This is an unexpected boost to our efforts. Come, let me show you around, and update you on where I'm at in finding a cure. Can I get anyone a coffee, a glass of water?"

Gratefully, and still breathing hard, they followed him down the hallway. Young checked his gun to put the safety catch back on as they went. He found that he had miscounted his bullets; he had only one left.............

****

Billy Magee hurried into his office and shut the door. A man was seated with his back to him. As Magee entered the man rose, turned, and shook his hand.

"Welcome to our research facility Senator" Magee said. Can I get you a drink? Your arrival is timely as we have something to celebrate."

"Sure I'll have a whiskey, what's the big occasion?" asked Senator Anton Carmody. He looked like a man who had not slept in some time. "It will be a pleasant surprise to hear good news at last. We are struggling to maintain control of the nation. It was only by an act of God that most of us and our like-minded friends were overseas at a conference and never got the chance to infest ourselves with those dreadful nanobots. If we had been infected then the nation would no longer exist."

"Then you will be delighted to hear that our scientists have finally created a working device that can reverse the effects of the nanobots! It's an electromagnetic pulse gun. We call it the Ghost

Hand."

"No way........ already!" the Senator exclaimed. "This is indeed good news, you've excelled yourself this time, my friend! You mean you can take a zombie and make it not a zombie?"

"We caught a live one and used the device on it. Within minutes it had lost its desire to gorge on our flesh, and it regained the rest of its human faculties within a relatively short time. Right now it's below in basement number one, under close observation by our medical team. Their last update is that he continues to improve steadily, although, as you can imagine, it will take days or weeks for the full effects of zombification to wear off. Here, let me show you the video documentary.........."

A short time later the astonished Senator asked for another drink. Magee then answered questions about how the device worked.

"With this device we can get our country back and restore family, friends and compatriots. What you have achieved here will never be forgotten. You do realise also Billy, that we can name our price from foreign governments for this technology? I'm not only talking about money, but we can lay out our terms on any number of issues, and they will have no choice but to comply? This thing can make zombies into useful people again, rather than having to kill them. This is huge, it's the game-changer that we have been waiting for."

"Yes, I know that the Ghost Hand changes everything. Those who were lost will be found again. No government can deny us and be seen to neglect their citizens, speaking of which, what are your plans domestically?

Carmody paused, wondering how much he should divulge to Magee. Eventually he decided that now was as good a time as any to lay it all out there, Magee was a like-minded individual. It was time to recruit him to the cause.

"During the last few years there have been a lot of people unhappy with the way they see the world heading Billy. I'm one of them, and correct me if I'm wrong but I believe you are too. All we've seen in recent years is a population explosion, mainly among people who have no useful contribution to make to society. No civilisation can afford to carry that many non-contributors and survive. In fact no society has. Do you think we're just going to use the Ghost Hand willy nilly, fixing every Tom, Dick and Harry we can find? No, of course not, that doesn't make any sense. We will only use it on people who have something to offer society. We have a civilisation to rebuild. We need people who can help us to do that, not people who will be a burden on the rest of us. The days of carrying the feckless are over. Any of these slackers who didn't become zombies had better learn fast to help out and pay their way will find themselves out in the cold very quickly.

There's a new order coming Billy, headed by people like myself. We have realised the flaws in democracy – everything grinds to a halt with over-regulation, idiotic policy, and pointless rules. It was taking too long to decide what course of action to take in any particular circumstances, and too long to then implement anything. The dead hand of bureaucracy had all but strangled the ability of western governments to operate efficiently, that's why we were falling down the ranks and others are poised to take over. We are people who see that democracy has had its day, it can no longer meet the needs of a fast-moving, dynamic world, where fast thinking and fast action gets the job done. Look at the way our national government worked up to now, taking years to get a piece of legislation out, and then, if something doesn't work right, it takes further years to correct it. By then the damage is often done, and we wind up looking like hapless idiots, just there for our expenses claims. It's time for a new paradigm, where we invest in helping people to be productive, not vast armies of welfare-dependents, who would bankrupt us in the end.

I belong to a group of people who have assumed control of the government Billy. We are looking to place power in the hands of clever people, who will rely on common sense and personal judgement to get things done efficiency. People who can come up with solutions to problems quickly, or immediately if necessary, without having to resort to years of squabbling and endless debates. The procrastinators and the ditherers had been leading us to oblivion and they have had their day. We are now entering the age of decisive leadership. This means that the system itself has to change and power has to be transferred to those who are fit to wield it."

Magee looked intrigued; "What about the President, where does he stand in all this? He's not going to just step aside and allow his authority to be usurped. Neither will the rest of them. They won't give up their power voluntarily, they would have to be forced out. We can help with that housekeeping if you like."

Carmody looked him right in the eye; "There is no President Billy. Last week the President became a zombie and ate part of the Vice President before he was shot in the back of the head by one of his own bodyguards. The Vice President sadly didn't survive being dined upon in such a manner. He bled too much and with the hospitals shut down, there was nowhere to take him. They were both buried secretly with full honours. Most of the legislature have suffered a similar fate. After years of arguing and back-stabbing each other they finally started to eat each other. The few who remain have seen the writing on the wall, and jumped to support our cause. They will have minor roles in the new administration. They will help to legitimise us but will be assigned functions where they can't do any harm. We didn't release the information to the general public as we decided it would make a bad situation worse. Inept and all as those politicians were, the general populace feel better if they think there's somebody who's in charge of running things, the way sheep feel reassured by the presence of a Shepard. It gives them a sense of stability. The President was an impediment anyway, he didn't see the reality as we see it. He was incapable of making a decision on the simplest thing without endlessly going through every conceivable option he could think of. Procrastination like that will cost you your freedom in these times. The way it's going to work from now on is that the country will be run by a supreme council of, say about twelve people, each of whom will have an area of responsibility. That is a flexible number though, we can add or remove people as we need them, provided that they have the right stuff, and they will all work in co-operation with each other, no more bickering and fighting each other while the country suffers. Each of these council members will have staff and advisors, who will assist them to get things done. Then each city and other areas can have their own council, who will run things on a smaller level, you get the idea. People, once selected for councils will remain there as long as they like, unless they prove grossly incompetent. What do you think?"

Magee was impressed; "I love it, every word of what you say is the way I've been thinking for years. We need strong leadership who gets things done in a reasonable manner and doesn't pussyfoot around. It will no doubt turn out to be a blessing that so many of our political opponents were turned into zombies while so many of our friends were spared. I would recommend that we refrain from using the Ghost Hand to restore those who would be hostile to our political philosophy, although I'm sure you don't need any advice in that regard."

Both men laughed.

"Something I would advise as well is strict individual punishment for criminals and deviants who break the law, not collective punishment for most people, while at the same time soft-on-criminals approach so beloved of the last government."

"I knew we could count on you" Carmody said, pleased. "In time you may be selected for a council yourself, I like your idea of punishing offenders rather than spreading the misery on people who have done nothing wrong, but now we have other matters to discuss. We need your expertise for other pressing issues."

He paused, and took another sip of whiskey; "I want you to start a new project Billy. Now that nanobots are here they will always be a fact of life. We have seen what these things can do and we want to be in control of that. We want Eclipse Enterprises to start researching ways to create more of these things, with other attributes. Say, for example, ones that could be used to make better soldiers, or more efficient workers, or even ones we could use en masse to incapacitate our enemies. Fixing zombies is one thing, but the next step is being to create them at will. Warfare is about to evolve into a completely new direction, and it is critical that we are ahead of the opposition. The wars of the future will be won by those who have the smallest machines, not by those with the largest, the same way that a virus can take down an elephant. We know our enemies are looking into research of this kind as well, but we must not allow anyone else to take the lead here. Do you think you can check out the possibilities?"

Magee was thoughtful; "There's no reason why we can't do that kind of work. In fact I'm happy to say that we have already been working on several different possible weapons applications for nanobots. We already have numerous samples of the Iasobots, as well as the rogue nanobots we have been taking out of zombies, to see how they work. It should be easy enough to replicate the process and then refine it to our specific requirements. There is a slight problem that has come to my attention recently, through my spies."

"What is this problem?"

"I have a man who does communications hacking for me. For years he's been an extra set of eyes and ears. Recently he had a phone call alert which automatically recorded a phone conversation between two men. The alert was activated by the use of certain words and phrases. Those two men were John Hodson and Alan Howal, they were plotting to get together to search for an antidote to the rogue Iasobots. Assuming that they have managed to team up, they are both probably working on the solution even as we speak. They have lost most of their team, and have limited resources, but with such brilliant scientists involved there is no reason to believe that they won't come up with some kind of cure themselves. Howal had already been working on something when this disaster struck. Obviously we cannot allow that to happen, as Hodson is racked with guilt and wants to undo some of the damage he sees himself as being responsible for. If they come up with some kind of cure they will distribute it as widely as they can, and probably for free. That would be disastrous for our operation, and our plans for the future. We would no longer be the only game in town."

"Where are they now?"

"The arrangement was to meet at Howal's laboratory. It's an old factory of some kind in the suburbs, he thinks no-one else knows about it but we've been keeping an eye on it for a while now. We spy on all his emails. The call was traced to the exact location."

"We could use these people, do you think we could recruit them to our cause?"

Magee mused for a bit; "Ummm hard to say. I have toyed

with the idea before but I can't make any guarantees. We did try to recruit Howal once previously, that time when he left Hodson's operation, but he's somewhat of a maverick, and wasn't interested. Would he now? I don't think so, a bit too ethical, wants to plough his own furrow, and I already told you about Hodson and his guilt complex, so somehow I doubt it. Sometimes we have difficulty in recruiting people who don't share our pragmatic view of the world, it can be quite frustrating at times, but we're up against years of cultural brain-washing by the traitors who, until recently, we nurtured in our own bosom. It can take time for people to eventually see the light."

Carmody finished his drink and rose to leave; "Assemble a team of your best men and send them to where our scientific friends are located. They will be made an offer to join us. If they accept well and good. If they refuse, then they will be captured and taken here to the basement."

"Why would we want to bring them here if they do not want to co-operate with us? Why not just take their work and eliminate them?"

"Because these are men of value and to waste them would be a sin. Genius does not come by very often and when it does, it is wise to encourage it and make the best use of it. I have faith in your imagination and powers of persuasion Billy. Bear this in mind; we are now the authority in this land, and we are on a war footing. You have the full support of myself and those I represent. How you get the job done is up to you, just get it done. Besides we will need guinea pigs to test our new nanobots on, and they will make ideal candidates............"

"I see, I like it, certainly in Hodson's case. There's something about irony that always tickles me. In relation to the Ghost Hand how many do you want to order?"

Carmody paused and gave Magee that probing look again; "How many of these things can you produce a week Billy?"

"At current production levels, I'd say one hundred per week, but that should pick up as we iron out any glitches. Production always works that way. The cost is ten grand per unit, a discount price for you."

"Ok we'll take all you can make for the next four months. That should cover our domestic requirements. Do not sell any to anybody else until we give the say so and only to approved customers. I will have one of the staff send you the list of countries who you may not deal with. They will probably get something similar by and by but they will be weakened as a result of the delay. By the time we release the technology to foreign governments things will be really bad, and I want them to be begging for our help. Even our friends must be taught the art of appreciation. That way we'll have more political clout and you can charge them what you like, so you win too. Happy?"

Magee nodded and raised his glass.

Carmody raised his too and finished his drink with a flourish. He liked doing deals and making things happen. Then he set down his glass and walked out, leaving a bemused Magee behind him.

8 AMBUSH

It was Brad who first noticed that the phones had a signal again. They had kept their phones off to conserve the batteries, but every now and then someone checked for a signal. It was a sign that there were people out there organised enough to make some things work once more. He wondered with a wry smile when the bills would start coming through. Immediately after this finding everyone started calling and texting friends and family, to see how and where they were. Some people answered………. but some didn't. Eventually Brad got through to his wife Christine. To his joy he found out that she had managed to escape to the country with the family. Tom's wife Caroline and family had gone with them. When the zombies had first begun their rampage the two wives had been on a shopping trip together with the kids. Realising quickly that the city was not a safe place to be, they had grabbed what they could in the way of supplies and fled. They had gotten out just in time, before the city roads became clogged and largely impassable. They were holed up in the middle of nowhere in an old farmhouse. They had chanced upon it while looking for a good place to shelter, and it was far enough off the beaten path to be reasonably secure. It's zombie farmer owners had had to be dispatched with, and now shared a grave in an out-lying field, but things had been quiet since and they were safe. They had kept a low profile and anxiously waited to hear from their husbands, and were sensible enough to stay at their haven until they heard news. They spent the time tending the animals, growing vegetables, and using wood from an old barn to reinforce the farmhouse, in case of any attacks of either the zombie or the human kind.

The friends on the road found a place to pull in for a break, and discuss the new information. It was a small side road, which had originally been made to service some forestry operation or other, and it looked like it hadn't been used for some time. Grass and weeds were growing up through the stones and gravel and the odd bramble had started to creep out from the ditches on either side. Ann and Josh were still with them, not having reached their turn-off yet. They listened intently to everything that was being said. From the description of the farmhouse it was decided by the friends that it would suit their needs until the zombie situation was resolved. For now they would forget about the cabins in the woods. The cabins would be a backup, in case anything went wrong and they needed another bolthole. They were happy and relieved that their loved ones were safe and that they would not now have to conduct a dangerous search of the city looking for them, but there was still a problem to be resolved; two of Tom's children had asthma. In the frantic rush to get out of the city there had not been time to locate backup supplies of medication. What they did have had now run out and the children were getting sick. Caroline had asked him to try and find some emergency supplies before he came out to be with them. After the phone conversation Tom said he was prepared to go alone to look for some, but to the others this was out of the question. The group would stay together, no matter what. They decided to try and find a pharmacy or clinic, preferably on the outskirts of the city, get the medicine and anything else useful that came to hand, then get out of there as fast as possible.

Happy with this plan they realised that the hour was getting late. Since they seemed to have found themselves in a safe spot they decided to camp for the night. Brad and Scott patrolled the surrounding area looking for any signs of trouble, while the others pitched the tents and collected water from a nearby river. They failed to see any zombies, but did notice that there were signs of some fresh logging activity about half a mile away. Whatever work had been going on here seemed to have been finished though and they saw nothing to indicate that there were any people in the area. On their return they told the others that the place seemed clear, but they would remain on alert, just in case. Figuring that there was small enough risk of attracting attention, they lit a small fire and cooked some food. Their campsite was a little clearing in the forest, naturally made by a semi-circle of dead and fallen trees, surrounded by fairly dense foliage. They completed the circle by the way they arranged the vehicles. These served as a wind-breaker, and gave them a sense of security. After some quiet conversation they turned in for the night. With an early start in the morning, Josh and Ann would make their turn-off by mid-morning, and the rest of them would make the city by mid-day and hopefully not attract any attention. They would make their way in on foot, scavenge what they could, and leave quickly. If anything unexpected happened, they would just have to deal with things as they came. And so one by one they fell asleep.

Scott was on first watch, since he usually had trouble getting to sleep anyway. He sat with his back to a tree and pondered how everything they knew had changed so suddenly. All the old certainties were gone. It was frightening but curiously liberating at the same time. If the phones were working again he took that as a sign that civilisation was attempting to repair itself.

Who knew what else was getting back to normal? He wondered how his kids were doing. He had not had much contact with them in recent years. The words were never said, but he knew they part-blamed him for the death of their mother. He should have been with her the night she died, and who knew what might have been different? If only they hadn't had that stupid falling-out things might have been different. It had been their first real argument and over nothing really. He couldn't remember now what had started it. Now his kids phones were out of service and neither had replied to his texts. He wondered if they were dead. He heard Scout and Keeper growl softly. They had been unsettled all evening and he didn't like that. Rising silently he took his gun and did a perimeter check, slowly scanning the area as best he could without using a light. Even though he had gotten a rifle and two pistols from the gun store, he still favoured the pump action in a situation like this. With a full magazine of buckshot in that thing he knew he was a match for anything that might come his way. Scout stayed at his master's side, but Keeper had joined him on his perimeter check. She whined a little and sniffed around anxiously, staring into the forest. He knew something was bothering her, and he could feel the unease himself but there seemed to be nothing moving anywhere though he strained his eyes to see. The moon was waning and it was hard to see anything among the gloom of the forest. He listened intently but heard nothing apart from a few normal forest sounds. Maybe it was coyotes or wolves or some other forest animals attracted by the smell of their food? These places were always full of prowling animals who knew how to stay out of sight, masters of stealth. Finally he returned to the camp and quietly woke Brad, who was up on watch next. He told Brad about his concerns and Brad promised to be extra vigilant. Brad had been having a bad dream and was happy to be woken. He quietly wandered about for a while, as Scott had, and watched and listened for anything unusual. Nothing stirred as the night settled in even further. Having been asleep earlier, Brad had a hard time staying awake. He passed the time wondering about what kind of world his children with grow up in. He wondered if they had witnessed many bad things as they had made their way out of the city with their mother, and if this experience would change them much. Only time would tell. He was glad when it was time to wake Josh so he could go back to sleep. The tension of the last few days had exhausted him.

The zombies stood as motionless as statutes in the woods. There were about fifty of them. They had all been loggers and foresters, recently arrived to finish clearing an area that had been left some years before. All had gotten the Iasobot vaccination before the job started as time lost to colds was money lost. When the solar storm had hit they had all been affected. There had not been suitable prey for them out in the middle of nowhere, so they had waited around in a state of confusion. With the passing of time their brains had recovered a little from the initial shock, enough for some rudimentary thinking and planning. They had seen the trucks come down the logging road and heard their engines. They had been just outside of the area Scott and Brad had checked, in dense forest, and so the friends had failed to detect them. They had smelled the tantalising smell of meat and it made them drool, but they knew it was not the time to attack……….not yet. It was not a conscious decision, but some primitive instinct that made them wait, despite their hunger. So they had stood motionless for hours and waited and waited for darkness to fall and the prey to sleep. They were hungry as hell. As the night wore on they knew the time was near, and then the time came…………

Josh threw some logs on the fire, then sat against the same tree as Scott had, cradling his rifle on his knees. The night had grown cool now and he was glad of the cheery fire. It was four in the morning and he was weary. He thought about the friends he would see no more, some of them killed by his own hand. He wondered if he would ever see the village again. Something told him no. Even when all this trouble was over that place now held too many painful memories and in its streets wandered too many ghosts. They would have to look somewhere else for a place to live out their final years. At least he and Ann had gotten.........he heard a twig snapping somewhere among the trees........what was that? He heard something move behind him, then more rustling coming from all around. This was not good. Cursing his bad knee he struggled to his feet and turned. There were half a dozen zombies coming towards him through the gloom. Now that they had been seen they charged forward, trying to overpower him quickly.

The others were woken by the dogs barking frantically. Something was out there! As they scrambled out of their sleeping bags and tried to remember where they had put things they heard shots ring out. Then Josh started screaming, cries of pain and fear, an unholy sound in the still night air. Everybody had gone to sleep fully clothed and they were out of the tents in seconds weapons at the ready. Each also had a headlight, to see with and to identify each other. The lights picked out a scene of horror. There were zombies closing in on them from all directions. There was not much time to mount a defense. The dogs were going crazy and started attacking zombies, who lashed out at them trying to shake them off. Going back-to-back the friends fired their weapons with all they had. Zombies dropped everywhere howling and moaning. Josh had been overpowered and was screaming with his last breath. Ann emptied her gun into three attacking zombies and then struggled to reload, dropping bullets into the damp grass. In the confusion some zombies got between her and the others, and she ran to where her husband was.

"I'm not leaving you Josh!" she shouted. Throwing the rifle away she drew a pistol from a holster. She got off a couple of shots but it was not enough to stop them. Even when badly wounded the zombies were extremely dangerous and tenacious.

A large zombie grabbed her from behind and sank it's teeth into her shoulder. She cried out and tried to struggle. Then there were more of them clawing at her. She dropped her pistol and tried in vain to break free from their grasping hands. Seeing her plight, Brad and Doug tried to concentrate their fire on the zombies that were around her, but it was not enough. There were too many of them and eventually she could offer no further resistance. She fell beside her husband, who was silent now.

The friends were aware that Josh and Ann were probably lost to this world, but they were too heavily surrounded themselves, and barely able to hold off their own attackers to make sure. Both Scott and Doug got bitten on the arms in the battle. After using up all the buckshot from their shotguns, only rapid fire from .45 cal pistols eventually drove the zombies back. They finished off the last of them and ran to where Josh and Ann lay. Both were confirmed dead. The friends were devastated, especially Scott. He knew he had missed detecting the zombies when he had done a check of the area earlier. He blamed himself for not doubling the guard, especially when he say how the dogs had been unsettled all evening. The others told him there was no way of searching the entire forest in such a short time with only two people, and that they all had estimated the risks to be low. How could anyone have imagined that there were so many of them? Despite their reasoning he was inconsolable. Eventually he calmed down enough to let them dress his wounds, some nasty bite-marks, to which they liberally applied disinfectant. They assisted Doug with his wounds as well. None of them were badly hurt, a small miracle given the ferocity of the attack.

They noted that the zombies had had enough cognitive ability to lie in wait to ambush the camp, that they had a basic ability to plan the attack and basic use of strategy, by surrounding it to maximise their chances. These were very worrying developments. What made them smarter than the zombies they had previously encountered? Had they gotten a different dose of the radiation, or had the passage of time allowed them to adjust and recover somewhat? Perhaps they had even established a hierarchical structure, and a leadership of some sorts? It was hard to tell. If the zombies were getting smarter, but were still craving human flesh, then no good could come out of that.

There would be no more sleep tonight so they got shovels and dug a grave a short distance away. They then gently laid the bodies of their friends there, in each other's arms, as they had lain so often in life. Brad gave a short prayer, blessed them on their way, and hoped they would all meet again. Then they covered the two with a sleeping bag and filled in the grave, their hearts heavy. Going through their belongings, Tom found the contact details of their son in an address book in Ann's purse, and he kept it for future reference. They siphoned out the fuel from the couple's truck and took whatever else was of use. They still had to look after themselves and their families. The zombies would be food for the animals of the forest and were left where they lay. They were victims too in all this, but there were too many of them to be concerned about, and there were matters involving the living that required their attention now. Finally, after a last sorrowful look around at the carnage they headed out for the highway. The events of that night would stay with them for the rest of their lives.

****

Tara Mahoney woke with a start. She had been dreaming

about being chased and eaten again. She told herself that these dreams had better stop, or she would go mad. She looked around the hospital storeroom and realised that there was still a very real nightmare to contend with right here and now. Her friend Beverley Shenton was still sleeping in the makeshift bed that they had rigged up. Tara wondered how Bev could sleep so soundly with all that was going on. Beverley hadn't missed an hour of sleep since the whole thing had started, something that amazed Tara. When the zombie apocalypse had started they had been at the District Hospital laboratory, near downtown, running tests on blood samples. Their job was two-fold; to monitor how the Iasobots performed long term in people and also the development of the afore-mentioned kill-switch which Hodson had talked about with Howal. They had been making good progress when all of a sudden people had started attacking each other and the hospital went into melt-down. Patients turned into zombies and attacked staff and vice versa. Those who weren't killed fled, and panicked people arriving for treatment found the hospital a warzone.

Tara and Beverley saw the reports on the television in the lunch room and quickly realised the scale and implications of what was going on. They had no access to weapons and the screaming that went on all day at the hospital was enough to deter any inclination on their part to go anywhere. They barricaded themselves into the laboratory and prepared to wait for a safe time to emerge. They were lucky in a number of ways; there was light and power in the lab. First the backup generators kept them going, then power from solar panels on the roof kicked in. There was also a bathroom there. Critically, the lab adjoined the hospital store rooms, and someone had had the good sense to put an adjoining door there. They had enough canned food and bottled water to last for quite a while. They did their best to keep noise and any signs of activity to a minimum, there was no point attracting attention. As well as the zombies to content with, there were reports of armed gangs going around looting and pillaging. They were two unarmed attractive young females and there was wisdom in staying off the radar of trouble.

Every now and then they heard noises in the hospital that terrified them. There was the shuffling walk and the animal-like sounds that they had learned to associate with zombies. There was also occasional gunfire, looters coming to take drugs and other things, fighting the zombies. A few times someone had made a concerted effort to gain access to the laboratory, probably correctly assuming that there were potent drugs there. The two friends had listened with dread as the doors had been struck with the juddering blows of some kind of battering ram. Fortunately the specially strengthened doors did their job and kept the intruders out, but those times had been especially frightening. Then the zombies would return, drawn to the hospital for some unknown reason, perhaps aware that there was human meat hiding there.

Communication with the outside world had been cut off because a fire had destroyed the main switchboard, and up to now, their cell phones would not work. They tried every day to get a signal and today being no different, Tara switched hers on. To her joy and surprise there were signal bars on it – it was working again! Not wanting to wake her friend with false hopes she went into the bathroom to try to make a call to Hodson. With bated breath she heard it ringing...........

"Tara, is that you?"

"Yes."

"Oh my God you're alive, where are you?"

"At the District Hospital with Bev, we are holed up in the lab. We were working here when everything blew up and it made sense to stay put. What the blazes is going on out there?"

"We put the Iasobots out there too soon and they've turned rogue, it was that blasted solar storm that caused them to mutate. They turn people into zombies, they steal their minds and make them want to feed on other people. It is the worst case of bad timing in history. I should have listened to you and Howal, but we're trying to do what we can to deal with things. Listen, I've teamed up with Alan Howal again, I'm at his laboratory as we speak. We're trying to come up with a kill-switch now as a matter of urgency and we need you and your work here asap, is there any way you can get here do you think?" Hodson gave them the address of Howal's lab.

"Right now that's out of the question. This place is crawling with zombies and every now and then looters try to break in. We have no weapons to fight with so our best chance is to remain here unless something changes. Can someone come to get us?"

Hodson thought for a while; "I'm not sure what our options are there, leave it with me. I'm in no shape to rescue anyone unfortunately and would be a hindrance more than a help. We might have to look into hiring some vigilantes or something. We would need to send a truck because we may need some of your equipment as well and that involves a bit of planning. We lost Maxwell and Porter to the zombies on the way here so we're all that's left of the team; myself, Alan, and a guy named Eddie Young, who we picked up along the way, he has some knowledge of science and he's been assisting us with our work."

Mahoney stifled a sob; Maxwell and Porter had been dear friends of hers. It was horrible to think of how they had died and now she regretted ever having heard of nanobots. Now Howal wished to speak with her;

"Hi Tara, it's me, Alan. I'm sorry you had to hear the news

about Maxwell and Porter, Hodson says it happened fast and they died fighting valiantly. Listen, we don't have much time and we don't know how long the phones will stay operational, so I have some questions. Tell me about this kill-switch you were developing?"

Mahoney gathered herself and the professional in her came to the fore; "Having looked at a number of options I've eventually figured that, given the type of problem, our best chance for dealing with the Iasobots is to try and develop another type of nanobot, except that this new type would attack the rogue type. We can program the new ones to attack the membranes of the Iasobots, allowing the contents to spill out, thereby killing them. The remains would then be cleaned up by the body's own cells and disposed of in the same manner as any other cell waste. In essence we would fight fire with fire. In recent days Bev and I have been working hard on such a nanobot but we have some progress but have a ways to go yet. The delivery system would remain the same though: since zombies are hard to get near and don't tend to eat or drink anything except us, the new nanobots would be suspended in a solution same as the Iasobots were. This could then be sprayed into their faces, and then be inhaled by them, in much the same way as the Iasobots were. A little crude I know, but as a quick and easy fix it's a viable option given the equipment we have at our disposal right now."

Howal was pleased; "I knew your work would be outstanding. Keep plugging away at it until such time as we can mount a rescue. I'm not sure what myself, John and Eddie can achieve in that regard. We are not armed either. Eddie has a pistol but I think he's out of bullets. Right now we are studying the mutant nanobots from his blood, to find out a good point of attack. It looks like the solar storm caused some of their genes to mutate, turning them from benevolent helpers, into something resembling a viral parasite. Sometimes in nature it takes very little to turn something benign into something deadly and vice versa. We will have to be more careful in the future how we use these things or the next time there may be no saving us. Ok I will let you go now. Sit tight and if we can come up with a plan I will let you know. Give my love to Beverley. Take care and bye for now Tara……………."

Mahoney tidied herself a little in the mirror and was happier than she had been in days. Her strawberry blonde hair was a bit tousled but there was a new light in her blue eyes now. Excitedly she went to wake Beverley and tell her the news.

****

Not very far away, hunched over his electronic gadgets, Billy Magee's man carefully noted the details of the conversation for his Boss. Magee was going to find this very stuff very interesting……………..

****

Beverley woke with a start when Tara gently shook her; "Whaa?" Despite the fact that she was sleeping relatively well she was also suffering the psychological effects of their predicament and having bad dreams. She had a moment of fear that their location was under assault again, but today Tara was smiling and happy.

"Hey, guess what? I just spoke with John and Alan on the phone!"

The news slowly registered in Beverley's mind. She pulled herself into a sitting position; "You mean John Hodson and Alan……."

"Yes Alan Howal! They're back together again and attempting to find a solution to cure the zombies! They're at Alan's laboratory a few miles from here, and they want us to go and join them, to help them with their work." Tara became more solemn now; "Obviously we have to figure out a way to get from here to there first though."

Beverley was more awake now, and the implications of this news was beginning to sink in. "That's the best news I've had since all this madness began! Do they have a way of helping us to escape from the hospital?"

Tara shook her head; "Sadly no. They're there with some guy John came across who got bitten by a zombie but that's all the resources they have. If you were going to assemble a swat team neither Alan or John would be among your first choices for it. John mentioned hiring vigilantes but, even assuming that you found some, then other persons of dubious trustworthiness would know of our location, and maybe even something of our work. Remember John is a household name now and anybody would recognise him. Somehow we're going to have to make our way to where they are by ourselves, and that thought scares me more than I like to think about. Right now, with no weapons and the place swarming with zombies and looters I have simply no idea how we're going to get out of here."

Beverley had been thinking about this since day one; "This place had been good to us; we have food and water, heat and light and a reasonable degree of security. We were probably luckier than a lot of people when this disaster struck, who were caught out in the open, but we can't remain here forever. I've been realising, even before we heard from Alan and John that the time must come when we have to leave. This place is too prominent, and it will keep attracting criminals and looters. Eventually someone might get in and then it's all going to be bad."

Tara sighed. These things weighed heavily on her too. "I know, that's what scares me. In the absence of much hope of rescue we will have to rely on ourselves. Our work must go on and it must succeed, much relies on that. The only thing I can think of is that we wait until nightfall and make a run for it. We could only bring what we can carry. It would take about two minutes to get to our cars outside and then we would simply drive over to where the others are. What do you think?"

Beverley grimaced a little. "It's probably as good a plan as any in the circumstances. Things quieten down at night. I don't know if those things sleep or not but they must rest in some sense sometime. We could bring knives from the lunch room I suppose, there's not much else to use as weapons around here, and you're right; with a clear run we could get to the cars pretty quickly. It would probably be best to go separately in case something happens to one car, we would have a back-up. I don't know what it's like out there, but I imagine it's been pandemonium."

"Yes" Tara agreed. "It would be nice if there was even one window in this place, so we could peep out and get an idea of what's going on out there. As it is the place sometimes gives me the sensation of being in a tomb."

"Oh no, don't say that!" Beverley exclaimed. "Don't think bad thoughts like that, try and be positive! We still have each other, to the very end, whatever happens. We'll stick together no matter what."

The two had a hug for a while and felt blessed that they had each other.

"Ok so the plan is we make a run for it. When do you say we go?" Tara asked.

"We've achieved almost as much as we can here, without access to fresh work supplies." Beverley said thoughtfully. "Now that I know that there's a worthwhile destination to go to, I suddenly feel the need to get out of here as soon as possible. I think we should make a break for it tonight after night-fall, whaddaya think?"

"Ok, I'm already nervous thinking about it, but I believe you're right, we should go soon, and not wait for more trouble to show up. We'll lock the place up behind us and if something bad happens we can try and make it back here. At least we will have gotten a sense of what's out there and we can look at it as a practice run."

"Great, I feel a bit better with our minds made up. I'm hoping that we make it out on the first go." Beverley said. "We can spend today wrapping up our work and organising what to take with us. Now let's have a big breakfast of tinned food to celebrate!"

9 CAPTURED

Eli Draks watched the District Hospital through his binoculars, scanning back and forth from his vantage point in a building about two blocks south and facing there. It was about ten o'clock later that same morning. Every now and then he paused when he thought he saw movement at a window. The place was crawling with zombies. Why did they gravitate to this place? Maybe they were looking for a Doctor he wondered to his own amusement? Maybe they thought there was some guy in there that would make them better again? He laughed softly to himself. He always liked his own jokes. Eli was a city boy, having been born and raised there. He was a failure at school and never worked a job. He thought such things required too much effort and too little reward. He still wanted a life of plenty and as he was not intelligent to do it the legal way, he naturally saw crime as the way forward, specifically drug crime. There was a vast market out there, huge profits, and relatively little chance of getting caught especially if you were fond of using other people to do the risky jobs, as he was. He was a great believer in having people about to take the flak instead of himself, and that's why he always made sure to have a large gang of associates around him. Whenever something went wrong Eli made sure someone else took the fall. If they took the fall willingly their loyalty was rewarded financially or with drugs. If they were a little less willing, then they felt the full force of his wrath, which made them change their mind. Eli was a large, heavyset man with a taste for violence and other people's property. He had a flat face and a snub nose which gave him a pugilistic appearance. Eli had been involved with several gangs over the years, and members came and went. He was presently the leader of a gang of misfits called 'Crime Machine'. Thirty five in number, they were a heavily armed outfit, mainly into drug running, but always open to new possibilities if they presented. When the zombie apocalypse started, where others saw terror and chaos, Eli and his friends saw opportunity. Now there was no law to stop them doing whatever the hell they wanted. This was the law of the jungle and now they got to play by their own rules. Now they sold their products openly to the huge market that was still there and still desperate for their fix. Their normal channels of supply for drugs were broken down and they were running out of product fast. Bearing in mind what they wanted to keep for personal use, the supply was about to dry up fairly soon unless they sourced a new supply soon. Now they were urgently attempting to make contact with suppliers and explore some new avenues for doing business. There was a large market out there for the right kinds of drugs and even though few people were using currency for now there were other ways of getting paid...........whoever had those drugs would wield a lot of power.

Eli knew there were large stocks of some of the drugs that they wanted in the stores at the hospital. He had known a janitor who had worked there who had an alcohol problem. For a bottle now and then, he used to steal drugs for Eli in the past; small quantities that would not be missed. However from his reports Eli knew roughly just how much of each drug was there, and now there was little to stop him getting what he wanted, which was he entire stock. They had made a couple of attempts to get in already, having had to battle their way through some zombies, including the former janitor himself, but had failed due to the strength of the security doors. Now they had returned with power saws and this time there would be no mistakes. He assumed the people who were locked in there were the two pretty little scientists that Brent the Janitor had told him about. Well, he had big plans for them if that was true. He was watching the zombies who wandered the halls and corridors where until recently busy nurses and doctors had gone about their daily business. Perhaps they liked pretty women too he thought. He laughed again. That was another joke. Maybe they had zombie boyfriends and girlfriends? That was damn funny! Zombies didn't trouble him too much, not with the numbers of his gang and their firepower. He was more concerned about reports he had received that the remnants of the police and army were making an effort to re-organise and clean things up. A state of martial law had been declared when the situation had looked hopeless and there was a standing order in place to shoot criminals and looters, who threatened the weak and the law-abiding. Some people who he worked with occasionally had been killed by soldiers two days ago, as they tried to blast their way into a bank vault, so it paid to be wary. Funny how, even in the middle of a zombie apocalypse, the banks got priority treatment, he'd thought. Eli knew there were still sacred cows around that you were better off not trying to slaughter. He was also on the lookout for any rivals that might turn up. He had enemies who wouldn't hesitate to steal his stash if they could. There were looters everywhere and places likely to contain drugs were attracting them like magnets, so there was some sense of urgency about getting in there now.

Eli summoned Tyler Theorn, his second in command:

"Ok there's no-one 'round except zombies. Here's the plan; you take ten of the men and cover all the entrances near the lab. Ten should be enough to hold off any zombies and watch for trouble. We'll also have ten circle the wider area around here, to deal with anyone who might hear the gunfire and come to investigate. There are several groups of vigilantes operating in this neck of the woods, basically idiots with nothing better to do, and I don't want any turning up and interfering. Anyone or anything that comes near, just kill them. I will take the rest of the men inside and we will deal with those damn doors. When we get inside I will call you and you will have to bring the trucks up to the main entrance, there's so much stuff in there, we will spend half the day getting it out. When this succeeds we'll have enough drugs to last us a year! Understand?"

Tyler nodded, it sounded straightforward enough. Tyler was a small, hyper-active, untrustworthy worm of a man, who would sell his own mother to save himself if he had to. He naturally gravitated to a violent gang which he could use to satisfy his need to intimidate people he would normally run scared from. "I hear rumours that there are some nice-looking women in there, is that true?" he smirked at Eli.

"That's what Brent used to say anyway, a blond thing and a brunette, he used to fantasise about them on his breaks, the dirty old bastard!" Eli laughed. "If they are in there then that will be the icing on a very nice cake. We shall see, we shall see……………Ok let's go………….."

****

Tom slowed the pick-up truck on the road. They were

close to the city and he had just remembered something. He was looking at an old mechanic's workshop a little way off the main highway. It was a small premises, in a state of disrepair. The rusting old cars lying around gave it the appearance of belonging to a bygone time.

"What's up, see something?" Scott was tense and edgy.

"I just remembered something about that workshop Scott. I have some dynamite hidden there."

"No kidding. You certainly are a man of mystery, where did you get it?"

Tom briefly told him the story of his dismissal from the mining company and the anarchists.

"Jeez, you're a bit mental Tom. How come you didn't give that stuff to the police? You do realise what could happen you if you were caught with illegal explosives?"

"I'd just lost my faith in the criminal justice system, so I just said 'screw it'. Anyway, I was careful enough not to get caught and if they found it by accident I could explain my DNA on it by the fact that I had worked at the company at the time it was stolen. My DNA was probably all over the place. Do you reckon we should get it?" he smiled, "It would not take long to retrieve it and that kind of stuff could come in handy if we run into major trouble in the city."

Scott thought for a bit; "Sure, we should stop for a quick bite before we enter the city anyway, who knows when's the next chance we'll get. If we run into problems it could be quite a while. There's no knowing what we may encounter there. I'll signal to the others that we're stopping."

They pulled in and explained to Brad and Doug what was

happening. The others had just been thinking about having a bite to eat and they were happy to stop and stretch their legs. A quick check showed the area to be zombie free, so they all went into the old workshop. While Brad and Doug prepared some food and drinks, Scott and Tom pulled some work benches aside to reveal a trapdoor in the floor. It was an access for various utilities, and had remained forgotten for years when the business closed. Tom wriggled his way in, with some degree of difficulty, and sneezed from the cloud of dust he had disturbed. He's been a little slimmer the last time he was here, and he made a mental note to be more watchful of his eating habits. He finally got to the four boxes of dynamite which had lain undisturbed all that time. Further effort was required to pass each one up to his waiting friend. Then he climbed out again; "This place was owned by a friend of my father's when I was a child. I often hung out here when dad came over to get work done on his car. I always knew about that hiding place and it really came in handy for me. I must say I never thought I'd hide dynamite there though!"

He closed the trapdoor and pulled the bench back into place. Then they clustered round and examined the dynamite and Tom gave them a quick lesson on how to use it. During the years of storage it had remained in perfect condition. It was important to know how to handle that stuff safely as once it went off it would not discriminate between friend or foe. Fuse type blasting caps were used to detonate the sticks. Tom showed them how to insert the fuse, and crimp it, and then explained how long the built-in time-delay lasted until the dynamite would explode.

Everyone was impressed with this new addition to their arsenal and each of them got a box for his own use. Then they all relaxed and had something to eat and drink. The conversation was casual but the atmosphere was tinged with a slight air of concern about what might lie ahead. When they finished eating they hit the road again and shortly they could see the tallest city buildings in the distance. Now a tense nervousness came over each one of them; the city would be full of danger, and not just from zombies. They had seen several other trucks on the road recently. Everybody who was moving was armed to the teeth and travelling in groups. None of them were friendly, but regarded them with suspicious glances. There had been a few times when they thought they were going to be attacked, but the danger had passed. If things got much worse people would destroy each other before the zombies got a chance to. Each time it happened made them feel a little more fraught. This is what it looked like when anarchy reigned, and taken-for-granted securities no longer existed.

Eventually they came to the last wooded area before the city, and quickly turned down a dirt road towards it. There did not seen to be anyone about. This was where they would leave the trucks, concealed as best they could. It was a gamble that no-one would find them, but they could see no other option. Splitting up and leaving someone to guard them seemed like a bad idea, especially with communication being so unreliable at the moment. At least together they had a greater chance of success, and if they lost the trucks they could just acquire more. They concealed their vehicles as best they could with camouflage covers and loose tree branches, took their weapons and the dynamite, and set off at a brisk walking pace for the city. The area here was fairly hilly, and they kept to the low ground to avoid being seen by anyone.

When they reached the outskirts of the city they could see something of the carnage that had taken place there. Crouching behind a burnt out SUV, the four friends scanned the area through the scopes of their rifles. There were crashed cars and trucks everywhere. These had eventually blocked all the roads out of the city, and the panicked people trying to leave had had to abandon their vehicles and try to leave on foot, blocking the roads even more. This evacuation had not gone well and thousands had been attacked and killed by the many zombies who were everywhere. The remains of these people lay in the dirt without ceremony or memorial, the victims of a feeding frenzy they had never seen coming. Birds and wild animals had begun to feast on anything the zombies left in their wake, and the friends marvelled at the speed with which nature was moving into the vacuum left by humanity. There were still zombies wandering among the wreckage, watching for any signs of people and these would best be avoided. The normal hustle and bustle of the city was gone, and now it more resembled a graveyard. Whether it would ever regain its status as a habitat was uncertain to the shocked observers. One thing was certain; no-one was going to expect them to show up for their old jobs anytime soon. All the paperwork and stuff that had seemed so important up to a few days ago, was now just a pile of dead trees that meant nothing to anyone.

After their initial reconnaissance had been completed, they moved cautiously through the ruins, on the lookout for a pharmacy or a clinic that had somehow escaped the inevitable looters. After some time it became apparent that this task was proving difficult. Every place they came to had been stripped bare in a remarkably short space of time. They surmised that there were lots of people hunkered down in their fortified homes and other buildings, who were waiting for the crises to pass. It was a safe guess that these people would be armed to the teeth, and very prone to shooting first and asking questions later. These would be the persons who had stripped bare the local stores of supplies, hoping they would last as long as they needed to. Eventually the friends stopped to think of ideas for what their next move should be. It was pointless looking for more pharmacies and clinics as they were obviously all looted. It was Doug who thought of the District Hospital. He had worked at all the hospitals in the city once upon a time, and it was the closest one to them. He knew every inch of the place, and he knew where there were valuable drugs, not just for the children, but for anybody who might be ill in the coming while. If they got lucky they might find supplies for them all there. Not wanting to remain in the city until nightfall, the others readily agreed that this was an excellent idea, and Doug led the way.

****

It was Beverley Shenton who first heard the members of Crime Machine returning. She had been running some computer simulations of a new type of nanobot when she heard the first gunshots and laughter, as the gang cleared the area of zombies. Horrified she ran to Tara Mahoney to warn her. Both had a bad feeling about the situation, so they hurriedly saved their most important work and hid the data sticks. Then they heard the power saws start up. Now they had to fight off a wave of panic that came over them. There was no way of knowing who or what was trying to come through those doors. They pushed all the heavy furniture they could up against the doors to slow down the invasion. Then they climbed up into the roof space to hide. It was the last resort in the circumstances, and now they prayed that they would not be discovered. Crouched in the near darkness they could only wait and comfort each other against the dreadful fear now gripping them both.

Eli's men had had a fun time clearing the area of zombies. Being well armed and so many it was an easy enough job to pick them off. What they didn't notice was that the zombies were gradually learning from their mistakes. As Scott and friends had suspected back in the forest, as time went by and their brains adapted and recovered more and more of their cognitive ability, they were getting smarter and more cautious. They realised that they were not going to get a meal from the intruders, and eventually slunk away into the shadows to hide and await a better opportunity. This left Eli's men alone to concentrate on cutting through the doors of the hospital laboratory. Cursing and swearing they took turns with the saws. It was hard work and some of them were not the fittest of men, sweating profusely from the exertion. Gradually they were making progress and this spurred them on to keep going.

Meanwhile outside the four friends had reached the back of a building across the road from the hospital. Moving with the same caution as before they saw some of the members of Crime Machine guarding the outside with Tyler Theorn. Recognising them as looters the friends decided that there were too many to engage with, and were about to move away, when they came under fire from behind them. The other members of the gang who had been circling around the area and had spotted them arrive. Thinking they were a threat to their operation, they had opened fire without warning. The friends scattered and took cover as bullets thudded into walls and ricocheted off the ground around them. By luck and fast reflexes none of them were hit. They fired back from behind what cover they could find, but more of the gang members were now running to the scene, blocking off their escape route. The situation was looking perilous, but Tom managed to break in through the door of the closest building and they all ran inside, laying down suppressing fire as they went. The building had been an electrical repair shop, and they found lots of tools and equipment with which to barricade the door. Bullets whizzed in through the windows, as the members of Crime Machine closed in on them. Crouching low Tom covered the front of the building and Doug covered the back, returning fire as best they could to hold off their would-be killers. Scott and Brad sprinted to the stairs and made their way up onto the flat roof of the building.

From there they carefully tried to get a picture of how many their enemies were and where they were clustered, without being seen themselves. Their attackers seemed to be equally divided between the front and the back of the building, gathered behind damaged vehicles for cover. From there they poured volleys of shots into the building. There was only one way to deal with this. Scott and Brad quickly inserted fuses and crimped those using a small pliers, preparing the dynamite for use.

With Scott taking the front and Doug the back, they each took a few sticks of dynamite, judged the distance and then threw them at their attackers. They spaced them out to maximise the blast zones and do as much damage as possible. There were several loud explosions in quick succession as the dynamite went off, then all four friends opened up on the stunned survivors. Gang members fell everywhere as the blasts ripped through them like ragdolls.

"Let's get the hell out of here!" shouted Scott, "There are more on the way!"

They raced out the back door, having to empty their guns into a couple of gang members who were still standing, looking dazed. Then they raced down an alleyway, the dogs excitedly racing in front of them, and took several turns to evade any possible pursuers, taking them far enough away to stop to catch their breath.

Tyler Theorn had seen the gun battle taking place, but had remained guarding the hospital entrance as he had been asked. He was confident that their men would overpower the strangers right up until the explosions had surprised them all. He did not know it was dynamite but thought that hand grenades had been used against them, and now he was worried that rogue soldiers were in the area, no doubt after the same drugs as themselves. He called

Eli on the radios they carried and gave him a report. Some of the men were making their way to investigate, angry that someone else might be trying to muscle in on their operation. Eli had heard the gunfire and explosions but ordered him to remain in place until he finished getting through the doors. They were nearly there and he wasn't giving up now. Whatever was going on outside, they would just have to deal with it. Tyler called the men back to their posts around the laboratory and left the others to their fate. Meanwhile, zombies had started arriving in greater numbers, attracted by the activity. They snuck around in the shadows, more cautious of humans now, but finding the smell of fresh blood irresistible. They flung themselves on the dead and dying members of Crime Machine and began to feast upon their flesh. That's when the wounded gang members started to envy their dead associates, and their terrible howls of pain and fear became the soundtrack to the devil's banquet.

Eventually Eli's men succeeded in breaking through the hardened doors of the hospital laboratory. Then, with a lot more cursing and swearing and effort, they finally cleared the other objects the girls had blocked the entrance with. Then they swarmed into the place, guns at the ready, and turned it upside down, searching for the occupants. Tara and Beverley held their breath, and observed the men below through chinks in the roof panels. This was the nightmare they had been dreading. Why could these bastards not have shown up a day later? Underneath their hiding place them Eli and his men conducted a search of the laboratory and the store rooms. They quickly found the bed and other signs of occupation, and they knew the pair were in there somewhere. One of the gang members sniffed at the bed and knowingly informed the others that it smelled "Like bitches". Having failed to find them on the ground level or in any nooks and crannies in the store room, Eli paused to think about his next move. He was cunning enough to narrow it down to where they were most likely to be. Standing in the laboratory he took a pistol and called out;

"Ok bitches I know where you are, come on out!"

There was no reply. Then he started randomly shooting an occasional shot into the ceiling. He aimed mainly at places he hoped they would not be like the corners; he did not want to accidently shoot them, just scare them.

"I'm going to keep this up until you either come out or I shoot you!" he called. His men watched with anticipation. Mahoney and Shenton were in a dilemma. The last thing they wanted was to come out, but those bullets were getting closer. Someone had to preserve their work and make sure it got to Howal and Hodson in order to find a cure. They both would rather die than be taken prisoner by these wretches below them but there was so much more at stake now. They were going to have to make a terrible sacrifice. Having no option, they decided with heavy hearts to surrender.

"Ok we're coming out" Tara called resignedly. "Don't shoot".

They pulled the panel back and were helped out of the crawl space by Eli's grinning and leering men.

"Well now what have we here?" Eli smirked at them. "Why didn't you want to come to old Eli, don't you want a boyfriend?"

His men laughed loudly but the two scientists recoiled with disgust.

"Brent the Janitor was right, you really are a pair of beauties!" Eli continued. "It's like my birthday and Christmas all at once. Search them boys."

Some of the grinning men jostled their way forward and the girls were given an uncomfortable pat-down by them. They quickly found that each of them was carrying a concealed kitchen knife on their person.

"What have we here then?" Eli cried. "You weren't thinking of hurting somebody were you? That's nasty! Still, I like that. I like feisty women, it's more fun when they have some fight in them!"

His men laughed while Beverley and Tara flinched from this odious individual.

"You and you, secure them and take them to my car. Make sure nothing happens to them until I'm finished up in here. Then it's party time!" Having gotten their orders two of the men sprang forward to comply.

"I'll come for them when we've cleared this place out. Business before pleasure. Now I will tell Theorn to bring the trucks over so we can load them up. I don't want to hang around here forever, who knows what scumbags might show up and spoil the show!"

Tara and Beverley had their arms tied behind them and were unceremoniously escorted out through the building. They were now very worried. As they were brought out and pushed towards a waiting car they were stared at by the other members of Crime Machine, now busy bringing vehicles up to the entrance for loading. The two scientists did not need to be geniuses to realise that they were in an extremely perilous situation, and they had no clue as to how they were going to get out of it. Again they mourned their bad luck with the timing of this, and wondered what fate had in store for them now. When they reached the outside of the building and saw the devastation it felt like a different world to them. They saw how fragile a thing was civilisation and what happens when it crashes down, and now they were the latest victims in this hell. What they did not realise though, was that there were four other pairs of eyes watching from a distance away. The four friends had had a quick discussion about their options after the firefight. Figuring that the looters would not stick around forever, they decided to find a place to wait until it was safe to return to the hospital. Then they would return and look for the drugs that they needed. They correctly surmised that the looters would be looking for different drugs to themselves and made a calculation that the things they needed would be there when they went looking. All they had to do was wait. Then they would get out of the city as fast as they could. They had seen enough of the place to realise that it was a lawless hell on earth.

They found a vacant residential high-rise and climbed enough floors to get a good view of the hospital. They watched proceedings with interest, again using the scopes of their rifles, and saw every move the gang members made. When they saw trucks being brought up they correctly guessed that the gang had found what they were looking for. Then they saw the two bound females being brought out and that changed everything............

"Oh my God, they've got prisoners!" Doug gasped with horror. "They must have been holed up inside somewhere. They look like some sort of hospital staff, they must have had a hidey hole for themselves somewhere in there."

"Damn, I wasn't expecting this development. Looks like we have more work to do here than we imagined" Scott agreed.

They all knew that they were going to attempt a rescue. That's the kind of people that they were.

10 THE OFFER

Hodson and Howal were busy in their laboratory, carefully analysing the rogue nanobots that had come out of Eddie Young. Eddie himself was there as well, acting as their assistant. He had been a science teacher by profession, and that made him a useful person to have around as he had a good general knowledge of what they were doing. Hodson peered at some samples through a microscope;

"I can see the changes the electromagnetism has made to them, but I just can't figure out why they behave the way they do" he said in an exasperated manner. "There doesn't seem to be any rhyme or reason to their behaviour."

"We need to focus on any weakness" Howal suggested. "The new nanobots we make will have to have a definite point of attack. Since the Iasobots are already in the brain cells of the victims, we need to program the new ones to enter the cells and somehow disable the old ones. This is where we need Tara's work. She has identified the weak point that we can use to switch them off but we still need help with the precise method of doing so. I still have no idea how we're going to get her over here, we may just have to go and get her ourselves, and risk everything. I will be honest though, the idea of running around the city being pursued for supper by hungry zombies isn't one I'm exactly enamoured with. It's been a while since I did the one hundred metre dash."

Eddie had been on his way with a tray of fresh samples when he glanced at one of the monitors covering the area around the building. He saw the place outside swarming with armed men in a dark military-type uniform, and he almost dropped his samples in surprise. Running into the laboratory he alerted his new colleagues:

"Come look at the cameras, we've got company!" he gasped.

With alarm Hodson and Howal ran to view the monitors. What they saw made them very concerned.

"Who are they, some kind of secret service? That's not an army uniform" Eddie asked his startled colleagues.

Hodson and Howal looked at each other worriedly. They recognised the uniforms and knew the implications.

"No, not army" Hodson explained to him. "Those are the uniforms of the hired goons of a private company called Eclipse Enterprises. They make, among other things, bio-weapons for the army, and other customers. Both of us have had dealings with them in the past. They must be here to steal our work."

"Quick, we don't have much time!" Howal exclaimed. "We must hide anything useful before they get in here!"

He began to save their work and instructed the others on

what to gather up. When they had collected the vital parts of their work, Howal led them to an unused room deep in the building. Once there he rummaged around at one of the walls, and opened a section of the wall using a hidden latch.

"When they put the furnace in, they were going to brick up this old chimney, but I got the idea that it would make a very useful hiding place if I ever won a Nobel prize." He managed a joke even in that situation. "It's all sealed up now, and you would have to do a lot of looking to find this place."

They quickly stashed all their work in the chimney space, locked it and hurried back to the laboratory.

"Now to leave a clue for Tara if she ever gets here" Howal said. "It may be our last hope."

He looked around him, and then left a clue only she would understand.

"How do you know they'll get in here?" asked Young. "This place is built like a fortress."

Then there was an explosion, and the locks were blasted off the front door. Some further activity with crowbars was enough to dislodge the heave door bars, and the building was breached. The uniformed men rushed in, bristling with machine guns and looking like they meant business. Hodson, Howal and Young waited calmly for them to reach the laboratory.

The men came in and assumed control of everything and the leader ordered his men to frisk everyone thoroughly. They found the 9mm pistol on Eddie Young, and took it from him.

"What do you want? How dare you burst in here like this!" Howal exclaimed angrily. "There is still a law in the land, and you are in flagrant disregard of it! You can't just start blowing the doors off places and pushing people about on private property. When this is all over Eclipse Enterprises will be facing a major lawsuit, mark my words!"

The Sergeant laughed; "No, we are the law now. You are in flagrant disregard of it, because we say so. You may as well try and sue the crows as sue us."

"I know Billy Magee thinks he can do what he wants, but there are lines even he cannot cross. Leave here now and we will consider the matter dealt with" Hodson suggested.

"No can do. We are taking you and we are taking your work back with us, so do not resist or it will be worse for you." Then the Sergeant asked them where their work on the nanobots was. He was met with stony silence. He shrugged and ordered his men to tear the place apart until they found it. His men weren't scientists so they didn't really know what they were looking for, so they grabbed anything that looked important with the intention of bringing it back with them. The Sergeant had been instructed not to destroy anything, so he ordered his men to fix up the doors as best they could, so they would leave the place secure. They might have to come back for something. Then the unhappy scientists and Eddie Young were brought out to a waiting vehicle for transportation back to the headquarters of Eclipse Enterprises. The trip was made in silence as each of them pondered the implications of this new development. There was no point speculating about what was going to happen. All they could do was to wait and see.

When they arrived at the imposing Eclipse complex, they were brought to a cell in the basement near to where some zombies were kept. This was not by accident. They could hear the grunts and other noises made by the zombies, and wondered what fiendish scheme Magee was up to. They gloomily guessed that he was trying to come up with his own cure for the zombies and wondered how much progress he had made. Not long after Billy Magee himself came to see them. He studied them for a moment with a thoughtful look on his face, then greeted them;

"Gentlemen, welcome to Eclipse Enterprises, the leading centre for zombie research in the world right now."

This was met with scowls from the three captured men.

"Why what's the matter, not pleased to be here?"

Still no answer.

He stared at Eddie Young; "Who are you, I don't know you?"

Eddie wasn't sure how to respond, so Howal spoke;

"He's just a person who sought shelter with us when the zombies started attacking everybody. He's a science teacher and he was acting as our lab assistant. He knows nothing of our work, so he is of no use to you. There's no point holding him here."

Magee thought about this; "Hmmm, I'll think about that Alan, I'm sure he knows some things, in the meantime let me explain the situation here. I want you to know where things stand, and your possible place in all that. This is important.......We have developed a device that can reverse the effects of the zombification process."

The three men gasped. Magee carried on. He was enjoying this.

"Yes, that's right, we have developed a device we call the Ghost Hand that can kill the Iasobots. Then, with a little time and some nursing back to health, we can get a person back on their feet in a few days. Here, let me show you: There was a TV screen mounted on the wall across from them and he used a remote control to play the video of the time he had first used the Ghost Hand, the same video he had played for Senator Carmody. They watched with fascination.

"What do you think, impressed?" he asked with a grin. "I know that you haven't got that far with your own exploits, but no matter. You will have ample time to prove yourselves in the future."

"Interesting" Howal was fascinated by what he had seen. "How long ago was that, what condition is the man in now?"

"That was three days ago Alan" Magee answered. "Why don't you ask him yourself? Lee, come here please."

To their astonishment a man walked into the room on cue. He looked and behaved like a normal man, but there was no mistaking, he was the man in the video who had previously been a zombie.

"Lee, why don't you tell these gentlemen about your recent experience please?"

"Yes, no problem. Well, when the cold vaccination first came out the wife and I thought it was a great idea and we both signed up for it. Everything seemed to go fine for a while but one day it seemed like a heavy fog had descended on my mind. I could not think straight. I forgot who I was and all I could feel was an insatiable hunger to eat. I think you all know what was on the menu. All I vaguely remember about the next few days is wandering around trying to eat people. Then I was captured by Mr Magee's men. I know that but I don't remember it. Then I had the Ghost Hand device used on me. Gradually my mind began to clear and I returned to normal. I still don't know where my wife is."

They listened, stunned. At least they were now sure the zombification process could be reversed. They felt an unusual mixture of defeat and relief for which there was no word to describe. Hodson in particular felt a weight slip from his shoulders, at least many people could now be saved from certain death. Magee was loving their amazed looks.

"You may take it gentlemen, that we have succeeded where you have failed, and we have the salvation of mankind in our hands!" he said triumphantly.

"I salute your success" Hodson conceded. "You have done a remarkable job, I won't deny you that, and I'm happy that you have made this breakthrough, but that does not explain why you have kidnapped us. There are consequences for breaking the law in this manner."

"No, that's where you're wrong John, there are no adverse consequences, at least not for us. We are the law now so we can do what we like, especially when we're acting in the national interest. I could have you killed and thrown out on the street if I wanted, and no-one would know or care. The day is gone when the state will allow its own enemies to enjoy the hard-won privileges and liberties which it provides, in the name of some perverse idea of freedom. The needs of the many and the freedoms of the many will no longer be threatened by the reckless actions of the few. I am however hoping that men of reason such as yourselves will not drive me to do drastic things like that though. I am hoping you will come to your senses and join the winning team."

"Are you asking us to come and work for you? That's something like what that Sergeant said when he, er, took us into his custody back at my laboratory, but he refused to elaborate much, perhaps you can. Where do you get the authority to act as you please and deny the rights of others as you see fit? Right now this is kidnapping, which is outlawed in all but the most corrupt banana republics of the world." Howal knew something was afoot and he wanted to know what. He knew the tentacles of Eclipse Enterprises extended far and wide and he wanted to know how far.

"Yes, it's like this, the country is now being run by a Council of Senators, answering to no-one but themselves. They are all people of intelligence and wisdom, carefully selected by and from their peers. One of them is the head of the armed forces and another is the highest ranking policeman in the land, and they are both loyal servants of the new republic. The others come from all walks of life and are experts in their fields. Don't worry though, the Council's will be a firm, but fair leadership. The age of incompetence, corruption and cronyism is over, and the age of just rule by carefully selected people has begun. People will have rights, sure, but they will also have responsibilities and the rights they have will be earned, not handed out like candy to the worthy and the unworthy alike. If someone refuses to carry out their proper responsibilities, like for example, refuse to assist their country in a time of emergency, then they will have their rights revoked, and be considered renegades. What you call kidnapping your country sees as proper utilisation of its own resources. To refuse to help us will be seen as an act of treason, and dealt with accordingly. This company and myself are allies of the Council and we are acting on their direct orders. Therefore we can do with you as we deem appropriate."

"What about the President, and all the other politicians? They're not just going to step aside and allow what is essentially a coup. There could be a civil war!"

"They're all either dead, or trying to chew on other people as we speak so don't worry about them. They're certainly not interested in politics anymore and won't be running for re-election,

I'll put it that way. Let me answer your other question, the reason we brought you here is that we had to stop you developing your own cure and mass producing it, so that anybody could be restored. The future belongs to the chosen ones Alan, and we will decide who gets to be chosen. Nature shows us time after time that an ecosystem can only carry so many organisms and after that the numbers are culled, starting with the weak ones. Mankind kept the numbers up through artificial means, and something had to give. If old Hodson here hadn't come up with his Iasobots then something else would have happened. We had been heading down the road to self-destruction. Do you realise that there are countries where virtually nobody got the vaccination? That means that their populations are still fully intact. Do you think that we can afford to restore people who will only ever be a burden on the rest of us when we have to compete with the rest of the world? No, that cannot be allowed to happen. That is why we had to stop you, and there is no limit to the means we will use if we have to. There is no more carrying of the feckless, from now on we are interested in the welfare of the talented and the productive. By that I mean people who are prepared to make a reasonable contribution to the good of all. It doesn't mean they have to be rocket scientists or something, but simply people who will carry their own weight. As you can imagine, when this is all over, there will be a massive clean-up operation. Do you really believe that we are going to let you restore lazy, idle shirkers, so they can lounge about, while the rest of us re-build? No, those days are gone, washed away by the blood of the zombie apocalypse. We are now in a major push to mass produce the Ghost Hand, so it can be distributed from coast to coast. As we speak we are recruiting teams of sweepers who will go through every town in the country, selecting who will be restored, and who will be destroyed. This country will go from strength to strength when we aren't dragged down by supporting huge populations of people who don't want to give anything, only take and take and take."

Everybody let this news sink in. It all made sense now. Magee and friends were building a new world, in the way they thought it should be, and this wasn't being put to a popular vote.

"So what now?" asked Howal.

"Well I looked through the data my men brought back here from your little operation, and I know it's worthless. That means you hid your real work. I'm sure you have made several interesting discoveries while you were holed up there that you are hiding from us. I am sending more men back to go through that place with a fine tooth comb. They will find what I want eventually. In the meantime I will cut right to the chase. Working independently you are a threat to this organisation and to this country. That will not be tolerated. These are your choices; join forces with us and work to the greater good, or else,…………well let's say you will be put out of commission. That is me being honest. You would have a good life here, we look after our people well. You would even have an influence on national policy through the council, that must be tempting for you. We can use brilliant scientists like you here, mankind can use you, and it would give you the chance to redeem some of the mistakes you have made. I know that you John, are particularly keen to undo some of the incalculable damage that you have done. We also would have no problem employing your friend Eddie here."

The three men looked at each other astonished.

"We need time to consider your offer. We want to weigh up the pros and cons of everything. As you can imagine this is a lot to throw at us all at once" Howal said eventually. He knew they had to buy time to figure out a manoeuvre. Magee was full of surprises, and was proving a more than worthy opponent. He would not be defeated easily.

"Certainly, that's understandable" Magee commented. "I will give you a reasonable amount of time to talk it over among yourselves. I will have food and drink sent down here to you, and I look forward to a positive response to our generous offer. Tomorrow I will return and I will let you know if we have found Tara Mahoney and her lovely friend at the District Hospital."

With that bombshell he turned and left. It looked like he held all the cards.

11 THE RESCUE

The four friends were moving again, walking quickly in single file towards the District Hospital. After having had a quick discussion they had decided to strike right away. If they did not rescue the two female prisoners now, they had no way of knowing where they would be brought to and then the chances of rescuing them were close to zero. Also they did not have any vehicles with them and if there was a car chase they would have to rely on luck in finding suitable vehicles nearby and more luck that they would have sufficient fuel. They also did not know how many more gang members were inside the hospital, but there seemed to be lots of them coming and going. They needed to counter the numbers imbalance by using the element of surprise. The time for action was definitely now, and they would have to worry about getting the medical supplies at another time. Tom ordered the dogs to stay put at a rendezvous point they selected. He didn't want them getting caught in a firefight, and they could be picked up later when all the shooting had died down. They were well trained and would wait for his return. The zombies did not express any interest in animals for some reason so they would be ok by themselves. On the subject of zombies they noticed to their alarm that there seemed to be lots of them accumulating in the area, they could see them all around and hear the terrible animal-like sounds they made. They seemed to be holding back for now though, waiting for something, perhaps for their numbers to grow stronger.

When they got within fifty yards of the hospital, in accordance with the prearranged plan the friends now split up. Keeping out of sight, Scott and Doug circled around to intercept the car containing the prisoners, while Tom and Brad covered the storeroom entrance. The target car was parked in the front parking lot of the hospital, faced toward the exit for a speedy departure. A low boundary wall ran about ten feet away from it, which separated the hospital grounds from a small park that was beside it, and it was behind the cover of this wall that Scott and Doug stole quietly forward, using the odd tree as extra concealment. They could see the two guards standing by the side of the car casually chatting. Both carried assault rifles. Discovery now would be fatal both to them and to the mission, and a cold sweat was on both their brows. Closer and closer they approached, their hearts pounding, but they were not seen or challenged. One of the guards on the car was watching his cronies carry out boxes and wondering what kinds of drugs were in them when he heard a noise behind him. Turning around he saw the muzzle of a shotgun pointed straight at him, the owner leaning behind the low wall.

"Put your weapon down and walk away and no-one will get hurt!" Scott hissed at him.

"Hey man we can cut you in on this, there's no need for any aggro......." the man said, stalling for time, assuming that some looters had shown up, probably suffering from cold turkey and desperate for a fix.

The other guard turned and now the two of them could see another gun pointed at them a short distance away.

"Listen to what he says!" Brad urged them. "We have got you surrounded! Give us the women and you will live to see another day!"

The gang member looked at his friend, and they slowly looked around for signs of more strangers. Contrary to the bold claim of these jokers, all the gang members could see were two of them; they must be bluffing.

"What do you want with the bitches? Do you know them?' One of the men called, hoping to distract them while they thought of a plan to get help.

"None of your business what we want with them, this is your last warning." Now Scott's voice had an air of deadly menace about it. He knew they couldn't risk others of the gang noticing the commotion and coming over to investigate. "Put the weapons down and walk away or in three seconds you will both be taking a full load of buckshot!"

The guards weighed up the options. They were both drug addicts, and they badly wanted their share of the drugs that their colleagues were in the process of stealing. If they lost the two pretty women, Eli was not going to be pleased at all, and especially to just these two chancers. He would at the very least refuse them their reward of drugs, and both of them were having a bad withdrawal right now. This laid the foundations for some very poor reasoning on their part. They gave each other a knowing glance, instantly communicating their intent to one another. They had been in a situation like this before, and each knew what to do. They would quickly dive for cover and hope not to get shot. When the other gang members heard the shooting they would rush over, and easily overpower the strangers.

"Ok, you know you do have a point....................." the

guard bluffed as he nodded to his cohort.

Simultaneously they both dived for cover behind the car, gambling that they would get there in time, and also that the strangers would not risk hitting the two females that they were trying to rescue. Their plan may have worked before in similar circumstances, but on this occasion they were up against tougher opponents than street punks, strung out on crack. While they were still in mid-flight, two shots rang out, and they were both cut down in their tracks. Then Scott and Doug raced to jump into the front of the car while a very surprised Tara and Beverley watched, start it up and drive pell mell out of there, before more gang-members could arrive.

Tom and Brad had been waiting anxiously, and hoping things would go without a hitch. They were concealed behind the wall that ran along the front of the hospital. It was the same height as the low wall at the side, and it provided pretty decent hard cover from where they could observe the front of the buildings. Neither wanted to risk not seeing their families again, but they were willing to carry out the mission as it was a just cause. They were prepared for the eventuality that things would not go to plan. Since Tom was the explosives expert he was manning the dynamite, while Brad covered him with several loaded guns. They had calculated that a massive display of force would deter the gang members from mounting a serious pursuit when things began to get interesting, until they too could get out of the area. Both also kept a watchful eye on the nearby zombies, who were still growing in number, waiting for their own signal, but not being threatening right now. Then they heard the gunfire coming from their left hand side. Tom crimped some blasting caps and ran forward to a position behind a truck from which to launch the dynamite. Brad raised one of his rifles in readiness. Things were going to hot up big time…………

Eli and the other members of Crime Machine had been in a

good mood. They had gotten into a treasure trove of powerful drugs before anybody else, and had gotten two fine prisoners as well. They were completely engrossed in getting the drugs out as quickly as possible, when they heard the gun shots outside. They paused and listened for more but heard none. Then Eli called the guards on the radio. There was no reply. He swore repeatedly. He shouldn't have left the prisoners with those two idiots! He ordered his men to investigate, his anger tempered by his usual caution. Dropping everything gang members rushed to the entrance, determined to fight off whoever had disturbed them. Slowing to look out at the entrance, they saw their car with the prisoners drive away at speed, and what was left of the guards lying prone on the ground, already attracting a swarm of waiting zombies to feast on the remains. They did not see Tom and Brad when they rushed out through the doors, and then they saw a stick of dynamite arcing through the air towards them, and heard the gunfire as Brad opened up on them. The first explosion ripped through them, cutting them down like a scythe in the confined space. This was quickly followed up by another explosion as Tom threw another stick of the dynamite right in through the hospital doors. Then he retreated back behind the wall again. There he grabbed a rifle and commenced firing at the survivors. Gang members fell everywhere and the rest retreated in confusion. Brad emptied one gun and picked up another and when that was empty, another. The gang were no longer in a position to threaten anyone having been killed or driven back by the onslaught. Seeing that they had neutralised the attack, Brad and Tom ran for it. As they went they heard the bellow of the massed zombies and watched them surge forward. This was what the zombies had been waiting for. Already the fallen individuals were being devoured, and the remaining members of the gang turned and fled back into the storeroom as the hordes pursued them, maddened by the smell of blood. As they withdrew Tom and Brad noted that the zombies were moving faster than they had seen them move up to now, another sign that they were slowly changing.

Tom spotted a motorcycle lying near a lamppost, a perfect getaway vehicle for the cramped conditions on the roads. The remains of its leather-clad rider lay nearby. The keys were still in the ignition and it started first kick. Brad hopped on, and Tom gunned the powerful 1300 cc engine. Then he headed off to where they would meet the others. They did not see the group of men in uniform, who had been watching the battle through binoculars, observing them from the roof of a nearby building.

Inside the hospital there were few remaining members of Crime Machine. Eli was among them, running for his life. This was going so, so wrong. Who were the men who had attacked them? He did not know, but he did know that he had to do some quick thinking, or he was going to be zombie food very shortly. He fired a couple of shots at some chasing zombies behind him and looked at his surroundings. There was only one entrance out of here, and they were being chased into a dead end. This was not good. Almost at the point of panic, he suddenly had an inspiration, the crawl space where those two bitches had hidden! He quickly looked around, how did they get up there? He saw a filing cabinet in the corner, that was it. Using a chair, he climbed onto the cabinet, not without some difficulty. One of his men helped him. They could hear the zombies getting closer. The caught some of his men and dragged them down, eating them alive like animals in the wild. There screams filled the air and echoed in the hallways. More would be upon them in seconds if they did not hurry. Frantically he pulled over the panel and climbed up, gritting his teeth from the exertion. He had never been much of a gymnast. Finally he managed to haul himself up into the crawlspace. The other man tried to follow him but Eli knew the zombies would see him. He drew a pistol and shot the man in the head so he fell back.

"Sorry, only room for one" Eli muttered, and pulled the

panel back in place. Just as he did the zombies swarmed in and fell on the last two of the gang who were still standing. They tried in vain to defend themselves but the zombies were too many, and more screams filled the air as the flesh was torn from their bodies. Then Eli waited tensely as the zombies below him settled down to devour their food. They did not scent him over the smell of the gore in which they presently wallowed but he was still in a very precarious place. It was uncomfortable in the crawl space and already his knees were getting sore from the narrow joists, but he had to bear it until he could work something out…………….

****

Doug killed the engine and opened the car door to listen for his friends. Scott followed suit. They had collected the two dogs to the surprise of Tara and Beverley, and they now jumped about and scampered around the car. They all listened to the sounds of battle and stared in that direction. After a short time the shooting stopped and Doug and Scott now had a tense wait on their hands. Would Tom and Brad succeed in getting away without harm? Then Scott remembered the two women in the back and he went to cut their ropes off. The two had been silent all along, wondering just exactly what was going to happen to them now. Who were these men? Were they good guys or bad guys?

"Are you two ok? " Doug asked.

"Ah, sort of……. Yes I …….think so" Tara answered. If their ropes were being dispensed with that was a positive sign. "Who are you if you don't mind me asking?"

Doug explained their story briefly and explained that they

had come to the hospital looking for medical supplies when they had seen what was going on.

"I'm Doug by the way, and my friend's name is Scott."

"We can't thank you enough for rescuing us from the clutches of those evil bastards" Beverley said. "It makes me shudder to think what would have happened to us if you guys hadn't come along. I'm Beverley and my friend's name is Tara."

She told them about the work they had been doing at the hospital, and how they had hidden there before the gang had broken in.

"With the benefit of hindsight it might not have been a good idea to stay where all those drugs were, but we didn't know what the alternative was. We had planned to leave there this very night but as you saw yourselves, that plan was rudely interrupted."

"It was probably as good a place as any to wait out the storm, but you were unlucky with the drugs alright. Sooner or later the supply of drugs was going to attract various elements to the hospital. It was what brought us to the place however, so it wasn't all bad!" Doug told them.

They waited for a few more anxious moments, and then heard the noise of a motorcycle approaching.

"This is probably them" Scott said hopefully, but they had their guns ready nevertheless. Then as the bike got closer they were relieved to have their feeling confirmed, and Tom and Brad gave them a cheery wave as they approached. Further introductions were made and Tom and Brad were updated on the girl's story.

Tara thanked Tom and Brad for their role in the rescue; "Today it is safe to say we have seen both the worst of men and the best of men. I am happy and relieved that we are now in the company of men who fall into the latter category. There's still hope for mankind with people like you around. Things could have been so much worse. I hope I don't have nightmares over this whole business to add to the ones I've already been having."

Now the friends wanted to know where they could bring Tara and Beverley where they would be safe, while they carried on their own mission. The girls explained that the one place they needed to be was at their friend's laboratory, so they could continue their work on the new nanobots. Intrigued the friends asked for more information about their work, and were astounded to know that they had been part of the team that had invented the Iasobots.

"Let me get this straight" Scott said to Tara. "You know this guy John Hodson, and you have planned to meet up with him to make nanobots that will be able to kill the original nanobots? Are you sure that's even possible?"

"Theoretically it's perfectly feasible. However we badly need to get organised with our colleagues, to marry up the different components, as we have been working on different aspects of the project. Now we need to put the whole thing together to make something we can use."

They told the friends where Howal's laboratory was located, and asked to be brought there. Doug wanted to know where their data was, as he did not fancy the idea of having to go back into the hospital, crawling as it was now with blood-crazed zombies. Tara however, explained that their work was hidden on their persons. During their time living secretly at the hospital, when they had feared that they might have to make a run for it sometime, they had made secret holes in the soles of their shoes. Their precious work was saved on data sticks, hidden in these holes. The friends were impressed at this ingenuity, and relieved at not having to go back to the hospital. They agreed to provide them safe escort to Howal's lab, and then they would continue on their way to their families. Tara tried calling Howal to say they were on their way, in case he had mounted a rescue of some sort, but there was no reply. Nor was there a reply from Hodson's phone. They exchanged worried glances. Scott decided that they had best proceed with caution, there were a lot of people disappearing these days.

****

Billy Magee was holding another meeting with some of his scientists. They had results in their quest to create more nanobots. The head of the team got the presentation going with a slideshow during which he presented the facts about their latest discoveries. They had found during tests that the Iasobots could be modified to deliberately attack the cerebral cortex of the human brain, reducing the victim to a mindless automaton. This automaton could then easily be manipulated to obey any command given by its master. The new nanobots could be easily delivered into the human system, and even ingested unwittingly. They called the new nanobots they had developed 'Slavebots' because they stole the free-will of the person and made of them an unthinking slave.

"So what you're saying essentially, is that these Slavebots can reduce anybody to a mindless, programmable robot?" asked Magee.

"Yes, that is exactly what they will do" the scientist answered enthusiastically.

"Have you carried out any trials on humans, as opposed to simulations in the lab?"

"Yes, we have. First we took one of the captured zombies. We restored her using the Ghost Hand. After carefully monitoring her recovery for a few days, we then injected her with some Slavebots, telling her it was some health-restoring electrolytes, and waited to see the effects. The Slavebots worked perfectly, and she became a completely mindless robot, prepared to kill her own mother if we asked her to."

Magee was impressed; "I love it, with this weapon we could turn entire nations on each other, and sit back and watch them tear each other apart. Domestically it would make a very useful workforce for menial jobs, say, using criminals and political opponents. Also, with an army of these things no force on Earth could stand before us. Is there a way to reverse the process, say if we wanted to bring someone back?"

"Yes, that's the beauty of it. We then reversed the process in the woman using the Ghost Hand again. It will disable the Slavebots just as well as the Iasobots because they are both susceptible to the same radiation. With your permission we will now release the woman because we figure she has been through enough at this stage."

Magee could see no harm in this, so he consented to her release. He ordered the scientist to keep up the good work and then went back to his office to receive an update from some of his men just back from the field.

The Troop Leader entered his office and sat down when invited.

"So tell me Sergeant, what news of the lovely Tara and Beverley, have you brought them here to me yet?"

"No Sir, when we got to the hospital there was a full-scale gun battle going on. Shenton and Mahoney were in the company of persons unknown when we last saw them. What their fate may be is anyone's guess, I don't expect that they knew either of the parties involved."

The Sergeant then told Magee about the firefight between the strangers and the members of a pack of human hyenas, who had been attempting to raid the entire hospital of drugs. He told of how he had seen these strangers rescue two females matching the descriptions of the wanted scientists, and then decimate the gang members, before they were presumably finished off by zombies. It had been too dangerous to enter the hospital to search for survivors who might have information, so they had returned to headquarters.

"That was probably the best option" said Magee thoughtfully. "We know where they were planning to head anyway; straight to Howal's lab. That's a good place to pick up the trail again. I want you to return there and watch that place, see if they show up. This time do not rush in arresting people, only do that if they show signs of leaving. Remain in concealment and do not under any circumstances alert them to your presence. Give them time to complete their work, it's easier than forcing or threatening them. When the time is right they will want to test their results on zombies and I want to see what technology they may have produced. Go now, bring double the manpower. These strangers sound like they know what they're doing, I want to know who they are and if they are a threat to us."

The Sergeant saluted and left.

12 HOWAL'S LABORATORY

Eli shifted his weight around in the crawl space as quietly as he could. The zombies had finished dining on the other members of his gang and had drifted away. Eli was still very nervous; even he knew theirs was a hunger that could never be satisfied. He could still hear some of them moving about in the hallways, recent arrivals picking on the leftovers. In the room below him there was blood and bones and tattered clothing everywhere. He knew it was time to think about escaping from the hospital. When the blood dried the zombies might smell his presence and return. He did not think they would be able to reach him in the crawlspace, but the idea of having a room full of them waiting below him was not exactly appealing. He guessed that they could wait for a lot longer than he could. He checked his pistol and reloaded it quietly. All he had left now were twenty bullets. He cursed himself for not being better armed. It had not seemed that important when he'd had thirty four armed gang members around him. Things were different now, he was alone and quite justified in feeling sorry for himself. His feared gang was no more, taken from him in the space of an afternoon. How the hell did that happen?

He quietly searched his pockets to see if he had anything else of use on him. He cursed when he realised that he didn't even have his damn phone. Where had he left it? Then he remembered, yes of course! It was in the glove box of his car, the one the strangers had driven off in. This gave him a glimmer of hope for the need for revenge that was building inside him now. His phone had a GPS built into it. If he could find the phone he might find the car, and then the strangers would not be far away. They would pay for destroying his gang and for making him have to spend hours hiding in a crawlspace while his legs went to sleep. He was feeling a little better now, revenge was a good motivator. He would build a new gang and start again. A new Crime Machine would rise and make those strangers wish they were never born.

He listened carefully once more for sounds below him. The zombies seemed to have shuffled further away. It was time to start moving. While he had been in the crawlspace his eyes had adjusted to the dim light and he had noticed that the space extended over the hallways of the building. If he could follow along the hallways it might lead him to somewhere that he could safely climb down out of there and bolt for it.

Slowly and stiffly at first he crawled along, trying to stay on the joists. It would not do for him to accidently put his weight on the flimsy ceiling boards and possibly go crashing to the ground below. His knees protested every time he moved and his right leg was driving him crazy with pins and needles, but he persisted. To remain would mean certain death. He finally got to the smaller space over the hall and cautiously crept along, all the time watching for zombies through the narrow cracks in the panels. The slow journey seemed interminable to him and drops of sweat fell from his face to spatter in the dust. The hall seemed to go on forever, and when he finally got to the end of it, he found himself at a T-junction. Which way should he go? He could only see a few feet in front of him in either direction, so there was nothing to guide him. He tried to visualise where he was, in his mind. If he had come north from the storeroom, he should be somewhere over the lab by now. The entrance was on the west side of the building, so that meant he should go left! He moved laboriously on, hoping he had picked correctly. The thought of having to retrace his steps was a dreadful one, this hallway seemed even longer than the first one. He soon forgot about this when he saw the air vent up ahead. Daylight! Crawling faster now he made his way towards it as a thirsty man in the desert makes for an oasis.

When he eventually reached the vent he saw that it was barely big enough to let him through. Barely would be sufficient. Peering outside he looked as best he could for signs of zombies. There were two not far away. Crap! They seemed to be watching something over to the right, outside of his line of vision. He waited and waited but used the time to look for anything outside that might aid his escape. When he got out through the air vent he would need a speedy escape as the noise he would be making would surely draw a swarm of zombies on himself. He did not relish the idea of being chased alone through the streets by a pack of zombies, with their growls and cries drawing every other zombie for miles around. He wasn't interested in the parked up vehicles along the street; these would be more than likely locked and without the keys in them. He was looking for abandoned vehicles on the road as there was a better chance that these would have the keys in them, essential for a quick getaway. There were two pickup trucks he could just about make out, over on his left. Both had the look of vehicles that had been left in haste by their owners. When he got out he would head straight for these.

Finally he watched the two zombies move off. He waited a while longer hoping they would keep moving. It was now or never, further waiting would do no good at all. He tried to push the grille away with his hand but it was surprisingly solid. More force was needed. He moved his position around and pushed his feet hard against it. Still no movement. The quiet way was not working, so he did what he had to do. Dispensing with silence he angrily began to kick at the grill. After three or four kicks it gave at one corner. Two more kicks and it came off, clanging loudly on the concrete path below. Cursing the noise he quickly turned onto his stomach and wriggled out through the hole. Then he was hanging on by his hands. A short drop and he was on the ground again. He landed well despite his tired legs and suffered no injury. The cool evening air was welcome on his hot face but he knew the sound would bring the zombies like flies.

He turned and ran as fast as his legs would carry him for the nearest trucks. Behind him he heard a snarl. He looked back and saw that the two zombies had returned and were now in full pursuit. He drew his pistol and fired twice, aiming for the central body mass where he was more likely to score a hit. It did not kill them but they were slowed enough for him to just keep running. He had to spare his bullets. He got to the first truck just as he heard more howls. Having heard the gunfire every zombie who was in the area was now on their way. Frantically he clawed at the driver's door and ripped it open; no damn key! He turned and scrambled for the other truck. This one had to be good or he would have to start running a lot further. Eli wasn't a very fit man, and he knew if he didn't obtain mechanical assistance soon then his chances were slim to poor. One of the first two zombies had dropped to the ground , pouring blood from a chest wound, but the other one was still mobile and Eli was forced to use another bullet on it before it got too close. Reaching the second truck he wildly looked for the ignition. The key was there! He jumped in and locked the doors. There were zombies closing in on his position from all sides. The truck was old and beat up and he grimly hoped the previous owner had at least maintained the battery. He turned the key and the engine spluttered lethargically into life. Throwing it into gear he reversed away from the wall, then into drive and he floored the accelerator, partly ramming the other truck out of the way. There were two zombies in the back and one clinging to the front, hanging determinedly on by the wipers. Speeding away for two blocks Eli suddenly hit the brakes hard. This caused the zombie to fall off, and then he drove over it, leaving a mess on the road. The two on the back were pounding on the rear window trying to get in. It would not hold much longer if they kept that up. Once he'd put some distance between himself the rest of the pack he slammed on the brakes, stopped, got out and quickly shot them both in the head. He was getting tired of being hassled. Now he was down to fifteen bullets, but he had a bit of open road in front of him. He jumped back in again and drove off, veering over and back around obstacles with the two dead zombies still in the back. He headed straight for the clubhouse. He was tired, hungry and he desperately needed a beer……..

****

Scott and the others parked up their vehicles a few blocks from Howal's laboratory and reconnoitred the area quietly on foot. Moving in a wide circle around the area they didn't notice anything untoward, just the occasional zombie wandering about. They moved in closer and had another look. Still nothing. Tara had tried calling and Beverley had tried texting John and Alan again and there was still no response. Something was wrong. They decided to go right in, whatever had happened to their friends, they would not find out any other way. It was getting well into the evening now, and dark in the absence of streetlights, when they got to the front door. It had been boarded up, and showed signs of forced entry. The girls gasped, something had happened John and Alan! Brad and Doug got tyre irons from some nearby abandoned vehicles, and while Tom and Scott covered them, they removed the boards as quickly and quietly as they could. Once the doors were open they moved inside, watching for any signs of defenders. Tara and Beverley called out for their friends, but they were only met by silence. They knew at least one of the residents had had a gun and it would be bad luck to get shot in these circumstances. No-one came to greet them though and they could sense the air of desertion about the place. They secured the doors as best they could and then began to explore.

Many of the rooms could not be seen from the outside, so they were able to turn some lights on in the building. Like the hospital, it was equipped with its own generator. It did not take them long to confirm that the building was empty, or that the previous occupants had left quickly. There were half empty coffee cups and a sandwich with one bite out of it in the dining area and other signs. The girls entered the laboratory, followed by the others. The place was in disarray, it had been thoroughly gone through by someone looking for something.

"I think we can assume that your friends were disturbed here and either fled or were taken against their will" Tom finally said gloomily. "Given the fact that you cannot reach them on their phones I'm sorry to say they were probably kidnapped and given the state of this place it is apparent that whoever did this wanted their work also. Do you have any idea who might have done this?"

"It could have been a number of entities" Beverley answered sadly. "Their work would be highly valuable to numerous governments and other organisations. During the Iasobot project we were all approached by shady characters from time to time, looking for the secrets of our work. Everyone from corporate spies to foreign government operatives. They were willing to pay a lot of money for the technology that we were working on. It's anyone's guess who might have done this."

"If they took your friends, I think it's safe to assume that you yourselves will be a target" Scott said softly. This situation was turning out to be more complicated that he had first thought.

"I wonder if it had something to do with that gang back at the hospital?" Brad wondered.

Tara thought about this; "Humm, it's not beyond the realm of possibilities, but no I doubt it in this case. They were just ordinary criminals looking to score a lot of drugs. The type of people who did this would be more interested in a research paper than they would be in a truck load of drugs." As she spoke her eyes were wandering around the room. Suddenly she saw something that made her gasp………

"Oh my God……………" The others looked at her, startled.

"What do you see Tara?" asked Beverley.

Tara walked to a marker board on the far wall. It was covered with mathematical equations, and chemical formulas, but that was not what had made her gasp. Down at the very bottom of the board, near the left hand side was written the words 'Molly keep warm' in very small letters.

"What does it mean?" the others asked.

"It's a message from Alan!" exclaimed Tara excitedly. "He knew we were trying to come here to help him and he must have left it just before he was taken away! Molly is a nickname he had for me, long story, never mind, the 'keep warm' bit refers to a hiding place he once showed me years ago. At least I think it does. I'm guessing that's where we'll find his research!"

She led them through the building to the room where the chimney used to be. "Now where was that switch?" she murmured to herself. It seemed so long ago since Alan had showed her. Then she remembered. She pulled back a false light switch and pulled the lever behind it. With a slight click the door to the hidden safe opened. Rushing to it she found to her joy all the work that had been left by Howal; papers, data sticks, bottles, samples and all the other equipment. There was a notepad written in Howal's neat hand as well, outlining all their work. He had written it specifically for Tara in the event that something happened to him, so that she would know how to carry on the work without him.

"Ingenious!" said Doug admiringly. "It's a brilliant hiding place, and there's no-one else on Earth who would have known what that message meant, even if they noticed it in the first place."

They brought everything back to the lab to have a more thorough look at it. They needed to see exactly what they had, and how much work there was left to do. While Tara and Beverley were doing that Scott and the others were quietly having a council of war among themselves.

"So what do we do now?" he asked. "It's obvious that these people are in danger. I am willing to stay to help them. Aside from the zombie threat, the city is crawling with every type of criminal and dirt bag you can imagine, these two could have a very uncertain fate without adequate protection. If they fall into the wrong hands again I don't need to draw you pictures of what problems may befall them. I feel bound by conscience to help."

The others thought about this.

"They're engaged in what is undeniably critical work" agreed Doug. "They told me this lab is the only place equipped to complete it. We can't just leave them here. They're two young women who probably can't even handle a gun. Like you said they'd be prey to every scumbag in the city right now. There is no law to protect them. We don't know who might be looking for them but they could turn up here at any time. I understand if Tom and Brad want to go to their families, but the fate of millions of people could rest on this. If these scientists have a chance of developing a cure for the zombies, the decision we make now could change the world. It would be criminal to walk away and desert them. I also will remain here to help them, it's the right thing to do and there is no-one else available to do it."

Tom and Brad looked at each other. This was indeed a conundrum. They desperately wanted to get to their families but if they helped these scientists, they might be able to come up with a solution for the zombies that would make the world a safer place for them all. Eventually they decided to call their wives to confer with them. They called Caroline and Christine, and explained the predicament that they were in. Caroline and Christine and the children were all fine. An Aunt and Uncle of the children had made contact when the phones started working again. They has been hiding in a small town not very far away. They had arranged to come out to the farmhouse as it was safer there, but they had raided a small dispensary on their way, so now they had all the medicine they needed. The house was fairly full now, but they had safety in their numbers. The Aunt and Uncle both had military experience so they knew how to defend themselves. Looking at the bigger picture, Caroline and Christine thought it was for the best if Tom and Brad stayed to help the scientists, after all it might help to cure a lot of the zombies. So it was settled. The friends would stay and be bodyguards for the scientists while they completed their project.

Scott broke the news to a delighted Tara and Beverley. They

knew the men had been on their way to their families and they were afraid of what would happen to themselves then. Now they had four bodyguards who knew how to handle dangerous situations. They all had a meal in the dining room to celebrate. The place was well-stocked with all the provisions they needed as Howal had seen the future and had left nothing to chance. Then they secured the front doors better by pushing large cabinets and other heavy objects up against them. If anyone tried to force their way in again, it would be a lot harder this time, and they would have plenty of warning. Tom noted that the locks had been blasted without doing too much damage to the rest of the doors. Whoever did this they knew what they were doing, they were not amateurs.

Scott convened a meeting in the dining room.

"I think we can assume that there are dangerous people who want to get their hands on the work that Tara and Beverley are doing on these nanobot things. Right now we don't know who these people are, but when we see what's at stake here it's a given that they aren't going to just ask politely for what they want. We must plan for the worst case scenario here, although none of us want to think like that. What are your ideas?"

Brad spoke first; "I suggest a twenty four hour guard on the building. We can double up, with two doing the day-shift and two doing the night-shift. Every gun we have can be kept loaded where we can get to them quickly and we keep the rest of the dynamite handy as a last ditch option. That would leave Tara and Beverley free to do their scientific stuff."

"Not a bad idea" agreed Tom. None of them wanted to talk about Josh and Ann right now, but the lessons had been learned. "I don't mind doing the night-shift, I don't always sleep too well anyway even when I'm tired. I can take Keeper on patrol with me. Whoever does the day shift can borrow Scout. If anyone comes near the place they will hear long before we do. They are trained to growl softly instead of barking so they won't give the game away."

"I'll do the night-shift too, if no-one minds" Brad said. "I haven't been sleeping too well either these days." No-one objected to this idea, so that was one thing settled.

Now Tara spoke; "We will hide anything we're not directly using at any given time, and leave everything in the chimney space every night. If we're attacked during the day we will run and hide what we were working on at the time. If the worst came to the worst, at least it would be safe there."

Everyone liked this plan.

Doug was struck by a thought; What do you intend to do if you find something that can cure this zombie thing? What happens if we don't find your scientist friends?"

Beverley answered him; "We were discussing this when you guys were talking among yourselves earlier. We have no way of knowing where our colleagues are, although we will keep trying to make contact. We have found enough information here to bring our work to the next level, I can tell you that already from a quick look over the stuff Alan Howal hid. Obviously we would make better progress with the others to help us, but we can still operate as we are. If we come up with a solution to zombification, we will disperse it to every medical organisation in the world. We will upload our work onto the internet and then it will be available to anyone with the knowhow to use it. We discovered the websites we need are working again. Obviously some things are slowly returning to normal, as people repair the damage that was done and get things working again. There are people like us out there everywhere, all fighting this apocalypse in every way they can."

"Great stuff!" said Scott. "I was wondering how you would get the information out there. It also raises a valuable other point; if you make your work freely available too soon your enemies will know how well you are progressing and may become desperate to destroy it. If that were the case they might just come and blow up the building or something. It's better to wait until the work is complete before you put it out there."

"Yes, good idea" agreed Tara. "We will do nothing until we make the breakthrough."

Brad now joined in; "I don't like the idea of being trapped in a building like this. Do you girls know if there's another way out besides the front and back doors? If we are attacked any easy escape is unlikely as both front and back will likely be watched. Did your friend Howal have any more secrets?"

They didn't think there was another way out. They didn't know of any, and if there was, it was likely that Howal would have used it himself when the doors were blasted in on him. The building was like a fortress. Howal knew the value of the things he was working on, and had the place reinforced to withstand most attacks. In addition to this there were no windows on the ground floor, and there were bars on all the other windows.

Brad had an idea; "While we were looking around earlier before we came into this place I noticed that there are brick buildings all along the street. Why don't we just make an escape route? We could get tools and knock a hole in the wall somewhere, big enough to fit through. If someone breaks in we wouldn't be trapped in here."

"That's actually a brilliant idea!" Tom enthused. "Brad and I could start doing that tonight when we start the night watch. It will give us something to do to pass the time!"

Everyone loved this plan. The girls told them about how they had been trapped in the hospital when the gang broke in, forcing their surrender. They didn't relish the thoughts of ever being in that helpless position again. A lot of animals, when making their burrow, will provide for themselves at least one extra exit. If a predator shows up and tries to get in, then they have a way out. Yes, a means of vacating the building in an emergency was an excellent idea.

"Ok so that's settled" said Scott. "It will break up some of the monotony and give you something to do for a while. Look for a place where we can conceal the hole quickly and easily, and I can't stress enough the importance of doing the job quietly, don't use any of Tom's dynamite!"

They all laughed at this joke, the idea that they would have a means to get out if needed had come as a great relief to them all. It took away the feeling of being trapped that they'd all had.

"One more thing" Doug suggested. "We should arm and train Beverley and Tara. I don't know what previous experience you may have but if things do get hot and heavy around here, it would be useful to have an extra pair of guns on our side. It will serve them later on as well, when we eventually leave this place. The one thing we're sure about the opposition is that they number more than us so a couple more guns on our side won't do any harm."

Neither Beverley or Tara had used guns before, so it was agreed that Doug and Scott would give them basic training during the day, when they took breaks from their other work. They would do as best they could without being able to fire some shots, there was no point attracting outside attention. When that happened it would not be training, but for real.

Leaving Brad and Tom to keep watch, and also to begin work on the escape route, they rest of them settled down for the night.

****

Meanwhile, in a building across the street, the Sergeant was on the radio again; "No Sir, they haven't come back out again. Looks like they are going to stay there at least for tonight."

"Have your men watch the front and back twenty-four seven. If they come up with a breakthrough they will try to contact Hodson and Howal again. I have their cell phones so I will know. Then I will give you the signal to go in and get them. Until then simply watch the place and do not let yourselves be detected. We should have bugged the place when we had a chance, but too late now. If at any stage they appear to be leaving, swarm the area and apprehend them. Try not to kill anyone unless you have to, and then notify me. Understand?"

The Sergeant understood. He quickly organised his own men into groups to watch the place around the clock. Then he bedded down for the night himself. He didn't like staying up all night, he'd read somewhere it wasn't good for your health.

13 BEING A ZOMBIE

Hodson and Howal looked up from an intense discussion as Magee entered the cell block. They knew from the smirk on his face that he had news which pleased him.

"Good morning gentlemen" he said with a grin. "I trust that you slept well? I want our guests to be comfortable!"

He was just too happy for their liking. Something was afoot.

"I wasn't sure whether to tell you this or not, but I feel I'm in a position where I can, so I might as well…………….we know where your friends Tara and Beverley are! As we speak they're at your laboratory, no doubt working like beavers to complete the work you were also working on. I assume that you hid the main body of your work, being clever people like you are, and I assume that your scientific colleagues will find it and find ways to develop it. I know that Mahoney seemed to have the missing pieces of the jig-saw, so all I have to do is wait until she delivers the goods, and then my men will swoop and capture everything."

Their hearts sank. Right now Magee seemed to be holding all the cards. He was cunning, they could not deny. They did not know about the four friends or how Tara and Beverley had managed to get to the laboratory, so they incorrectly had to assume that the girls were on their own.

Magee pressed on; "Now, having had time to consider my offer, and seeing as you do that we are the new power in the land, are you going to join us?"

"No we're not" answered Howal curtly. "Frankly we think that your plan stinks."

"And why is that?" asked Magee.

"Who are you to decide who gets the cure and who should not? It should be freely available to all. No-one did anything to deserve being a zombie, so everyone should get a fair chance to be restored" said Hodson defiantly. "The very idea of selecting people based on some perverse idea of a meritocracy, where you are the judge, is revolting."

Magee was somewhat disappointed; "I am not surprised at Howal's rejection, he's always been a bit pious, but I am surprised at you Hodson. You seemed like a man with ambition, and here you are, turning down a chance to work with the best. Remember your role in bringing us to where we are today? As far as I'm concerned, you have a responsibility to help us to repair some of the damage you have caused."

This stung Hodson. He was getting tired of this; "You and your plan are rotten to the core!" he exclaimed. He realised then that he was suffering a little from guilt exhaustion.

Magee was unfazed; "Rotten, really? I thought you gentlemen knew the way the world worked. When the farmer wants the crops in the fields to grow, he sprays them with manure, he doesn't spray them with perfume. The perfume might smell sweeter, but it won't fertilise anything and it certainly wouldn't be good for his crops. We are trying to build a better world here gentlemen. We have seen how fragile a thing is civilisation, especially when certain pressures are applied. No matter how good our machines and our systems are, it can all collapse in a matter of hours when disaster strikes. We need a more robust framework to clad our civilisation around, a new paradigm. You all saw how quickly the police, the army and even the government collapsed during this epidemic. Everyone thought those institutions were rock-solid, but they fell like a house of cards in a hurricane. We need to build the new society on solid foundations. Next time there might be no second chances. People need help and they need it quickly. They are in hiding all over the place. If their supplies are running out or if they get sick there is not much in the way of help for them. Once the supermarkets were emptied our way of life was on a countdown. That countdown is still ticking. Not everyone knows how to plant crops or raise livestock, even if they had the means. I am in the business of ensuring that our way of life survives and I do not have the luxury of prolonged philosophical or ethical debates. One final time, are you willing to join us?"

They looked blankly at him. Then Eddie Young spoke; "I will join you."

Everyone looked surprised.

"Why should I bother with you, I thought you were supposed to know nothing?" Magee was genuinely surprised.

"Because I have information that you need, not all of it but enough to point you in the right direction. I may not know the exact details, but I worked with them long enough to get a fair idea of what they were working on. I know all their ideas, your scientists will be able to fill in all the blanks."

"And why should I trust you?"

"I only tagged along with them because I wanted to see if they could come up with a cure. Now that they are prisoners here, they cannot achieve anything useful. All my friends were killed because of Hodson and his meddling with nanobots. I was even going to kill him once, but I was waiting to see if he could reverse some of the harm that he had done. Now obviously he has reached the end of that road, so I want to help the people who can. You have already demonstrated your technical know-how with the Ghost Hand, and that's good enough for me."

Magee had a think about this.......the man might have information, so it would do no harm to get that out of him. He would question him and have some of the men keep a close watch on him. As well it might lessen the resolve of the others if they knew some of their secrets were lost to them. He called the guards and had them release Eddie Young.

"Take him to Professor Larry Irvine." Magee ordered them. Then he turned to Eddie; "Tell the Professor everything you know. It had better be good, or you will be food for the zombies by lunchtime. If this is some kind of trick, or if you are wasting my time, I will feed you to them slowly. I will not be toyed with............."

Magee addressed Hodson and Howal again; "Well gentlemen, all your secrets will soon be ours with or without you. What have you got to lose from joining us? Just your ill-founded sense of righteousness and some peculiar sense of morality. In a different time and place you would have different beliefs, and think them just as valid, even if they totally opposed the values you have now. Why be so stubborn?"

"There is a universal concept of right and wrong that

overrides cultural belief systems." Howal argued. "We believe that you are effectively condemning millions of people to death, through no fault of their own, without even a proper trial. That is simply unacceptable to us."

"So you choose recalcitrance over co-operation. There are lessons in life that you have obviously yet to learn. Perhaps you have hung around universities for too long to understand that if life can't teach you through kindness it will teach you through pain. So be it, the die is cast." Magee answered ominously, his patience now exhausted. "Since you liken me to a Judge there is one of you whom I now cast judgement upon. Perhaps this will be a fitting punishment for your sins."

He called the guards and had them remove Howal from the cell and restrain him. Then Magee swiftly drew a dart gun from his jacket pocket. Raising it he fired it at John Hudson, the dart hitting him in the chest. He winced and pulled it out, but he could see that it contained a clear plastic capsule, now empty. Whatever had been in it was now inside him, and he had a feeling he knew what that was. Right now he wasn't feeling very confident.

"I have just injected you with some of your own rogue Iasobots, which we harvested from a zombie here in the lab Doctor Hodson. It is time for you to meet your worst nightmare, created by your own hand, the fruit of your own labours. In a very short time the nanobots will migrate to your brain, and then they will invade your brain cells, taking over your personality and reducing you to a slobbering zombie in a living hell. You were the architect of all this and now your penance is my final gift to you. This is where we say farewell."

Hodson was beginning to feel somewhat groggy.

"I believe I know the science involved, Mr Magee, but

thanks for the lecture anyway............."

He felt a slow fog descend onto his brain. His mind seemed to be emptying of its memories and it's personality. He was forgetting who he was and who the people standing the other side of the bars were. Desperately he tried to cling onto his humanity, as a drowning man clings to a rock, but now even the rock was moving, swimming in the sea of confusion and forgetfulness, and then he was swamped........

Howal watched in horror as his friend and colleague was transformed from a scientific genius into a slavering zombie, before his very eyes. The creature which bore some of his friend's features was now pulling at the bars of the cell, trying to attack them.

Magee turned to him; "As you can see Alan, there is a high price to be paid for lack of co-operation. This action has been sanctioned by the highest power in the land. It gives me no pleasure to see a great scientist reduced to a gibbering idiot, but you forced my hand. I will leave you alone now in the next cell. You will have more time to consider my offer while you listen to your old friend baying for your blood. I will return again tomorrow morning to see if you have changed your mind. Remember, we hold the means to release John from his stupor. You hold the key to his salvation as well as your own, all it needs is your co-operation."

Howal was placed in the cell next to the zombie and he would have a sleepless night listening to his friend going through the throes of 'zombie hunger' which only human flesh could satisfy.

****

Eli Draks had been busy since his escape from the hospital. He had driven several miles to where the gang's clubhouse was, and let himself in. After some food and a few beers he then went on the internet, and found the location of his cell phone, using it's GPS tracker. He did not know if the phone had been removed from the car, but he was willing to bet that it had not, because it had not moved in all the time since that he had monitored it. Wherever the phone was, his enemies would not be far away whoever they were. He was clever enough to guess that, like him, they would have parked up in a hurry, and then gone on foot to wherever they were holed up, so as to avoid attracting zombies and drawing them to the hideout. The next few days saw Eli begin a major recruitment drive, contacting old friends and associates who were still around, asking them if they wanted to join Crime Machine. Most of them asked where the rest of the gang were and he simply lied and said that they had become zombies after getting the cold vaccination. The reality was that, in the circles that they moved in, very few people were conscientious about things like cold and flu vaccines, leaving all that stuff to chance and relying on other people to bail them out of trouble. This was now to his advantage as he was able to recruit twenty new members in a fairly short space of time. They were men of varying quality and trustworthiness, and he had turned some of them down before when they tried to join the gang due to lack of intelligence and unreliability. These were changed times however and a man had to work with whoever was available and he really needed numbers around him for the goals he had set himself. Most of these cretins would be cannon fodder until he accomplished his mission, and after that he would worry about finding some people he wanted around himself long-term.

Their first outing had been a success. He had led the new

Crime Machine back to the hospital and retrieved most of the drugs that they had been in the process of stealing the time of his previous visit. Some had been damaged from Tom's dynamite attack, some to the weather, and some to the activities of the zombies, but most of the drugs had remained sealed in their boxes and were usable. They'd had to fight off a few zombies during their time there, but most of them seemed to have drifted off in search of new prey. There was still sporadic gunfire going on around the city, suggesting that other people were active doing various things, enough to attract hungry zombies. This had been an easy job however, and though the rest of them were beginning to think they were a serious force, Eli was under no such illusions. With enough men and firepower you could deal with huge numbers of zombies, especially if you had a strong defensive position. Zombies had limited intelligence, tended to be very predictable, and they didn't use weapons. Fighting other groups such as the military or those strangers with the dynamite was another matter altogether. A success was a success all the same however, and after making sure they had gathered anything of value the gang had returned to the hideout and had a party celebrating their success and the strengthening of their friendship.

Later on, using some of the drugs as currency, Eli and company had a rendezvous with an infamous gang of gunrunners that he knew. There they had purchased military type weapons and explosives including machine guns and rocket launchers. He had been out-gunned before and counted the cost, but the next time it was he who would have the upper hand. His enemies would pay and rue the day they had crossed him. Next he informed the gang of his plan to attack persons unknown, whose location he was not really sure of. They were a little mystified as to what this was all about but he concocted a story that these persons unknown were operating a drugs manufacturing plant. He said the chemists were two pretty females and they had a number of security personnel who knew how to handle themselves. This made sense to the gang and after their recent success and the acquisition of their new toys they were ready for anything. With the ground thus prepared, Eli outlined his plan. They would attack sometime the next day, when their hangovers had abated..............

14 A BREAKTHROUGH

During the night Tom and Brad had found a good place for an escape hatch. In the dining area there was a fridge in between the two built-in cabinets that spanned the entire length of one wall. It was a big old thing that hummed lethargically whenever the motor was on, and probably did not have much life left in it. They pulled it back and began knocking a hole in the wall behind. Using a sledgehammer and a chisel which they had found in a storage area under the stairs they set to work on the concrete between the bricks. They tried to keep the noise down by wrapping the hammer with cloth, but still made what seemed to be an outrageous dim. No-one complained though, so they carried on. Once they got the first few bricks out things became easier, and they could use the sledge alone to knock the bricks out. They did not know when an attack might come, so time was of the essence. As one did some chiselling and hammering, the other would patrol the building and keep an eye on the security monitors. Then they would switch places for a while so the work was continuous through the night. They were aware that they were working on a support wall, but they planned to keep the hole small enough not to compromise the building structurally. Sometimes when they changed roles they would chat about various things, partly to help themselves to stay awake. On one such occasion Brad chuckled softly as he handed over the hammer to Tom:

"You know, I was thinking as I was working just now........." he paused.

Tom waited patiently for him to continue.

"I was thinking about that conversation that we had on the river about all the things that used to annoy us about our jobs. None of that stuff matters now. The world we knew is dead and gone and all those worries died with it. What was it all for? What did it achieve? Makes you wonder why we worried in the first place."

Tom thought about this for a moment: "You know, you're right. It was about ten minutes after we had that chat that we saw our first zombies, and though we didn't know it, everything changed in that moment. The world as we knew it came to an end."

"Yes, that's what I've been thinking about all night." Brad smiled. "I realised that I spent years worrying about stuff that can never happen now, and I realise that I wasted my time. Where did it get me? I invested so much in a future that can never exist, and all that worrying was for nothing. From now on I'm just going to live day by day and not let things get to me, there's no point!"

Tom laughed. "I've often heard people say that you shouldn't worry about tomorrow, but it always seemed like something that was easier said than done. Maybe something people more philosophical than me did. Like some concept that only people like Monks can actually do in practice. Now that so much of the world we knew has been swept away it's hard to believe that it was even real in the first place."

"That's exactly how I feel as well!" Brad exclaimed. "I find myself wondering if it was all a dream. I feel like nothing real has been lost with the passing of that life. We were all just sleepwalking to the grave, we weren't really living. I have a guilty confession to make: these last few days have been the first time I have really felt alive since I can't even remember. I know that sounds bad, but it's the first real excitement I've probably had in years."

"Now that you mention it, I've felt the same" Tom said thoughtfully. "I think the others have too, I've seen the look in their eyes. It must be something about not knowing if you'll see tomorrow that makes you appreciate today much more. They say soldiers in a war feel that way. Strange that it took a zombie apocalypse to make us see that. It's a strange world."

"It is a strange world" Brad agreed. "In ways we were like zombies ourselves, getting up, going to work, coming home and going to bed, slowly dying of boredom. I know a lot of bad stuff has happened this last while, but maybe something good will emerge at the other end. I certainly know I'll be a different man. I see things in a new perspective. Different things have regained their importance for me now. Family, friends and taking the time to watch the flowers grow. Even this, what we're doing now; we're risking our lives to help strangers because it seems like the right thing to do. It seems like a noble thing. We don't know what enemies we may make as a result or what these people are capable of, but throwing caution to the wind and running with something has never felt so right."

"I'm glad we're together in this" Tom said with a grin. "I think it was no coincidence that we happened by just in time to protect Bev and Tara. We are on a mission that will help to save the world. Whatever happens in the next while we'll give as good as we get and give a good account of ourselves."

Brad nodded, picked up his shotgun and walked away to do his patrol.

By morning they had made good progress and had made a hole a grown man could slip through. A quick look around in the next building was enough to confirm that it was empty, but they would leave a more thorough exploration to the day shift.

When Scott and Doug came along to relieve them they were impressed at the progress and at the location for the escape hole. They added ropes to the back of the fridge and suggested bolstering it with some timbers in case someone happened to be prowling in the adjoining building. If anyone in the next-door building found the hole and tried to get through, the timbers would prevent them from doing so. It was probably unlikely but any exit is also an entrance and one never knew. In the event of intruders to their own building all they would have to do was exit through the hole, then pull the fridge back in snug against the wall using the ropes, and only the most thorough of searches would find the hole. By then they would almost certainly be long gone. Their biggest task now was to clear away the dirt and rubble from the area. If they left any traces of their activity then it would give the game away and cause complications as they made their getaway.

They decided that the best place for the rubble was in the adjoining building where no searchers would find it, and they worked at a steady pace to clear the area. Finally it was cleared and Scott swept and mopped the floor. No-one would have guessed what they had done and they were very pleased with themselves. Now it was time to have a better look around and they decided that Doug would do that. Scott handed him a shotgun and remained to guard the hole. Doug advanced through the neighbouring building, Scout trotting by his side, and had a look around. The building had probably once been a pub, but now it was the offices of some business, and the ordinary things of offices lay strewn about. Like so many other places, there were the signs of zombie attacks, and a hasty evacuation. Scout found plenty of bones to sniff at and Doug had to stop him from taking one as a souvenir. It just did not seem right. Doug was careful not to stray too close to the windows, in case he was seen by anyone or anything in the area. There was not a sound, apart from those he made himself. Watching for fallen office chairs he moved to the rear of the premises again being careful not to let himself be silhouetted against the windows. If he were watching a building he would have people both front and back, so he assumed that if they were being watched, then there would be someone observing the back as well. The office building was a long one. It looked like they had extended into the adjoining building at some point, so the back door at the very end was the equivalent of two buildings away from their own building. This was an excellent finding, as was the fact that the back door was one of those ones which, even when locked, could be opened by pushing on a metal bar from the inside. If they needed to make a hasty exit, all they needed to do was quietly push on the bar and let themselves out. The door was presently hanging slightly ajar; it had obviously been used as an exit when all hell had broken loose in the office. He could picture terrified office staff bolting out the door to escape been eaten by their former colleagues. He crept as close to the door as he dared without being seen, and peeked out. There was an alley running right beside it, perfect for a getaway on foot, if the need arose. There were several abandoned vehicles clogging it up, same as half the alleys in the city, but that would not slow them down while they were on foot, and indeed they would provide cover if need be. The alley ran for at least a couple of miles from what he could make out and this would be their escape corridor if and when the time came. Having seen all that he had, he personally felt that it was a matter of when rather than if, they would be making use of it.

Judging by the length of the building, he calculated that anyone watching from the building directly behind the laboratory would not be able to have enough angle to see this door, so he quickly looked out. His glance confirmed his suspicions, as there was another building blocking the way. It had a blank wall at the back so there was no danger from that side. Having made sure there were no zombies in the area to hear him, he stepped back inside and locked the door.

Armed with his new knowledge he returned to the hole in the wall as carefully as he had first come. Their work had left an ugly gash in the wall so he took the time to pull a desk over against it, to conceal it, if anyone did happen to enter the building. The desk had a high back to it, with a filing cabinet on top, which completely concealed the hole, but it did not weigh much. Then he returned to Scott with his findings. They were happy with their work and felt reasonably prepared for escape.

While Doug had been exploring some things had been going through Scott's mind and he felt the need to discuss them; "What do you think we're going to do when we finally get out of here?"

"You mean when we get to the farmhouse?"

"Well, yes that, but also longer term. It's not like we have jobs to go to anymore. Will we all have to become farmers?"

Doug pondered this for a moment; "It's hard to say, depends on how bad things get. If these people can come up with a cure then society could be pulled back from the brink. If not, then things will probably reach a tipping point, from which there may not be any swift return, certainly not in our lifetime. Then, you're right, people will have to start growing things or starve. When the goods lorries stopped rolling supplies were cut off and I imagine most people are relying on whatever canned goods they've hoarded or scavenged. When that runs out, and the electricity grid fails then it's all bad. When winter hits people will have to burn the furniture, assuming they have a chimney. There aren't enough trees around here to cut down for fuel."

"If the worst comes to the worst, then people will abandon the cities and migrate to the country" Scott mused. "The zombies may be gone by then, if they have nothing left to eat. I suppose the next few days and weeks will be the saving or the undoing of many people. I'd never have believed that we would possibly play a central role in that, but here we are!"

"Yes" Doug agreed. "We may just help to save the world, or at least our bit of it! Being optimistic I'm hoping that the girls can pull something out of the bag and start saving people. If that can happen fast enough, then we have a chance. Then we will have the essential skills to re-build a functioning society similar to the one we know. There will be lots of jobs available then, bearing in mind the huge loss of personnel we've had. If they don't find a solution, then it's off to be farmers we will have to go, scavenging off the remains of the old world, and having to defend ourselves from bandits."

"Crikey, that's what life was like a couple hundred years ago!" Scott exclaimed.

"Yes, that was life for most of human history, and we could well see those times again" said Doug. "At least one good thing is that, as human society recedes, the animal kingdom will expand to fill the vacuum, and there will be a lot more animals around to hunt. We still have our guns and a lifetime's supply of ammo."

"On the other hand, if we can turn things around in time we may see a new society emerge similar to our own. There will be some differences, I just know that, something like this will have profound consequences, but we will still have a technology based civilisation, as opposed to a hunter-gatherer one. There are still numerous places pretty much affected by the zombies and I'm hoping that they will have a positive influence on how everything pans out" Scott suggested.

"Oh yes, there will be enormous changes, I'm certain of that. What exactly they will be who knows, we will just have to wait and see. Different countries will have different population losses and there's no way of knowing how that might affect things" Doug said. "We will adapt to the circumstances as we find them. We're in a better position than a lot of people. Not everyone is in an armed, cohesive unit of loyal friends."

"I'll tell you one thing, if society as we knew it returns in some form or other, then I will be doing something that I really want to do, not just showing up and doing an occupation that my heart isn't really in" Scott declared emphatically.

Doug smiled; "That's the dream of a lot of people but it's sometimes hard to achieve in reality. Most don't make it. I hope you do. Did you have something in mind or are you going to see which way the wind blows you?" He was interested because he'd been having thoughts like that for a long time himself.

"I'm not really sure yet what I will do. As you said much depends on the world that will emerge from all this insanity. If the zombies win, then I would probably be happy enough to live off the land and commune with nature. If we win then I will have to wait and see what options and opportunities are out there. Who knows, I'm sure my talents can be used somewhere, but it will be something I actually enjoy doing, not just living for a pension that I might never see. What about you, will you go back to being a paramedic?"

Doug paused to have a think; "No, probably not. I've been

there and done that. Of course I will still help people from time to time on an informal basis, but to do it again professionally is not something I would consider. Maybe it will be a different occupation in the new world but my experience of old was of constantly giving and giving to people who for the most part only knew how to take. I could not go back to that again, that constant giving to people who did not deserve so much help, and who never acknowledged you or thanked you, and who frequently were the cause of their own misfortune. That's why I left it before, I'd had enough. What will I do now? Like yourself I will have to see what the next while brings and work it from there. I do know I've changed personally in the last while so who knows?"

Scott was intrigued; "How have you changed?"

"Well you may remember all that trouble I had with the law a while back and with my Grandmother dying and everything?"

Scott nodded gravely. He'd been angry about that too.

"Ever since that happened I carried a rage within me and a desire for revenge. I wore it like an Albatross around my neck and I let that simmer and fester within me, always thinking about the day I would get the chance to extract some revenge. I knew deep down that it was an emotional poison that was harming me, but I told myself I didn't care. Well I recently noticed that I have lost that desire for revenge. I just woke up one day and it was gone, and the anger is gone too. Maybe it's the thoughts of my own mortality and the possibility of facing eternity at any time, I don't know, but it's like the poison had been burnt out of me. I've moved on. I know the people who wronged me and Gran will face their own punishment."

"I'm glad to hear that. It's strange how something good comes of every situation" Scott said. "The zombies drove your demons away………."

With these thoughts in mind they went to see how the two scientists were getting on.

Things had been going well for Tara and Beverley and their research. Using the data that Howal and Hudson had created, combined with their own work, the two girls were on the cusp of the breakthrough which they were desperate to achieve. On looking at the work their colleagues had done, they realised that, being organic machines, the Iasobots were susceptible to any direct attack that would destroy their DNA strand. During their own work they had discovered that they could create a nanobot that could seek out the Iasobots and disable a strand of their DNA thereby causing the nanobot's membrane to fail. They then tested some of the new nanobots on rogue Iasobots taken from Scott, from the time he had been bitten in the woods, and they had performed perfectly. They had also modified their nanobots so they could self-replicate in the body, accelerating the process. This had been a breakthrough achieved by Howal and Hudson. To do this the nanobots simply harvested free-floating molecules in the body and used them as building material. Now they were working on an 'off-switch' and their work would be almost complete. Tara did not want to risk the new nanobots turning rogue in response to some other stimuli, so she was working on a means to let them die quickly once their work was done. After some hours working on it Beverley discovered that, by implanting an aging gene into the nanobots, it would give them a short lifespan. One more trial and they would know. Would the new nanobots destroy the Iasobots before they died? Their results showed that they did………..their work was done!

The two of them had been assigned a .45 caliber pistol and a rifle each. The pistols had been Josh and Anne's so it was nice that they would now protect their new friends. When Scott and

Doug came back from making the exit, they took turns going through the basics of firearms with Beverley and Tara, teaching them how to properly grip guns, shooting stance, aiming, and loading and unloading drills. They set up targets and practiced 'dry firing' where they would adopt the correct stance, aim, and fire an unloaded gun at the target. It was not the same as practicing with live fire, but it was the best they could do in the circumstances and a lot better than nothing. Both of the girls seemed to take to it fairly quickly, and there was a lot of laughing and teasing going on during their coaching. They all could feel the bonds growing between them and sometimes when they touched going through the drills there was no mistaking the sparks that were there. Tara felt it for Doug, and Beverley felt it for Scott, and vice versa. Stressful times tend to bring people together like that.

****

Alan Howal lay on the bed in his cell and listened to the growls and grunts from next door. Stage one of their plan had not gone smoothly, now Hodson had been turned into a zombie. That regrettable event had seemed unavoidable given the circumstances. Realising that they were in a trap with no hope of release Hodson and he had run with the only option the saw available to them. They had arranged for Eddie Young's 'defection' and he was able to make it convincing based on his earlier desire for revenge. He would feed Magee's people a good story about their work, without giving away the critical details and use the opportunity to look for a means of escape. With Hodson a zombie Howal now had to act alone. Come morning, after a night listening to his friends howling, Howal would also join Eclipse Enterprises, making it look like he was afraid not to. If he didn't seem to co-operate, they might turn him into a zombie himself and then all hope was lost. After a while of appearing to help them he would gain their trust and attempt to steal their technology from them. If he could get the blueprints for the Ghost Hand, he would send them to colleagues world-wide and the technology would be free to all. Then, while Eddie created a diversion of some kind, he would endeavour to restore Hodson and the three of them would mount an escape from the complex. It was a long shot and they hadn't thought of all the details yet, but it was all they had to go on. Their plan to hold out for better terms with Magee had backfired and now John was paying the price. They had known that Magee would be suspicious if all three of them agreed to join him at once, he was no fool, and they would be under too much scrutiny to achieve anything, so they had decided to stall for time, but they didn't count on him turning one of their number into a zombie.

It could have been any of them, but Magee had chosen Hodson. Howal was impressed with John's stoic acceptance of his terrible fate, and would have understood if he'd had a last minute change of heart. John knew there was no guarantee of being restored when he had calmly stood and taken the dart from Magee's gun. Now Magee would leave him a zombie to ensure the allegiance of Howal. Alan hoped he could rescue his friend and soon. At least John had little awareness so he would not suffer too much. Howal heard the door to the cell block opening and wondered if it was breakfast or Magee arriving. He also wondered when these cells had been installed and if the company shareholders knew about them. Footsteps came down the corridor. It was Magee.

Magee as always looked purposeful and focussed on something important. He paused at Hodson's cell. Hodson groped the air through the cell bars and snarled at Magee, who shook his head, as if in sorrow. Next he came to Howal's cell and wished him good morning. Howal returned the greeting. He had not slept much, and when he had he'd been haunted by zombies chasing him. He looked pale and had dark rings under his eyes.

"Now that you have seen the price of refusal, are you willing to join my team?"

"Yes I will join you. This is against my principles but if joining your organisation is the only way I can make a contribution to society, then so be it. You leave me with little choice and there are enough zombies in the world already."

Magee could not hide a triumphant grin; Very well, you will get your chance to prove your loyalty. You do realise that you will have to do much to prove that we can trust you? There are some things that you should be aware of, we have gotten much information from your former colleague, Mr Young. You will be questioned about that work, and I expect that you will be as frank and open as he was. I do not want you to hold anything back. We will know if you do. Understand?"

"Yes."

"Furthermore, you can consider yourself on probation. You will be closely monitored, and where you may go within the complex will be restricted. Any attempt to enter unauthorised areas or to escape or any other act of foolishness will incur a total loss of privileges."

"I understand what you mean by that."

"On the other hand, if you prove as valuable an employee as I expect you can be, then you will be handsomely rewarded for your efforts. We did not become the success story that we have by failing to reward talent. Indeed a lot of our best people left their old employers because they were not recognised and promises were broken. When we make a promise, we keep it, you see we do have our own morality."

"What of John.........?"

"John I'm afraid will have to sit tight for the moment. His fate is still in your hands. If you measure up to expectations there is no reason we can't restore him. Don't worry I will not string this out a moment longer than I have to......... loyalty will be met with reward. All this could have been achieved without any unpleasantness, but you had to be stubborn, but let's move on from that now. We are where we are. Once you have proved yourself perhaps John will see the light and join us too. That reminds me, I have to feed him."

Howal appeared resigned to his fate and nodded acceptance of the terms. Then Magee summoned the guard and had Howal released from his cell. On the way out he met another guard bringing in somebody's arm for Hodson's breakfast, and he had to resist the desire to retch.

Magee let him have breakfast, and then Howal was introduced to Professor Larry Irvine, who greeted him cordially enough, recognising a fellow professional. James McCullough was there as well holding a pen and paper. He was polite and business-like. They quizzed him in detail about the work he had been doing prior to his capture. He knew more or less what Eddie Young would have told them, and he tried to stick to the script. They obviously expected more details from him, but he pretended that they had stalled on a problem before reaching any significant breakthrough, blaming Mahoney and Shenton for not getting to his lab in time. Most of Hodson's work had been burnt before his tests had been concluded, so that had caused a major delay as well. He did feed them some good ideas though, realising that he had to satisfy them that he was worth having around. He didn't want them going back to Magee reporting that he was a waste of time. If Magee thought he was of no value then he might well become a zombie like poor Hodson.

Irvine and McCullough were pleased enough with some of his ideas for self-replicating nanobots and requested that he begin work on this immediately. They would set him up in his own laboratory, with a team of assistants, and everything he needed. He would have liked to have Eddie Young around as well, but he didn't dare ask, after all they were supposed to be enemies now.

Once he got back into a laboratory setting life was almost bearable again. This was where he was at home, and his mind needed to work after the days spent locked up. The staff were friendly enough, and knew their stuff, so things went as well as could be hoped. He gave the appearance of having accepted his place at Eclipse Enterprises but was constantly watching for anything of use to himself. He wondered where Eddie was, he never saw him in the lunch room or in the sleeping quarters, and he guessed that they had deliberately kept the two of them apart. There were several different zones in the huge complex, each self-contained, so you could spend a lifetime there and not run into someone from another zone, unless you had the freedom to move through the security points dividing all the different areas. Then he had a thought that gave him serious cause for concern; what if Eddie had out-lived his usefulness, and they had gotten rid of him? Then he would be on his own...........

15 ELI TURNS UP AGAIN

Eli logged into his computer and checked his phone's GPS one last time. He yawned and reminded himself again why he was up at this unearthly hour, usually he liked a good lie-in. Getting up early was for farmers and suckers who worked for a living. It was seven o'clock in the morning and the gang had a busy day ahead. The phone had not moved since he had first located it, confirming his suspicion that it was still in the car. That was a good indicator that the strangers were still holed up somewhere nearby. Once he found the car they would find the strangers, if they had to go through each building in the area one by one. Then those people would pay for what they had done. He had ordered that any men they found be shot, but to try and capture the bitches alive. He was still interested in their value. His gang had grown further since the arms deal, and he now had twenty five men, including some 'heavy-hitters' who could handle themselves in a tight spot. Word had spread in the underworld of their successful drugs acquisition, and this made them an attractive proposition for other criminals who were looking for a gang to join. He could have increased his numbers even further but that would have meant too many people to share their drugs with and lead to management problems. He had marginally increased the calibre of the man at his disposal but he was aware that smarter people required closer watching. They were prone to having ambitions of their own if the opportunity arose. Eli felt he had gotten the balance right though and now had enough manpower to deal with the strangers, especially with their new weaponry. He recalled his unpleasant experience crawling through the roof-space at the hospital and grimaced. He would not get caught out again.

He gave the order to move out and the men collected their equipment and ventured forth. They travelled in eight pick-up trucks, no-one really saying much because of the early hour. Each truck had an armed man positioned in the back to deal with any zombies who accosted them on their way. The city was functioning again on some levels and crews were out with tow-trucks, doing their best to clear the roads. There were not enough of them to take the vehicles anywhere, so they were pushing and pulling vehicles off to one side. It was an effective way of clearing the worst of the gridlocks in a short space of time, and even when they only cleared a single lane, it was enough for vehicles to get by. These work-crews operated in a particular place for a short time, then moved off before their armed guards found there were too many hungry zombies to deal with. This was a godsend for Eli and his gang, as it allowed them an ease of movement that they otherwise would not have had. It never crossed any of their mind's to lend a hand. That kind of thing was not their way and working was for fools. They carried on their way with a scornful glance at the road crews. Their destination was seven miles from their own base, and they shot at numerous zombies as they made their way along, even the ones who were not trying to get at them. This kept zombies from impeding their progress towards their target, but it had the unfortunate effect of attracting half the zombies in the city, who knew by now that gunshots meant fresh food, even if it meant dining on their own kind. The more watchful zombies didn't try to rush the vehicles, but followed along after, following the sounds of the gunfire. More and more of them gathered, biding their time to see if an opportunity arose to strike.

One of those zombies was Steven Grace. Since the day of his infection he had roamed the city looking for his lost soul. He had attacked the uninfected whenever he got the chance, and he bore the scars of those encounters. Every now and then someone would run out of food and be forced to leave their fortified hiding place to scavenge for food in other houses. Always they were armed and some were better able to defend themselves than others. He now limped from a bullet wound to his right thigh, and one of his arms was broken from the blow of a baseball bat. He had last fed two days ago but it had been on one of his fellow zombies who had gotten run over, and that was out of desperation. He wanted to dine on the uninfected because they were whole, but they were becoming scarcer, so he had to make do with what he could find instead. His clothes were tattered, and he was covered in dried blood, some of it his own and some not. He did not rest from his searching because he could not, driven on as he was by the desperation to be part of something real again. Now and then he collapsed on the road out of sheer exhaustion, but it was not a real sleep, it was more like a coma. When he would get up again his body was barely less tired than before. He had suffered massive blood loss through the wound in his thigh and he was weakened considerably, but that did not stop him. If things kept going the way they were going, Steven was not going to last much longer, but he was incapable of knowing or caring about this. Still he kept searching, though he knew not what for, but he had to keep going or he would be lost in the abyss forever. Something was out there that would make him whole again and he would keep going until he finally fell for the last time.

He had been wandering by chance near Howal's laboratory when he heard the sounds of gunfire approaching. By now his brain had managed to restore a little of his cognitive function, and he knew enough not to walk directly in front of the pickup trucks. Men with guns could kill zombies before the zombies had a chance to get close enough to taste the delicious meat, so he stayed hidden behind a burnt-out truck. He knew if he waited there would soon be other bodies to feed on, so he held back with some of the other zombies who were doing likewise.

Eli had the car's location marked on a street map. It did not take the gang long to find it and for Eli to recover his phone. He noted the presence of the motorcycle as well, parked up beside the car. He carefully looked around and there did not seem to be any other vehicles near these. He had not known the numbers of those who had attacked his gang at the hospital, but seeing only two vehicles gave him reason to believe that there were not many of them. When they had come to snatch the bitches they had just gotten lucky by having explosives, and by using ambush tactics. Now to find these strangers, where were they holed up? He again looked carefully around him and assessed the scene, using the same cunning that had guessed where Mahoney and Shenton had been hiding at the District Hospital. He calculated that the vehicles would have been left about two blocks from where the strangers were, three at most. This was enough distance to avoid attracting zombies but not too far to carry on to a hideout on foot. Fortunately for Eli this was a commercial area. Most of the buildings were big warehouse type buildings with one or two floors. It would not take forever to search them. Dividing the men up into six teams with an allocated area each Eli knew it was only a matter of time before they would locate the strangers. The teams had initially been ordered to proceed as quietly as possible, as he was worried about being attacked by snipers, but that became pointless after a while as there were now hundreds of zombies in the area, lurking around every corner. Every now and then some of them were unable to wait any longer and attacked the gang members. These were shot down with machine-gun fire and an occasional hand grenade was used as well. Most of Eli's men had taken drugs of some kind that morning as well as alcohol, to give themselves courage for the mission. The effects of this were beginning to tell, and they became sloppy and undisciplined. Every time Eli heard sporadic gunfire he got angry; the strangers would know for sure that someone was coming, and that was the element of surprise lost that he had been hoping for. Now there would be a major gun battle to deal with. Oh well, there was no going back now, after all they had rockets……….

Scott and the others had been having a bite to eat, before changing from the night watch to the day watch, when to their alarm they heard sporadic gunfire. It seemed to be getting closer, there was trouble approaching! Then they heard a couple of explosions. Scott knew the sound of grenades from his army days. Forgetting their meal and their casual banter, everybody ran to check the security monitors. There were lots of zombies collecting outside, a lot more than usual. Whoever was causing all that noise was attracting them. There was no sign yet of the gunmen. Tom an Brad had been up all night on patrol and had been looking forward to some sleep. They were a bit bleary-eyed but reasonably alert and calmly ready for action. Everyone checked their weapons and Tara and Beverley got ready for a quick departure if necessary. They hid most of their work in the chimney space but saved the critical information to data sticks, to bring with them. They had meant to upload their work onto the internet but there seemed to be a problem with the connection, and they struggled to do some fault-finding, while there was still time. Not knowing if events were going to overtake them, it was critical that they posted their breakthrough onto sites where it would be available to the right people everywhere. As this was going on they also gathered up all of their spray bottles of their new nanobots. They might soon be trying these out on the real thing. No one knew who was out there, or what they wanted, but by the sounds of it they were coming closer. Dividing up into two groups, the others began to push any available furniture up against the front and back doors. Added to what was already there, if anyone tried to get inside they were going to have a hell of a time. Then Scott and Doug went to the lunch room and pulled the fridge away from the wall, clearing the way for a hasty departure if one was required. A careful check of the adjoining building showed it clear, and Doug remained to cover the exit, while Scott returned to observe the monitors, trying to establish what was going on out there.

The Sergeant in the building across the street heard the commotion about the same time as Scott, and like him he had no idea what was going on. He too observed that the sounds were getting closer, and that there were unusually high numbers of zombies in the area. He radioed back to headquarters and asked for instructions on how to proceed. He was advised to sit tight and gather any intelligence he could from the situation. Headquarters wanted to know who else was prowling in the area and what they were looking for. They were always paranoid that foreign agents were active in the country, taking advantage of the chaos to cause sabotage and steal vital secrets. If some group were to attack the laboratory, then the Sergeant and his men were to engage them and destroy them, preferably taking a prisoner or two, to establish who they were. Reinforcements were on their way to help deal with whatever was going on. The Sergeant ordered the men to make the building as secure as possible, with defenders front and back. He had nine men with him, and another nine in the building behind Scott's building. He radioed these men as well, and told them of their orders, and to stay put until further developments. He had a feeling that this was connected to the scientists they had been keeping an eye on, and that they would shortly see action. Before long someone spotted the first of Eli's gang running around shooting at zombies. They did a lot of shouting and then kicked in the door of the building next to them. For several minutes they could be heard calling to each other before they came out again. They seemed undisciplined and off their heads on something, not a good combination with all the machine guns they were carrying. Now the gang were banging on the door of their own building. This had been bolstered with everything they could find, and it withstood the assault. Then someone tried the back door, with similar results. The gang members knew what this meant called their friends on the radio. They had found a building with someone inside!

Eli had just finished checking a warehouse a block away when he was passed the good news, and he hurried to that location. Those people were surely in there. This was his time for revenge! He ordered the building surrounded front and back while they all took cover behind parked and wrecked vehicles. No-one thought to check the building immediately behind them, and no-one noticed that the damaged doors had been wedged shut. Eli decided to try to charm his way into the building first; "Hey you inside! We just want to talk to you, no-one will be harmed, that I guarantee. Come out with your hands up!" he bellowed hopefully at the place.

People didn't tend to believe Eli when he made promises in situations like these and since there was no reply he tried again; "I said come out with your hands up! We know you're in there! We just want to talk, if you surrender now you will be unharmed!"

Still no reply, so he ordered a quick barrage of gunfire and a rocket straight into the front door. A little display of power might change their minds but not too much, since he did not want to kill the two girls. They were worth more alive. Glass and bullets flew everywhere inside and the Sergeant and his men sheltered behind anything they could. He was smart enough to guess that these morons were looking for the scientists for some reason, but that they had stumbled on the wrong building. He wondered who they were and what they wanted with a couple of scientists, hired mercenaries perhaps? The rocket badly damaged the door, leaving a gaping hole, but it partly held due to the amount of tables and other furniture stacked behind it.

Eli tried once more; "Hey you inside, this is your last warning! We have you surrounded. If you do not come out now you can expect no mercy! When we get you we will feed you to the zombies!"

His offer was met with a hail of gunfire from within the building. The Sergeant was getting angry now and had ordered his men to give their attackers a taste of their own medicine. He did not like being pinned down by a bunch of common criminals whoever they were, and he wanted to show that they had an impressive arsenal themselves. Bullets flew everywhere, pinging into the vehicles Eli and his men crouched behind, and thudding into the walls behind them. Eli's gang poured more volleys into the building. The new Crime Machine were really in their element now. A few ricochets had come close but so far none of them had been hit; they were well concealed and had superior numbers and firepower. The Sergeant had an ace up his sleeve and he decided that a tactical move was needed to break the siege. He ordered the men behind Scott's building to come to their aid. Calling on the radio he said to leave two behind to keep watch on the scientists and friends. He was worried that they might slip out the back while all this shooting was going on. The rest were to sweep out wide and come in behind the building where he and his men were. Most of Eli's men were out front and he figured that a surprise attack on those at the back would enable him and his men to escape via the rear. When reinforcements arrived in the area they would reassess the situation and possibly counter attack. He did not want to be still in this building when they started sending more rockets this way, that door would not take another hit.

Scott and friends were fairly surprised at the way things had developed, to say the least. Watching the security cameras

Tara and Beverley had recognised Eli and were able to tell them that it was the same criminal that had tried to kidnap them back at the hospital. He must have somehow survived the zombies there, and come looking for revenge for his dead friends. He was crouched behind a pick-up truck excitedly barking orders at his minions. Using the zoom function on the camera they confirmed it; yes it was him without a doubt. How he had found their location was a complete mystery to them, but a lot of strange things were happening these days so they just hoped they would figure it out eventually. When he had attacked the building in front of them, and had had gunfire returned, it became apparent that he had blundered upon the wrong building for starters, and also that there were armed men in the building across the street, probably the same ones who had snatched Howal and Hodson. It then became apparent that it was time to leave Howal's laboratory as a matter of urgency. Their security was heavily compromised and sooner or later someone would realise the mistake and then it was anybody's guess what would happen. The people outside were dangerous killers and only a fool would remain to negotiate with them. They quickly gathered their few belongings and prepared to move out. When all that was ready, Tara frantically checked the internet connection again. This time she found to her relief that it worked! She hurriedly uploaded the results of their priceless research onto the Internet while the others waited. Now it was accessible to scientists all over the world. The curing of the zombies could begin. All the work and sacrifice of themselves and of their friends had not been in vain. Then they all ran to their newly made exit, and slipped through one by one. Brad and Tom pulled the fridge back into place really snugly. The ropes had been a good idea. By the time anyone found that hole they would be long gone. Then they pushed the desk into place as well, in case someone searched next door looking for clues.

Keeping away from the windows, they ran through the

building with their heads down. An occasional stray bullet pinged through the windows from the firefight now in full swing. Doug flinched and swore as one got too close for comfort. Getting wounded now could be a disaster, there were no hospitals to go to. Across the way the Sergeant and his men were holding nothing back in their efforts to show the gang that they were messing with the wrong people. When they reached the door at the end of the building Scott paused. Tom checked the alley through the window. It was full of zombies, waiting for the rich pickings that the battle was sure to leave behind. It was a lucky thing that Doug had locked the door on his recent fact-finding mission or the place would have been swamped with them by now.

"What do we do now?" Beverley whispered fearfully. "We can't just waltz out the door into that lot, there's too many of them!"

"No we can't" Doug said grimacing. "Even if we fought our way through them, the gunfire would let everybody know that we are trying to leave the area. Using dynamite would clear them quicker, but that would still leave a slight noise issue. We're in a bit of a pickle here for sure."

"I don't see how we can go back either. Eventually the warring parties out there will figure out what has happened, and then they may both turn their attention on the lab. They might even come to a deal and join forces if they realise they're both after the same thing" Scott said grimly. "Maybe we will have to wait here until things quieten down, and then make a run for it?"

Tara had been thinking; "No, I have an idea. I have twelve bottles of our new nanobots. If we could use them on the zombies that are out there we might be able to restore enough of them to allow us to get out of here, assuming that it will work successfully. I don't know for sure how long the process will take but it shouldn't take too long. It looks like this is as good a time as any to find out."

The others had a think about this. If they restored some and not the others, they did not really know what might happen out there, but it was something that was going to have to be tested sooner or later, so they agreed that the plan was worth a shot. At the very least, it would allow them to see if they worked or not on real zombies. If it cured some and the others turned on them then there would be carnage, but desperate times called for desperate measures, so the plan was given the go-ahead.

There was a stairs leading up to a storage area above them, and up there was a window out onto the back alley. They piled wooden pallets up to reach the window, and Tara and Doug took a bottle each and leaned out. The range was a little further than they would have liked, but it would have to do. When the zombies became aware of them, they raised their faces to the window and began howling, making a perfect target for the spray. Aiming as best they could Tara and Doug began spraying every zombie they could reach with the stream from the bottles. They tried to get each of them just once, to make the spray last as long as possible and carefully watched for any signs of changes to their actions and behaviour, praying that the stuff would work and work fairly quickly.

After a while Tara noticed a male zombie on the edge of the main group. He looked in a bad way, covered with blood, limping and with one arm dangling brokenly beside him. She leaned out to try to reach him with the spray, but he was just out of range. Something about him was familiar, with his fair, curly hair. Suddenly she gasped; "Oh my God, I don't believe it! I think I know that one! Yes, he used to work at Gemini Chemicals, he's a chemist, what was his name? Oh yes, it's Steven Grace, he has a daughter with a woman I was in college with, Leanne Turner is her name. He looks like he's in a really bad way but he's just out of reach, I have to get to him! Steven.....Steven......." she hissed as loudly as she dared.

She leaned out the window so far that Doug had to hold her by the legs to stop her falling out. Tara paused, she was running low on spray and she did not want to waste a drop. He was getting agonisingly closer........Steven was slowly turning towards the building. He heard his name being called but it meant nothing to him. What attracted him was the sound of a human voice. Weakly he limped forward, hindered by the other zombies milling around, and then turned his face to the sound. He did not even notice the spray falling on his face like a soft May mist.......... and then he was pushed away by a surge in the crowd.

****

The Sergeant radioed for the location of the reinforcements. They were still too far away to be of use, and had started to run into lots of zombies, which was slowing them down. With time and ammunition running out, it looked like they would have to save themselves from this predicament. While his men laid down suppressing fire he called to Fernando the leader of the other group, and asked for their position. Fernando and his men had worked their way around to the side and could see the gang members waiting at the rear of the building. The Sergeant gave the order to attack, he wanted out of this death trap now. There were five gang members out the back, taking cover in various places and firing an occasional shot at the building, just to let the people inside know there was no chance of escape. Fernando and the six other men were capable operatives and had moved into position without being detected themselves. Now they had a line of sight on the gang members. When the order was received they responded clinically and opened fire on them. Three died instantly in the barrage, not knowing what had hit them. One took a bullet in the stomach and was sprawled screaming on the ground clutching his mid-section. The last one had better cover and was not initially hit but when he realised that he was under attack he fled as fast as he could around the front where he took a hail of bullets from his own side, who fired on him before realising that he was one of their own. Satisfied that the area had been sterilised, Fernando radioed the Sergeant that it was safe to come out, and he and his men poured out the back door and away from the scene as fast as they could on foot. Behind them several grenades went off in the building. A couple of the men had sustained superficial injuries, but overall they had gotten off lightly. In the confusion they did not realise that they were a man down.

Eli saw that one of his men had come around the front and he cursed, realising that there had probably been an escape at the back. He was getting tired of continual incompetence from the people he associated with. He still did not realise who it was that he had been attacking, although he had been surprised at the amount of return fire, and assumed that there were more of the strangers than he had originally assumed. He ordered another rocket to the front door. This time it was blown to pieces, and he sent half his men charging into the building, while the rest went around to cover the back. It did not take long to realise that the building had been deserted and reports from the men at the back showed no sign of anyone. He had been foiled again! He started kicking furniture and swearing with frustration, when someone saw blood dripping on the ground and found the wounded man hiding in a closet. They dragged him before Eli, who looked in surprise at his uniform. Who the hell was this? He was dressed like some kind of security guard. Had they got the right place? A quick search of the man turned up his card pass with his ID for Eclipse Enterprises. Eli had never heard of them. He needed answers and fast if he was to make sense of anything right now.

"Listen to me real hard my friend. I'm not in a good mood here. I can see that you're having a really bad day, but if you don't give me the answers I want it's going to get worse for you very soon, you know why?"

The man groaned with pain and shook his head.

"Because there are lots and lots of zombies out there who all look like they haven't eaten in quite a while, and right now you smell like fried chicken to them, and if you don't tell me what the hell is going on here, my men are going to hang you out the window so they can have a picnic with you, understand?"

The man nodded his head weakly. He was bleeding heavily and Eli knew he had to work fast.

"Who are you working for and what are you doing here?"

"I work for Eclipse Enterprises, and we were watching the scientists………"

Eli was getting places. The mention of the scientists could only mean one thing. Excitedly he shouted at the man; "Where are they, is it the women? Go on! Go on! Tell me!"

"They are in the red brick building across the street, it's some kind of laboratory. They were working on the nanobot thing there. Yes it's two women, and a few guys…………"

The man slumped, he was dead. Eli still hadn't the whole picture, he made a mental note to look Eclipse Enterprises up on the internet when he got back to base, but now he had a concrete lead. He assumed the man worked for some company that were looking to steal secrets from the scientists, they did that sort of thing all the time. These drugs companies were stealing stuff from each other and spying on each other constantly. Now he had to act fast. Hs enemies were not far away, they had probably been looking out the windows at him! He had to get in there, before they tried to escape. Shouting at his men to reload he led the way back out. He recalled the men from the back of the premises as well. As they left that place the ravenous zombies were already closing in to feast on the gang members who had fallen. Several piled into the building and fell on the Eclipse man too, tearing his body limb from limb. There were so many that they pushed and jostled each other trying to get at the feast, which did not last long.

Taking cover as best they could Crime Machine now attacked the front doors of Howal's laboratory. Firing rocket after rocket, and a whole barrage of machinegun fire, they eventually reduced it and the furniture behind it to a heap of sticks. Then they advanced in through the door emboldened by the fact that there had been no returning fire. Once inside the gang members quickly verified that this was indeed a laboratory, but a quick sweep of the building showed it to be apparently empty of human occupation. There were signs that someone had been there recently, but the occupants were nowhere to be seen. Eli's mind was racing; were they hiding somewhere in the building or had they somehow managed to slip out under the radar? He remembered how the females had hidden at the hospital, they might have done that again. If they were gone he wondered how recently they might have done so, but he had to assume that they had left under cover of his battle with the men from Eclipse Enterprises. The Eclipse men would not have been watching an empty building, so the females and the strangers could not be far away. He ordered half his men into the trucks. They would spread out and find the quarry if they were running for it. If they got away this time they would most likely escape him for good. He stayed with the rest of the gang and systematically began going through the building room by room. If there were hiding places they would find them.

16 RESTORATION

The creature that had been John Hodson grabbed a leg bone and gnawed at it, chewing at some muscle still hanging on it. It was aware of the man that had just walked in, but it knew by now that he was out of reach, so it just chewed on its bone and watched him should anything change. It did not pay much attention when the man raised his arm, then lowered it again, but just went on chewing at its bone. Gradually it felt something happening in its mind. It was as if a dark fog was slowly lifting from it, or waking up from a very deep sleep to realise that it had a terrible hangover. Groggily he stopped chewing on the bone and waited for the feeling to pass. The feeling did not pass. His head was getting lighter now, and then the spinning started. Dropping the bone he began to roll around on the floor. Then he slowly started remembering things, the humanity gradually returning to his tortured mind. Names and faces and recent events were remembered first, then older memories began to filter through. The Iasobots were loosening their grip on his mind as they died. Now he was remembering childhood memories, his parents, school, friends he had known. Then he remembered where he was and realised what was happening. He looked with disgust at the bones on the floor around him. John Hodson slowly rose to a sitting position holding his head in his hands. Even at that moment the speed with which the process happened was a wonder to his scientific mind. Billy Magee was standing in front of him holding a Ghost Hand device. There was no-one else there.

"Welcome back John" Magee said quietly. "How's the head?"

"Wha.......what's happening............?" Hodson asked weakly. He felt like a train had run over his skull recently.

"Right now or since we last spoke? Oh not much. Right now I have used the Ghost Hand to restore you too your senses, hopefully in more ways than one. Looking at the bigger picture, your two lady friends are still on the loose, that's a fluid situation, but Alan Howal is now working for us. In fact he's just had a wonderful breakthrough with his work on self-replicating nanobots. He's found a way to program almost the exact number of nanobots you want, through the programming of gene switches. As you can imagine this has all kinds of possibilities for us. I'm not going to dwell on the details just yet, you look dreadful, and I can only imagine how you feel. Apart from that news there's not much else. Do you want a painkiller?"

"Why did you bring me back?"

"Because I'm a nice guy and I wanted to give you a second chance John. If I'd had to condemn you to a living death forever then I would feel really bad. Now that you have known what it is like to be a zombie you have so much to teach us. I will summon the medical team here, to nurse you through your recovery. Then, after a few days of recuperation we can talk again. Just relax for the moment and don't stress about things. I will have the place cleaned up and have someone bring you a toothbrush."

With that he walked out, leaving Hodson to contemplate his recent experience and to wonder what plotting was going on now.

Magee walked back swiftly to his office and called for the

head of security. He wanted an update on the battle that was raging around Howal's laboratory. The head of security had just gotten off the radio with the men on the ground. The gang had just blasted their way in through the door of Howal's lab and it was anyone's guess what was going on inside. So far their men had not heard any more shots, which could mean anything. Perhaps those inside had surrendered quickly, although the Sergeant had doubted that, after what he had seen of these people at the hospital. They themselves had now joined up with the reinforcements who had just arrived, and were awaiting fresh orders. Magee thought things through quickly. His need was not urgent anymore, but he knew that Mahoney and Shenton would make a valuable addition to his team. If he could get them here they would yield to his demands a lot quicker than Howal and Hudson. Maybe he should have left Hodson a zombie a bit longer, to act as a persuader? Oh well, he would leave him now, there were other zombies to scare them with.

"Do we know yet who this gang is, that attacked us?"

"No Sir, we still haven't a clue who they are. The gang who raided the District Hospital were all killed, so I don't know if there's any connection there. Unless some of them escaped or it's friends of theirs who are looking for revenge perhaps? That would explain their motivation, who knows. Maybe they're just drug addicts who are desperate for their next fix and they think the place is full of drugs or chemicals. How they knew about the lab is a mystery though. Howal is a crafty beggar, there's only a handful of people on this planet who knew what he was operating out of there."

Magee made up his mind; "I still want Mahoney and Shenton. I know what they are capable of with their talents. I don't want them falling prey to a foreign government. I have had reports that there are enemy agents at work in the country, hell-bent on subterfuge. Neither do I want them getting robbed and killed by a bunch of stinking street scum. Order the men to attack this gang and finish them once and for all. Take Mahoney and friends alive if you can and have them brought here."

The Head of Security relayed the orders to the Sergeant on the ground, who moved into action with his men. By now the Sergeant had discovered that they had lost a man, and he was angry about this. He was still annoyed at having been attacked as well. It was time to deal with this riff-raff once and for all............

****

One of Eli's men had been watching the security cameras while the others tore the place apart with their searching. To his alarm he saw several uniformed men moving into position at the front of the building.

"We've got company!" he cried with alarm. "Looks like the other crowd are back, the ones with the uniforms!"

Eli rushed to view the bank of screens, swearing profusely from all the running around. What the hell was so important about these scientists that these people just would not give up?

The Sergeant had divided his men into two groups, front and back, and now it was Eli's turn to be under siege. The Sergeant shouted in to them and announced that they were surrounded by 'State Police' and that they were under arrest.

Eli was not amused. Who did these idiots think they were? State Police did not go around in the uniform of some private company. As far as he was aware there was no longer any police control of the city and the boss was the one with the biggest guns. He ordered a barrage of bullets in reply to the Sergeant's demand, followed by a few hand grenades lobbed from the top windows. Outside the security men returned fire, or retreated from the blasts. Then Eli ordered him men to conserve ammunition. If those 'police' wanted them, they could come in and get them. In the meantime they continued to rip the place apart, looking for their enemies.

****

Tara and Doug had used up most of their spray bottles on the assembly of zombies down below. It was with great relief and joy that they realised that the nanobots were doing their job well. The effects were already to be seen, as they began to have their humanity restored. They were jubilant that the cure was working, and that it appeared to take effect so quickly. Looking confused these people began to drift away from the scene, making room for more zombies to come along and be restored. The zombies did not seem to bother the newly restored people and the scientists surmised that until the Iasobots had fully died and maybe even were finally expelled from the body, the zombies would be fooled into recognising what they thought were their own. This would give the restored people time to find a safe refuge somewhere. As this was going on they had heard the battle raging out on the front of the other building. Then there had been a lull in activities, but now it had started up again. It was closer this time. When the rocket attack was launched on the door to Howal's building they knew the dynamics of the battle had changed and now it was time to go. The zombie numbers had dwindled enough to make a break for it. Before long more would accumulate and they would be trapped again, so it was now or never. After a last check on the alley, they burst out through the back door and ran for dear life.

Their plan was to acquire some vehicles and flee the city until the heat died down. There seemed to be too many people after them in the city trying to kill or capture them, for reasons they were not even sure of. They encountered a few zombies as they ran, but they clubbed them out of the way, so as not too attract attention by their gunfire. Out on the road they saw hundreds of other zombies making their way in the direction of Howal's laboratory, drawn by the noise and the smell of blood. The longer that fight went on, the more of them would be turning up there. After running a few blocks they came upon an SUV that was crashed in the back window of a shoe store. It was only lightly damaged, with the driver's door hanging open. The keys were in it, and it started first go, so they all piled in and took off at speed with Doug at the wheel. No-one seemed to be aware of their getaway so Doug headed out of the city as fast as he could, heading for the place they had left their trucks what now seemed an age ago. They had to stop to move a few vehicles out of their way now and then, but there were less and less zombies the further out they got, and they made fairly good progress. No-one appeared to be following them, which was a major relief as well. Finally they left the city limits and they could relax a little. After their night on watch, and their hectic day, Brad and Tom were in a state of near-exhaustion, and the others lapsed into silence when they realised that both of their friends had fallen fast asleep. Doug tried to drive as gently as possible into the night as the vehicle ate up the miles and took them further and further away from the city and it's dangers.

When they eventually got back to the wooded area where their things were hidden, they were happy to find that the trucks were still where they had left them and all their belongings were undisturbed. No-one had been up here in their absence. It was getting darker now so they decided to make camp for the night and decide what their next move should be. Traveling at night was a risky business because anyone could see your lights long before you might see them. Tara and Beverley now knew that their new nanobots could restore people from zombification, but they did not know the long term effects yet, so they did not know how much work was yet to do. Still, there was reason for them to be quietly happy with the result that they had accomplished. They wondered how their work was being received by the rest of the scientific community, and if anyone was making and distributing their new nanobots yet. Perhaps now people would stop trying to attack them? They also did not know where Hodson and Howal were being kept, or even if they were still alive. There was still no response to calls or texts to their phones so they were kept guessing. They wondered if the best thing to do was just go with their friends to their families, and wait until further developments.

Tom and Brad were looking forward to finally getting to see their families. Things had delayed for long enough as far as they were concerned. They had done their bit for humanity by helping the scientists and now they wanted to see Caroline and Christine and the kids. The less involvement they had with criminals or shady organisations from now on the less chance there was of one of them getting hurt or killed. As long as they didn't lead some of their new-found enemies to the farmhouse then things would be alright.

Things were a bit more complicated for Scott and Doug. There was a love-affair blossoming between Scott and Beverley and between Doug and Tara. It had started at the laboratory while they just had each other's company and there seemed to be few other people in the world who were not zombies. In the short time since it had developed into something so intense that it had to be taken into consideration when they planned their next move. They wanted the girls to just come with them to the farmhouse and start a new life there, but if the girls wanted to do something else they didn't want to let them go alone. Then they would be torn between their friends and their lovers. Nothing was simple anymore. They were still undecided on what to do when they turned in for the night, this time leaving Doug and Scott to keep watch. Perhaps a good night's sleep would bring some answers.

****

Eli was wondering how long he would be trapped in another building when one of his men found the hole that the previous residents had used to escape. He had been going through the fridge looking for a snack when the motor started up. It occurred to him that there seemed to be a strange sort of echo being made by the sound of the motor. Then he had noticed the slight scrape marks on the floor, left by the fridge being pulled around. Summoning some of the others to help him, their further investigations had discovered the means of escape.

"The cunning bastards!" Eli exclaimed when he saw how they had gotten away. He secretly wished he had some men who displayed the same levels of intelligence, but they were hard to find. It did not take him long to figure out what had happened, and that his quarry had probably slipped away while the battle raged outside and that they would be long gone by now. Still, they had provided a way out for him and his gang, and they would live to fight another day themselves. They fired a couple more rockets out front, to warn everyone away, then called for their friends to be ready to collect them. The zombies were gathering in the alley again and they did not want to attract any attention with a lot of gunfire so it made sense to plan for a quick getaway. Then they departed the building themselves, some of them having gotten through the hole a little more easily than others. They ran down the same alley as Scott and friends had not long before, and called again on the radios for the other gang members to hurry and pick them up. The ones who had been out looking for the escapees had nothing much to report. There was no trace of the people they were looking for. When the search had proved negative they had returned to the area and lain low, waiting for instructions from their boss. When he had unexpectedly announced that he was ready to meet up again they were relieved as they had been half-expecting an order to attack the uniformed men out front, and there were an awful lot of them there now. As it was there would be no more fighting for today, so they headed back to their base. Eli had been foiled in his plans, but all hope was not lost. When he got back he would do some research on this Eclipse Enterprises company. He might find out something useful that he could work with. They seemed just as interested in the scientists as he was, perhaps if he caught up with them he could do a little deal………

****

After a period of waiting outside, the Sergeant realised that things had gotten very quiet. The evening was drawing in and he did not want to be out there in the dark, especially with all the zombies waiting in the shadows. Weighing up the choices available to him, he decided that the only practical option was a frontal assault on the building. There was a gaping wound in the front of the place, where the doors used to be, and there were no signs of any activity within. After a quick consult with the men, he led the charge inside himself, believing that one should lead by example. Half-expecting to be met with a hail of bullets they rushed in through the front door and spread out. No-one was there to challenge them however, which was somewhat of a relief. After clearing each room they came to the conclusion that the birds had flown the nest. They quickly located the way the gang had vacated the premises. The Sergeant peered out through the escape hole in the lunch room and wondered how long the scientists and their friends had actually been at the laboratory. Had he and his men been watching an empty building? Then the Sergeant reported on the radio to Magee that the gang had fled, having used the same means of escape as the scientists had sometime before, possibly using the firefight as cover to get away. Now there was no trace of either group in the vicinity. The Sergeant did note that there were a lot of confused civilians wandering around the area, and that they were not being chased by zombies. He reported this also to his very interested boss. Unlike himself, Magee did not seem to be overly surprised by this development, but he did not elaborate why. The Sergeant just assumed that Magee knew something that he did not. The boss always knew stuff that no-one else did. With there being nothing more they could achieve this evening, Magee ordered them back to Headquarters.

17 A TRAP IS SPRUNG

Alan Howal poured himself another cup of tea, and returned with it to his chair to relax. He was in one of the cafeterias at the headquarters of Eclipse Enterprises. He had finished his work for the day and was preparing to relax for a while. The last few days had been spent working on any project that they sent his way, painfully aware that he was being closely watched and that any sign of subterfuge might be punished by zombification. He was working on making friends among the staff at Eclipse, and gaining their trust. There was no knowing when he might need allies. He did notice that they all seemed fanatically loyal to Billy Magee, and that they all subscribed to his world-view, at least in appearance, and this was rather worrying. He still had not seen any sight of Eddie Young, and he hoped that they had not done something to him, once he had outlived his usefulness. He was surprised at how much he missed his friend, but maybe it was his relative isolation here that did that to him. He was also very concerned about John Hodson. He did not know what the long-term effects of being a zombie were, but he was guessing that it would not be a particularly good thing. John wasn't getting any younger, and the long-term implications of having been a zombie were unknown. Finally he was worried about Tara and Beverley. He felt that he had failed them by not having come up with some sort of rescue plan. He thought now that he should have foreseen the possibility of something happening to himself and Hodson, and should have put something in place as a backup plan. He did not know where they were and he still did not know anything about the friends they had teamed up with. It was infuriating having to toe the line here and not have news from the outside world. Magee had hinted one time that he had been aware of their whereabouts, did he have people watching them? Was that assertion even true? Magee would say anything to get a result he desired. Maybe Magee had even captured them and was holding them somewhere without telling him? Knowing him anything was possible. He wondered then if the two had possibly tried to leave the hospital to try to meet up with himself, only to be attacked by zombies of some other dirt bags that were on the prowl. In a lawless world they would have been easy prey. Perhaps Tara and Beverley were dead, would Magee tell him if they were? He sighed with frustration; he was going to have to stop mentally torturing himself like this before he went mad. All he could do was to bide his time and wait.

Speaking of Magee here came the devil now, walking through the doors with some of his entourage. There was someone slightly behind Magee, who he did not at first recognise. Then he caught a glimpse of a familiar face, and his jaw dropped,..........no, it couldn't be, but it was! He could barely believe his eyes but it was true! There was John Hodson walking in behind Magee. He looked a little pale, but he was not a zombie any longer!

Overjoyed, Howal came to his feet as Magee led the group over to him.

"'Good day Doctor Howal, I hope you are well? Professor Irvine tells me you are doing a good job. Keep up the good work!" Magee was being really casual about this.

"Yes, good day.........." Howal was still stunned.

"Yes Doctor, as you see I have restored your friend and colleague here. This is a demonstration that I am prepared to be reasonable, and reward good work. Doctor Hodson, led by your own example, and penitent from his time as a zombie, has also agreed to join our team and work for a new world. As part of the trust-building process he insisted on seeing you. I hope it will contribute to his successful recovery. I will leave you to catch up with each other. No doubt he has a tale to tell you. He will have access to the same places within the complex as you and have the same restrictions for the time being. In time, and as the partnership between us increases, you may even get to work on the same projects."

Magee and his entourage left and Hodson sank into a chair. Howal quickly grabbed him a coffee from the counter and stuck it in front of him.

"Oh my God, John, how are you? When did you get restored?"

"Yesterday sometime, I'm not really sure, I had lost all notions of time and place. There was a fog in my mind that prevented me from knowing even my own name. When Magee restored me and repeated his offer to work from him, there was no more defiance left in me, I was broken like a dry twig beneath the wheels of a tank."

"You made a wise choice John. The alternatives are too dreadful to contemplate. At least this will buy us time, and who knows what opportunity may arise in the future for some kind of escape. What was it like being a zombie? Why did you want to eat people? Were you hungry all the time?

"The zombies don't eat people because they are hungry, it is because of the fear."

Howal was surprised; "The fear…….?"

"When all your mental defenses are stripped away you stand naked before the world, naked and alone. Then all that is left is fear, the fear of being incomplete. You wander the Earth like a shadow without a soul. That is why the zombies will walk through bullets to try to eat people, so they can somehow be complete again. Anything is better than the emptiness that defines you as a zombie, like a black hole at the centre of your being."

"So it is not a mindless craving for food?"

"No, in a way it's almost a quest for spiritual survival manifested by a physical hunger. That's why they don't attack each other, they can recognise the same lacking in other zombies. Only a normal human contains the parts they think will make them whole again. I regret the day I ever embarked on that research" he said sadly. "To think of all the millions of people still going through that awful experience!"

"You were not to know, your intentions were good, even though the timing was out" Howal consoled him. He had listened with great interest to his friend's experience, learning as much as he could along the way. "In a way it could have been worse. If that solar storm hadn't come early, a lot more people would eventually have been treated with some nanobot vaccine or other. With millions more zombies running around we could have reached a critical mass from which there was no pulling back. As it is it appears that civilisation is making a comeback, and although we may not like it, sometimes it's people like Magee that are making sure that it does. Sometimes it takes the single-minded, ruthless type to get things done, and he is that. Someday you will use your experience to transform the world for the better, all we have to do is wait."

Then he went on to update Hodson on his own news. It had not been so bad working for Magee, the staff were friendly enough as long as you understood where their loyalties lay. Working and living conditions were good, but it was a gilded cage all the same. He had not seen Eddie anywhere and he still had no idea of what may have befallen Tara and Beverley. Neither of them dared to say it, but there was a cold feeling in their hearts when discussing the two girls, there was a very dangerous world out there and no-one was telling them anything about whether their colleagues were still alive. Magee had previously suggested that they were at the laboratory, but that was a while ago, and he had refused to be drawn on the matter since. If they had been at the laboratory, why hadn't Magee kidnapped them as he had done with themselves? Perhaps if they did some good work he would reward them with information, Magee's men might be keeping an eye on them. In a way they hoped that Magee was keeping an eye on them, at least he might be able to keep predators at bay.

Hodson enquired if Alan had had any ideas on how to escape from the complex?

"I'm not sure. You being restored really simplifies things. Originally I thought I would have to steal one of their Ghost Hand devices and restore you. I've heard they are producing more of them in a part of the complex to which I don't have access. Then we would had to have somehow teamed up with Eddie, I wouldn't want to leave him behind, and somehow gotten out. I haven't laid eyes on him since the day he walked out of those cells. If he's still here they must be keeping him in a part of the complex where I'm not allowed access. I haven't dared to ask anybody because it would go straight back to yours truly. As you can see the whole thing is terribly complicated. The building we are in is built like a prison. All the doors need electronic access cards, and they know in the control room who is going where at all times. There's more cameras here than at a celebrities wedding. Even if you got out of this building, then you would have to cross the yard to the perimeter wall. It's too high to climb and the place is crawling with armed guards. No-one is allowed to leave the place without an armed escort, probably understandable with the situation outside I suppose, they can't risk a security breach. They also have armed patrols constantly on the move outside. Magee is completely paranoid about security and leaves nothing to chance. Now that you are yourself again I suggest you appear to co-operate, as I do, and use the time to build confidence. Eventually they will loosen their surveillance of us, and we may spot some way of getting out of here."

Hodson agreed with the plan; "I need a little more time to recuperate and get my head fully back to normal. I'm still getting crazy headaches and dizzy spells. One thing I will say; the plan will need to be foolproof before I will contemplate a breakout attempt, there is no way in hell that I am going to be a zombie again. Remember that they will be watching us at every moment in case we try anything."

With that thought in mind, they rose from the table and Howal started showing him around his new home.

****

Magee had been watching Hodson and Howal talking, using a camera that was covering the cafeteria area. He wondered what they were saying; plotting to escape, or resigned to their fate? Time would tell. Howal's work had been good so far, and Hodson had told him with his own lips that he would never wish to be a zombie again. Hopefully the lesson had been learned. The two of them would remain under constant surveillance and any hi-jinks would be swiftly punished. On the other hand, if they worked hard they would be well rewarded. Lots of people were initially hesitant to join them, brainwashed by years of liberal poison as they were, but when these people had been with the company a while, they soon learned a new, superior philosophy, and were happy they were now on the right side.

Happy enough to continue his gamble with Howal and Hodson, Magee turned his attention to other matters. The Sergeant had lost Mahoney and Shenton yesterday. Magee was not angry, the Sergeant was a good, loyal man, and he was up against a cunning, resourceful group of people. Magee still had no idea if these men were part of some organisation, or just talented civilians, but the strangers had proved yet again that they could take care of the girls. It was now up to him to adapt and try another tactic; if his men could not catch the girls out there, then it was time to get the girls to come to them. There were too many shoot-outs going on, each one increasing the likelihood of the scientists getting killed, so he needed to be creative. Now, how to proceed.........?

****

Brad stirred the small fire they had lit, and threw more food in the frying pan. Beverley filled the kettle again, to make more coffee. The others were packing up the tents and anything else that was not immediately needed. They were still in the little wooded area where they'd left the trucks, enjoying a relaxing breakfast. It was nice to be out in the open after their relative confinement in the laboratory and to see the open sky. The air was fresh and clear, and in the absence of the usual rumble of traffic they could enjoy some of the subtle sounds of nature they would have missed in another time. They still did not know for sure what their next move should be, and had more or less decided to head for the farmhouse where Caroline and Christine were, circling around the city to avoid more trouble. In the absence of other options it was a compromise decision. There did not seem to be much else they could do. At least they were out of the city, with all its madness and its mayhem.

Suddenly Tara's phone began to ring, disturbing their thoughts and causing them all to jump. After so long the noise seemed almost alien to their ears, an abrupt intrusion into their quiet morning. She grabbed the phone from her bag, and looked at the display; the caller name coming up was Alan Howal!

She quickly answered as the others gathered around with bated breath; "Hey Alan, is that you?"

"Hi, is that Tara?" answered a strange voice. "No it's not Alan, but I've got his phone. I'll tell you who I am. My name is Eddie Young. I had been helping Alan and John with their experiments at Alan's laboratory. Alan mentioned me the day you called him from the District Hospital, do you remember?"

Tara did remember, but she had not really thought any more about him since the day of the call.

"Ok, I remember he did mention you. Now what is going on and where are Alan and John?"

"It's like this; we were busy doing experiments at the lab not long after you called when armed men broke in and kidnapped us all. They belong to an organisation called 'Eclipse Enterprises' which you may or may not be familiar with. They specialise in hi-tech weapons for sale to governments, that sort of thing. They're now working for a new government that has taken over the running of the country. Obviously they were very interested in the work that Alan and John were doing, and since the two of them refused to join them, these Eclipse people came to steal their work by force. Just before we were overrun, Alan hid his most important work in the chimney space, and he left that message on the marker board for you to find. Well anyway, they hauled us back to their complex and we were kept there as prisoners. They tried to get Alan and John to work for them, but the two of them would not see reason. I have some bad news, Tara. They turned Alan and John into zombies, because they would not co-operate, they used the Iasobots on them!"

"Oh my God no!"

The friends looked on with alarm as tears started streaming down her face.

"Because I was not much use to them, they put me to work in the cell block, watching and tending to the zombies. There were others there as well, they do medical experiments on them, testing all sorts of drugs on them and stuff. It was terrible, I had to feed bits of people to them. Eventually I couldn't take it anymore, I knew I had to get out of there. Yesterday my luck came through. I hid in a dumpster, which was transported out of the complex and then emptied out at a landfill site. Then I ran off and hid in a disused factory. That's where I am now. Alan had given me his phone because he knew he would not be able to use it, and I looked up your number on it. I want to get Alan and John out of there, we have become very dear friends, but I don't know who else to ask for help. I don't know anyone else who can assist me now."

Tara struggled to regain her composure. Could she trust this stranger? He knew some details that no-one else would, unless someone had since found the hiding place, who knew? All she did know was that her friends were in a terrible predicament, and only she could help them, she still had two bottles of the new nanobots, more than enough to restore Alan and John. She needed more information;

"What do you want me to do?"

"If you can come to the disused factory and meet me, I'm hoping we can come up with a plan of some sort. I don't know what to do on my own, but if we can team up, we will be stronger together. All my friends are dead. They were either zombies or killed by zombies. If I hadn't met John that time I would probably be dead myself by now. I owe him, and Alan too, and I want to help them as they helped me. I know the layout of the complex and how the guards operate, so that might be of some use."

Tara was not sure how to proceed so she wanted time to consult with her companions.

"I will need to discuss things with my friends. I will let you know presently what we decide to do. The only advice I can give you now is to lay low. Anyone wandering alone in the city would be easy pickings for the zombies."

"Please do not leave me waiting long. I have no food or supplies, and no weapon here. If I get attacked I have limited options as regards defending myself so please hurry. Where are you guys now, are you safe?"

"Yes, we are safe. I won't however tell you where we are, you do not need to know that right now."

"That's understandable, I should not have asked. Please help me, I will be waiting. I will text you the address of the factory where I am hiding. One more thing, I do not have a charger for this thing, so please communicate by text from now on as I need to conserve the battery. If it runs out I will lose you……."

Then he was gone.

Tara sat down and sobbed with grief. Beverley sat beside her and put her arm around her shoulders, trying to comfort her friend in her despair. The others waited patiently until Tara was ready to speak. When some minutes had passed Tara gave them the distressing details of the news she had just got. They were all taken aback by this turn of events. They knew they were dealing with dangerous people but they had not known the scale of what they were up against. This added an element of danger into the equation that they had not really considered before.

Scott was the first to speak; "I gather that you don't know this Eddie Young guy?"

Tara rubbed tears from her eyes; "No, John Hodson mentioned him the day I called the lab and said that they'd bumped into him somewhere, and that he was assisting them with their work. Apart from that I couldn't even tell you what he looks like."

"It sounds sketchy to me" Tom murmured. "Think about it, those people had us under surveillance, waiting for a chance to pounce, and the day after we give them the slip some guy suddenly makes contact with some story about how he escaped from a mysterious complex where they do experiments on people. The whole timing of this is a little too co-incidental for my liking."

"Let's look at what we do know" Doug suggested. "We do know that Alan and John were kidnapped, along with some guy who may or may not be the person who just called Tara. We know they are probably alive because if they just wanted to kill them, they could have done that back at the lab. That leads to the conclusion that Alan and John have some value to them. Because these same people were watching the lab when we were there we can infer that it is the work on nanobots that interests them. So far, a lot of it does add up."

Beverley now spoke; "There is an organisation called Eclipse Enterprises, and they do all kinds of shady dealings involving bio-weapons among other things. I was there some years ago for a presentation, they were trying to recruit people for their science team and I was fresh out of College and looking for work. I didn't take the job because there was something about the place that creeped me out, but I remember lots of armed goons running around wearing uniforms. The whole place had the feel of a military camp and I didn't like it. You couldn't get anywhere within the complex without a door card and the whole thing made me feel claustrophobic. In the years since I have heard them mentioned a few times in scientific circles, always in the context of some dodgy weapons technology or something but it's always been vague information. No-one seems willing to discuss what they really do."

"Humm, so some of it does add up" Brad mused. "It still looks suspicious though. The best lies always contain elements of truth, that's what they say."

"We don't know for sure that your friends are zombies" Scott said, addressing Tara. "All we have is this guy's word for it. I think the only thing we can assume to be true is that it was someone from Eclipse Enterprises who snatched them. That part makes sense. Now whether this guy is genuine, or whether he's trying to lure us into a trap is anybody's guess. We don't have enough information to tell. We don't know the exact circumstances of how Eddie Young came to be in their company either. For all we know he might have been a planted spy from the beginning, who pretended he was looking for help. Once he had gained your friend's trust they'd have a man on the inside. It's an old trick."

Tara was struck by something she had just remembered; "Oh, I almost forgot, he said something about these Eclipse people working for a new government that has taken over the country. Not exactly a minor detail but all I can think about is my friends………"

This was news that stunned the others.

"A new government? Holy crap what the hell does that mean?" Tom wondered.

"I don't know, he just said that a new government had taken over the running of the country and Eclipse were working for them. He wasn't forthcoming with more details and, to be honest, I was too shaken and preoccupied with other things to question him further. Perhaps I should have."

"Interesting" Scott said thoughtfully. "While we have been cut off from the rest of the world, who knows what has being happening elsewhere. Now that I think about it, while we were holed up at the lab I never heard from any of our politicians on the radio. I assumed that they were all in some kind of bunker somewhere waiting for the storm to pass and letting others deal with the fallout. It is entirely plausible that there has been a takeover of some kind."

"Who would have done that, there must be remnants of the police and army around to prevent that type of thing. Surely it could not be done so simply?" asked Brad.

"It depends" Scott answered. "I can only guess here, but if a lot of our leaders were zombified when this all happened the government might have been unable to carry on functioning and have fallen. Throughout history natural disasters have frequently precipitated the fall of kings and emperors and various different rulers. In past times a famine or an earthquake or a plague could destabilise a society and cause it to happen. There are always other individuals or groups waiting in the wings to move in and fill the vacuum. I don't know if you'd call the zombie apocalypse a natural disaster exactly, but it contains all the elements of chaos and disaster to create the conditions for a power transfer to occur."

"Maybe they were all murdered" Doug suggested. "Like you said, there are always certain elements biding their time and hungry for power in any society. The zombie plague would have provided the perfect opportunity for those elements to seize that power. With the entire country in meltdown there may have been a coup and no-one even noticed, too busy trying to stay alive. It seems incredible because we have always known one form of government, but it could happen. As Scott alluded to with earthquakes and plagues and that, extreme events cause extreme changes in a society. Assuming that this is true it alters the dynamic of our situation drastically."

"So we can assume that this new form of government will be very different?" asked Tom.

"Yes" said Scott. "If there has been a coup, these people, whoever they are, do not believe in democratic values, so whatever form of society emerges from all of this, it will be radically different from the one we knew. From our point of view it makes the situation even more tenuous than we previously thought. Along with this mysterious company who are after us, we may in fact be fugitives from the government. We may be up against forces greater than we ever thought. That's a reality we haven't even contemplated."

There was silence while everybody digested this information. No-one was sure what to say. If this Young guy was genuine then the implications of his information were enormous.

"I have to find out" Tara suddenly said. "I don't know for sure who we're dealing with but if Alan and John are zombies they need help. I know our cure works and I'm not leaving my friends like that."

"I second that" Beverley said. "Alan has been like a father to me since my parents died in a car crash, and I'm not leaving him to his fate. John is also a dear friend of mine. We have to do something. To fail to act would be a betrayal and I could not walk away and live with myself after that. I don't care if we are fighting some new government."

Everyone else looked at each other, what to do now?

Eventually Scott spoke; "If you want to try and rescue your friends, then I will help you. I do not expect anyone else to do so, especially Tom and Brad, whose families have been waiting long enough as it is. My family are grown up and they barely speak to me, I don't know if they're alive or dead today, so I am willing to take a risk or two for my friends."

Beverley hugged and kissed him proudly.

Doug was next; "I have no family that I keep in contact with. I have a few relations but none of them visited me when I was in prison or even called me, so I haven't bothered with them since. In fact they may all be zombies for all I know, they were always very conscientious about getting flu shots, so I'm in too."

Tara smiled for the first time since she got the phone call. She was happy to be in love with a good man.

Brad and Tom looked at each other. What to do now? This was an unbearable predicament. They were longing to see their families and this seemed like the biggest danger so far, but these were their friends, and they had come through so much together the last while. They had seen Tara and Beverley restore zombies successfully and they knew they were trying to save millions of other people. These Eclipse Enterprises people and their cohorts might be up to any kind of badness. They would not desert their friends now and leave them to face such mighty odds on their own.

Tom shrugged his shoulders; "Damn it, I know this is crazy, but I'm in as well. Just make sure you save a bottle of that spray stuff in case we need it. Being a zombie is the last place I wanna be!"

"Me too" Brad said with a grin. "Someone has to look after the rest of you!"

Now there were smiles and hugs and handshakes all round, whatever was going to happen in the next few days, the team was still going to be together. Now all they had to do was to plan their approach to the unknown dangers facing them.

18 THE REUNION

Steven Grace awoke and realised that it had not all been a dream. He was still trapped in a living hell, wounded and alone, and with no recollection of what bizarre events in his life had brought things to this pass. He was lying on the floor on some borrowed coats, in a strange building in the industrial sector of the city, shivering. He did not know why someone had shot him and why he had a broken arm. The day before he had been restored and found himself surrounded by people acting like zombies in an urban wasteland, in the middle of a gun battle between a street gang and some kind of private army. Added to that he was suffering injuries he did not remember getting, famished with the hunger and parched with thirst. Realising that he was in dire trouble he had dragged himself away from the scene as fast as his wounds and his weakened condition would allow, then he had gotten into an empty building from which he could still hear the sounds from the gun battle. It was an unoccupied warehouse. There he found a sink and drank some water until he was full. It was the first time since his zombie infection that he had drank anything other than human blood. Then he had used some discarded clothes to dress his wounds and splint his arm. It was not a perfect job and very painful, but he did the best he could. Not long before all this he had spent two very boring days doing a first aid course the company had made him go on, but he was glad of the knowledge he could put to good use now. When that was done he had found some canned food in the cafeteria, which he opened and devoured. Then he had barricaded himself into an office, made what he could in the way of bedding, and collapsed on the floor.

****

Billy Magee took Howal's cell phone back from Eddie Young.

"That was a very convincing act you did Eddie. Maybe you should have been an actor."

Eddie was not flattered. He was being used as a pawn in a game, as bait for people he didn't even know, for the sake of people he did know and for himself, and he wondered if this game was eventually going to destroy them all. For one crazy moment he wondered if he would be able to kill Magee with his bare hands and try to rescue his friends, regardless of the cost. Magee must have seen something in his eye, for he leaned back in his chair, and fingered a rather sharp looking ornamental letter opener which he played with in his hands. Eddie regained his composure and the moment of madness passed. If he got killed or zombified he would be of no help to anyone.

"Why did you turn my friends into zombies? There was no need to do that to two brilliant scientists!"

"I do what I have to do to get things done" Magee said, still toying with the letter opener. "Why are you so upset, I thought you wanted to kill them yourself not that long ago? You weren't trying to fool me were you?"

"I was angry with Hodson once, that is true, but then I got to see that he was in more pain than most men ever know, and I saw how he tried to reverse as much of the damage as he could. As for Howal, he did no harm to anyone. Now that I've kept my side of the bargain, will you use the Ghost Hand on them and restore them?"

"You know what Eddie? I'll do something even better. I'll tell you now that neither Hodson or Howal are zombies. I restored Hodson a couple of days ago, and I never even had to change Howal because he had the good sense to join in our enterprise. He saw what happened to Hodson and that was enough to make him see reason. I just told you that to help you to put up a good act for Tara Mahoney. If you didn't believe it, then she might have picked up on that and the ruse would have failed. A lot of women are very intuitive like that. I still could turn you all into zombies, but I choose not to. You should be happy with that."

Young was stunned, he had been tricked into luring more victims into Magee's web, and now they would soon be tied up in all this as well. He felt the anger rising in him again, but seeing Magee carefully watching his reaction, he realised that a wrong move now could cost them all dear in the end. As a plan formed in his mind he felt the anger subside.

"Ok, I have to hand it to you, you fooled me good there, Magee! I thought Hodson and Howal were right now trying to eat people! You shouldn't fool people like that, it isn't right! What are they doing anyway?"

Magee relaxed somewhat; "Right now they're doing the sensible thing, and working on projects which will benefit the new society which we are helping to create. When Mahoney and Shenton arrive here, they will become productive members of the team as well. They have the potential to do amazing things and we have the resources and the infrastructure. Together we can save our civilisation. Right now we are in the process of finalising a number of deals to sell the Ghost Hand to various governments and organisations around the world. Members of our new government are conducting intense negotiations with these people. Part of the price for the technology is a number of political concessions. For example some will have to have the type of government or certain people who we want in power, others will have to give up claims to certain territories, others will supply us with cheap resources, that type of thing. Needless to say, these places are desperate to buy, so they will do almost anything we demand. Mind you, we must get the right balance of pragmatism and charity when it comes to our friends. We don't want to extract too heavy a price and create future resentment. As for our enemies, they are being denied the technology, there's no point helping them. Sure, they will get our technology eventually, even if it's through theft or piracy, but they will be weakened in the meantime. Every cloud has a silver lining Eddie!"

"Very clever, I must admit, it looks like there's no stopping you now. I realise that I am not really in a bargaining position here but may I ask a small favour that will cost you nothing to grant?"

"That depends on what you're asking for my friend."

"Since I was brought here against my will I have worked very hard on the factory floor, and caused no trouble for anyone. However I have been very lonely. The people here are ok but I have little in common with them and am still viewed as somewhat of an outsider. I'm not part of any of the cliques that always form in these places. Is it too much to ask to be allowed to see my friends, even to just chat over a cup of coffee?"

Magee had a think about this; Hummm, it was not a very big favour. Young would tell them about the plot to lure the girls to the operation, but there was nothing they could do about that. Sooner or later they would all be working together anyway. He decided it could do no harm. In fact it might even be a good thing. Once he had dealt with this whole business and put a lid on it, he would have more time to deal with other matters.

"You know what Eddie, I will grant you your request. Do you know why? Firstly, as you said, hard work deserves a reward and the reports from the foreman on you have been excellent. Secondly I want you to tell Hodson and Howal that we are going to rescue their friends from an uncertain fate, living in a lawless society, never knowing when they are going to be attacked by criminals or hordes of zombies. They have been lucky so far, I think they must have joined forces with some mercenaries or something, but that luck could still run out. We will bring them here, where they will be safe and secure. You have done them a favour Eddie, you should know that. Now go to your friends, I will have the guard escort you."

Eddie was feeling a lot better now. Yes he had unwittingly helped to lure these people into a trap but at least when he saw the others they might be able to figure a way out of all this mess together. He was about to leave when he was struck by a thought; "Before I go I have a question for you. That device of yours that cures the zombies, why do you call that thing the 'Ghost Hand'. Does that name mean something to you, or is it just some random thing you thought up?"

Magee looked at him for a moment, wondering what would be the most appropriate way to reply. Then he looked at a framed photograph which was sitting on his desk with a far-away look in his eyes and replied; "Got any family Eddie?"

"Uh yes, my parents are still in England and I have brothers and sisters scattered around in some of the smaller towns near here.

I'm hoping that they have been safe during this disaster and will make contact with them as soon as I can."

"The only family I ever knew was my mother. She raised me all by herself when my father walked away from us. We only had each other and I tried to be the best I could be for her. Growing up one of our greatest pleasures was to go for long walks in the countryside, just me and her. We could not afford trips away or foreign travel, but we didn't need that. We were lucky to live near a place that had lots of forests and hills, and we would pack some lunch and roam for miles and miles and never see another human being. She used to hold my hand and we would chat about anything and everything, or sometimes just walk in silence, enjoying the beauty of the world around us."

Eddie listened fascinated, wondering where all this was leading. It was a human side of Magee that he had not previously seen.

"Well anyway Eddie, all good things come to an end, and God for some reason saw fit to take my mother from me when I was seventeen. She died of a massive stroke and the only mercy for me then was that she went too quick to suffer much. We never even got to say goodbye, something that caused me pain on top of all the other sorrow. Well anyway I joined the army shortly after that and was soon sent overseas on one of our government's more futile and pointless foreign adventures. I was part of a specialist unit that was sent in to clear insurgents from a mountainous area where they were dug in and fortified so well that regular units or airstrikes could not dislodge them. One day we got a tip off from some local traders about the location of a cave network that some insurgents were using as a base for launching attacks on our troops. They'd managed to ambush some of our guys and kill several of them and the powers that be saw a need to counter some of the negative publicity back home with a big success story. Our unit was dispatched to the location under orders to clear the place and kill or capture as many insurgents as possible. What we did not know then was that the enemy had spies who warned them of our approach. They did not run, but laid an ambush and prepared to fight and die like fanatics. When we entered the cave network they let us get so far in and then trapped us in there by detonating explosives behind us, which caused a big rock-fall. Them they opened up on us with everything they had and my comrades fell around me without knowing what had hit them."

Here Magee paused, remembering fallen friends. Eddie did not interrupt but waited for him to continue.

"Miraculously I had remained relatively unscathed despite the barrage of gunfire and explosives going off all around me. It was pitch dark in the caves but there was enough light from the gunfire to see a tunnel nearby. I emptied my gun in the direction of our attackers and then I ran like hell down that tunnel and then used my flashlight to try to navigate my way out of there. The tunnel was narrow and wound left and right all over the place. I had no idea where it led but all I knew was that I had to keep moving until I could find a way out of there. There were other tunnels and caves leading off in different directions and needless to say I was hopelessly lost. As chance would have it, in my haste to escape I tripped and fell over a rock and my flashlight flew out of my hand and got smashed on the ground. Now I was alone in the dark and I was already half-blinded from the dust and half-deafened from the explosions. I was running blind and did not know where my enemies were or where I was. I had begun to lose hope when all of a sudden I felt a hand take my hand in the darkness and gently lead me along as if they knew the way. I felt no fear and I knew that this was a hand of a friend. I thought that maybe one of the others had survived and was leading me out of there. We carried on through the tunnels as if my guide knew the place like their hometown, and I following trustfully along. I was too weary to speak and thought that any conversation could wait until we were safely out of there. Eventually I felt a breeze on my face and I knew we were near an exit. Finally we made it out and then the hand slipped away from mine. It was nighttime and I still could not see properly as I had damaged my eyes with dust and dirt. I called for my friend to come back but there was no reply. I thought then that they might have gone back in to try to rescue someone else. My radio was damaged and I was exposed in the open so after a while waiting I made my way slowly down the mountain to make contact with our side and get help. Not long after we sent reinforcements in there and cleared the whole place. We found that all the rest of my team had died in the initial ambush. Their bodies were all together in that first cave. I was the only one who had gotten out. No-body had been sent in after us and no-one could explain who had guided me through those tunnels. The army medics thought I had been delusional from all the trauma I had experienced and they tried to give me medicine for my head. I was sent on leave to recuperate and it was during that time, when I was looking through some belongings that I found this old photo. I had never seen it before and must have packed it with my things when I left home without noticing. It was then that I realised who had led me to safety through those tunnels..............."

Magee handed Eddie the photo which had sat on his desk. It was a photo of a woman and a young boy and had the feel of a photograph that had been taken some years before. They were standing on a country road somewhere, hand in hand. On the bottom of the photograph was written the words: "To Billy, I will always hold your hand. Love Mother."

"That is why I named the device the Ghost Hand. When we created something that could lead the zombies out of the darkness I named it after something that had once led me out of the darkness……….so now you know."

Eddie had listened enthralled to the story and now he was stunned. He stared a while longer at the photograph and then handed it back to Magee, who gently placed it back in its place on the desk.

Then Eddie left the office and left Magee to his thoughts. He followed the guard into a part of the complex where he had never been before and was told to wait in the cafeteria.

Hodson and Howal had been busy working on various projects under the supervision of Professor Larry Irvine. He was warming to the two of them and they did not find him a disagreeable sort to work for. He did not have any of the professional jealously or the ego issues that many people in his profession had, and this made him easy to work with. Soon it was envisaged that they would be put in charge of their own projects with minimal supervision and they were looking forward to that. They wondered what the guard wanted when he came looking for them. He was a dour, taciturn man, who did not give much away in the form of details, but simply said someone was here to see them. They had been a little anxious at first, but that soon turned to joy and relief when they saw Eddie sitting there waiting for them. Howal gave him a big hug, but John Hodson felt he had to be a little more reserved, aware that there were cameras watching them, so he just gave a handshake, as if to bury the hatchet.

"I don't believe it, Eddie! How have you been?" Howal asked excitedly. "We often wondered what had become of you, and were worried that Magee might have fed you to the zombies!"

"They put me to work on the factory side, making among other things, the first version of the Ghost Hand they're putting out. When this mess is cleaned up I'm going to have a lot of money to spend!"

"That must have been interesting work?" Hodson suggested.

"Oh it wasn't too bad, after the initial training was completed they pretty much left me to my own devices. All I did really was monitor the equipment. It's the easiest job I ever did. What was it like being a zombie?"

"It sucked big-time. Fortunately the part of my brain which stores memories seems to have been temporarily disabled, and I don't remember much of the whole thing. Mostly it was like watching a primitive version of yourself do mad things. When the Iasobots die they seem to take their memory with them, which is a blessing, otherwise I'd never sleep again. I'm more or less recovered from it now thankfully. If anything I'm more at ease with myself than I had been. I don't know why but it's a side effect that I won't complain about."

Howal wanted to know why Eddie had been allowed to see them all of a sudden, and so he recounted the bad news about how he had been tricked and coerced into setting a trap for Tara and Beverley, a trap it looked like they were going to fall right into.

"Well, at the least the good news is that they are still alive" Howal said thoughtfully. I was afraid for a while that his tale that they were at my lab was another bluff of his. I couldn't figure out how they could have made the journey from that hospital, through all the zombies and gangs. They've done well to survive out there with all that's going on. I wonder how they did it?"

"Magee sort of hinted that they had found allies to help them" Eddie answered. "During our conversation he inadvertently said more than he meant to. He thinks they have teamed up with some armed men who are protecting them for financial reward. That's why he's sending half his men to intercept them if they do turn up at that disused factory he was on about."

"That would explain why they have survived when so many others have fallen by the wayside. I hope their isn't a massive firefight if and when the two sides collide. Did they say where they are now?" asked Hodson.

"No, Magee hasn't a clue. He wanted me to get it out of Tara, but she was too clever for that. His trump card was me pretending that you two are zombies. That may just cause them to overrule their suspicions and walk into the trap. That's when I asked if I could see you two, I was hoping that we might be able to figure out a way to warn them."

"It's difficult to know what to do. Right now Magee appears to be in full control, that's why he allows us to get together and chat like this. It's his way of demonstrating his power over us, he knows there's nothing we can do and if we cause trouble he can punish us again. I think he's enjoying this little battle of wits because he thinks he can't lose." This was the stark assessment from Alan Howal.

"In a way you're right" agreed Hodson. "What could we do? The best scenario would be for all three of us to escape and somehow meet up with Tara and Bev and go somewhere else, and I suppose carry on our work. The problem with that is that these people have taken over the government, who in turn control the resurgent police and army. We would be always be fugitives, looking over our shoulders and scavenging for scraps to survive. We don't even know where this factory you mentioned is and I don't have my phone anymore. At least if they were here we would all be together, and they would be safe until the zombie apocalypse is over. At first all I wanted to do was to get out of this place, but gradually I am settling in here."

"I have both their numbers memorised" Howal murmured. "That wouldn't be an issue if we could get our hands on another phone. There have been long periods when theirs were the only numbers I ever called. However I can't help but wonder if you're right John. They would be safer here than wandering around in a crime-ridden wasteland. As they roll out more and more of the Ghost Hand devices the zombie threat will subside. Eventually it will be over. Then these people will be in control, and what then? As John said, you can only survive on scraps for so long. We may not like all the politics of these people, but the more I think about it, a lot of what they say does make sense. Recently I have come to realise that a lot of what I previously took for granted was wrong. I don't agree with everything they say and do, but I didn't agree with everything the last government did either. We will have a lot more influence working from inside, than being fugitives on the outside. I think we're in a better position than a lot of people. At this stage it might be better if we let Magee bring our friends here, where we can work together, and all be safe. Who knows, somewhere down the line things might change, and we can re-evaluate our position. Until then it's probably best to play the game here."

Eddie was surprised. He had been expecting fighting talk about a daring escape and starting all over in another laboratory somewhere, but then he realised that he was talking with two scientists in their sixties, not a couple of commandoes who were going to blow a hole in the wall and then have a gunfight with everybody. Now he realised what Magee had known all along, these were beaten men whose fighting days were long gone. They had lived their whole lives pottering around with their test tubes and their slides, and that was where they felt at home. Now they were willing to trade freedom for security and trade independence for a place at the fire. Maybe they were right he thought? Maybe they should all lie low here and wait the whole thing out? They had complete security, taken care of by other people, all the good food they wanted, recreational facilities, and productive employment. Events bigger than themselves were taking place outside. Maybe it was time to make the best of it and embrace their fate? He looked up at the security camera and it seemed to twinkle back at him.

****

Eli was enjoying a few beers with some of the other gang members at their clubhouse. He had spent a couple of hours researching the company called Eclipse Enterprises and now he knew all that was public knowledge about them. They seemed like an outfit who would have a lot of spare cash lying about, but more importantly they had planes and pilots at their disposal. Eli was dreaming of setting up an international drugs importation empire, and he needed a small passenger plane and someone who knew how to fly it. If they could set aside their past differences there was no reason why himself and these Eclipse people couldn't work together, after all that whole shoot-out thing had simply been a misunderstanding. He needn't tell them what he wanted a plane for, just make up something, and go from there. Of course all he needed now were those scientists, otherwise he would have nothing to bargain with. He would capture the scientists, kill their friends and then the deal was on. Tomorrow he would present himself to whoever was in charge of the company, and offer his terms.

After an early night he rose when the first birds were

singing in the morning. Since there was little in the way of traffic in the city there days there seemed to be birds singing everywhere. Noisy little critters. He got up and dressed and had porridge for breakfast. Then he assembled his gang and they prepared their weapons. Even though he was going to present a business offer, the last time he had met these people there had been a gun battle, and the gang had killed at least one of them, he didn't know if that would be held against him. Also there were still lots of zombies wandering the area, and also other armed gangs and vigilantes. It was safer to travel in numbers just to be on the safe side.

When all was ready they piled into their trucks all twenty six of them, and set off for the main complex of Eclipse Enterprises. They were all cheerful and most of them were still drunk from the night before. Many of them were drinking now, as a cure for their pounding hangovers. Occasionally one of them would spot what they thought was a zombie, and they would pop off a shot at it, much to Eli's annoyance. He was trying to keep a low profile and did not want to show up at Eclipse Enterprises, trailing a horde of zombies after him. He got angry and shouted at them over the radio to desist from drawing unnecessary attention onto themselves. The crew would stop for a while, but they were in a jovial mood and sooner or later discipline would break down again.

Eventually they came in on the approach to the complex, with its high walls and watchtowers, and they were met by a large number of Eclipse security, who had been monitoring their arrival and were wary that it was an attack. Eli was in the foremost truck, waving a white flag out the window. When they rolled up to a checkpoint he introduced himself to the Sergeant in command and asked to be given an audience with whoever was in charge. The Sergeant was not very helpful and refused to pass on his message without more information. Eli conceded and told him of their plan to capture the scientists and deliver them to Eclipse, in return for fair payment. To strengthen his hand he exaggerated a bit and pretended that he was aware of where the scientists were right now. The Sergeant was well aware of the importance of the scientists, as he was the self-same one who had been assigned to watch them at Howal's laboratory. He also figured out that these were the criminals who had attacked him and his men and killed one of them. He did not reveal this information to Eli, who he had no interest in enlightening. Realising that this bunch of misfits might do a lot of harm if they were not controlled the Sergeant agreed to pass on his request.

He had Eli carefully searched and brought alone into the complex. His men would have to wait outside and drive around to avoid zombies. The Sergeant would speak with the boss, and then let Eli know if he was interested in the gang's proposal. Eli was not overjoyed at being disarmed and isolated from the rest of the pack, but he figured it was a temporary inconvenience while he set up the deal. It would be worth it in the end, so he went along with things. That was what being a leader was all about.

Magee was on the phone to Senator Carmody when the Sergeant arrived at his office. Finishing the call he invited the Sergeant in; "What is it Sergeant, something important?"

"I'm not sure Sir. You won't believe who's just showed up at the front gates. It's the gang who attacked us back at Howal's lab!"

"Are they looking for more trouble or something, what do those people want anyway?" Magee was getting irritated by these meddlers.

"No Sir, not trouble. It looks like they want to make a deal with us. Their leader, some 'Eli' character, is saying that they know where those scientists you're looking for are, and he wants some sort of payment if he brings them in."

"Did he actually say where they are?"

"No, he refused to tell me, that's his bargaining chip. I don't believe him anyway, this guy is a pathological liar if you ask me."

"What sort of payment does he want, did he say?"

"He was very vague about that, he said he wanted to discuss things with you in person. The guy is a big bluffing idiot but when he mentioned the scientists I thought I'd make you aware, just in case he did know something."

"Yes you did the right thing there Sergeant. This guy Eli and his gang are more trouble than they're worth. They're more likely to botch a kidnap attempt and kill Mahoney and Shenton than capture them. From what we've seen of their antics so far, we'd be better off sending a few of the zombies off looking for our scientific friends. He must think he's dealing with a bunch of fools. Where is he now?"

The Sergeant smiled at this; "I brought him in alone and made him wait in the front compound Sir. The rest of the gang are waiting outside getting increasingly pissed from booze and taking pot-shots at the occasional zombie that strays too close. Needless to say the sooner we get rid of them the better."

"Humm, well we certainly don't need to do a deal with these morons, I agree with you, if he knew where the scientists were he would have tried to catch them, so he would have a proper bargaining chip when he showed up. However I have just been struck by a very interesting idea. Perhaps the arrival of these idiots may turn out to be a fortuitous event in the end. Sometimes opportunity initially presents itself as a problem until you change your perspective. Go back down for him and take him to testing room number three. I will meet you there shortly."

The Sergeant went back out and informed Eli that his boss had agreed to meet him to hear what he had to say. He then led Eli to another part of the facility under the pretext that he had passed the first level of clearance. Eli was feeling in a congratulatory mood with himself. He was about to meet the boss of this whole operation. He had been impressed with the way things seemed to work here, and he envisaged that the boss was probably someone just like himself, someone who lived by their own rules. He was happily imagining a long and mutually profitable partnership when Magee and a couple of his scientists entered the testing room. Magee was an excellent judge of character and could read most people pretty quickly. It only took him one glance to confirm all he needed to know about Eli. Here was a bandit, trying to hit the big time. He'd seen men like Eli often enough before, and had nothing but contempt for them. They were parasites, petty criminals who had nothing to offer society, except to prey on others so they could live their drug-addled lives work free. This was the type of low-life scum that previous governments had pandered to and enabled to live a life of crime. This type of waster had profited from years of pseudo-intellectuals trying to frame their criminal behaviour in terms of some kind of failure by society, instead of lack of moral fibre and personal responsibility, and sheer badness. It had made people like this think that everything they did wrong was someone else's fault, and that everybody else owed them a work-free lifestyle. These dogs had no place in the new society. Magee could almost smell the sense of entitlement from where he stood and it made him feel sick. He hid his contempt behind a pleasant smile for now though, old Eli was shortly going to pay his debt to society, albeit unwittingly:

"Good morning Eli. I am Billy Magee, I'm the man in charge of this operation. I hear you have a business proposition for me?"

"I certainly do Billy. I am in charge of my own enterprise. We are interested in making the most out of the chaos and disorder that has emerged as a result of so many of our citizens trying to eat each other. I hear that you are interested in finding a certain two good-looking scientists who up to a short time ago were holed up in some kind of science lab out in the west end?"

"Indeed, the zombie plague has been a most unexpected development and one that will shape our world for the next century, maybe the next few centuries if we get the foundations right. It started off as an apocalypse and had the potential to send us back to living in caves, but lately I've been seeing it as like a cleansing forest fire which burns all the dead wood away, and makes room for a new forest to grow. Tell me, what do you know of the two female scientists that we are looking for?"

Eli knew that he had to really sell this part so he adopted a really sincere expression that he always used when he wanted to bluff people; "Yes, we've been tracking those two ever since we first came across them at the District Hospital. We were just going to hang onto them but now that we realise that you have an interest in them, we reckon we could do a deal. If and when we catch them, and it's only a matter of time before we do, we are willing to trade them for half a million dollars and the use of one of your planes for a week. I have twenty five armed men under my command, and there is nothing and no-one in this city and beyond that we can't reach. Some of my men have relatives in another country that they want to visit. Er, that's why we want the plane. We can insert ourselves into an area, neutralise whatever resistance we encounter, extract the wanted personnel and have them here by tea-time. Once our net closes around someone, they have no hope of getting away from us. We can operate like a surgical strike-team. That kind of talent comes at a cost, but it will save your men from getting hurt and get the job done cleanly. Those two scientists have acquired bodyguards that know what they're doing, not just anyone has the goods to handle them and win."

Magee could barely hide his incredulousness at the sheer stupidity of Eli's ruse, and his brazen attempt to make a deal based on an empty lie, but he did not let him know that. Struggling to conceal his utter contempt for the man, he tried to appear intrigued.

"Sounds like we might be able to do a deal, we are indeed interested in those two scientists and the money and everything else are just details. However, I need time to think about this. Why don't I leave you with the Sergeant while I make some phone calls? One of these other men will bring you a drink while you're waiting. A guest should be offered refreshments, what would you like?"

Eli wanted a coffee with some whiskey in it, so one was soon brought and placed before him. He was in a jovial mood and tried to make conversation with the taciturn Sergeant who already disliked him immensely. This moron was responsible for the death of a good man and friend of his. It was hard to stand there listening to his grandiose yapping, and resist the urge to throttle him. Well it was nice to watch some revenge taking place.

Eli sipped his drink and wondered who Magee was calling. Probably some secret bank these business types used for themselves. Wheels within wheels and all that stuff. This Magee guy had seemed impressed with his negotiation skills. He was pleased with the way things were going and the way he could handle himself around important people. Then he suddenly began to feel strange. He was trying to boast some more to the Sergeant about some of his daring exploits when he began to lose track of things that he was saying, then forgot where he was in a sentence. Then he couldn't remember if he had finished his previous sentence or not, but couldn't quite say it from start to finish again. Then he began to forget who he was or where he was or what he was doing there. What was this place? Who was that man looking at him? Then his mind went blank and he ceased to care. The Sergeant noted with considerable satisfaction that he had finally stopped talking.

Magee and the scientists came back in. They had been watching developments from behind a two-way mirror in the next room.

"It looks like he's totally succumbed to the Slavebots" one of the scientists said, peering closely into his eyes. Eli did not react in any way to this treatment.

"Eli stand up" the scientist commanded. Without hesitation Eli stood up.

"Now jump up and down!" Eli jumped up and down.

"Eli, stand on your head." Eli ponderously stood on his head, and stayed there.

The demonstration was enough for Magee; "Looks like this idiot will do anything we tell him to. Those things are an amazing invention. How many of his men are outside? I forget what he said in amongst all his other blathering about surgical strike teams."

The Sergeant was able to report that there were twenty five more of these fools outside, in varying states of sobriety.

"Ok offer them all a beverage containing the Slavebots. Tell them the negotiations with their leader are at a critical stage and we don't know how long it will take to seal the deal. When they are in a similar state of mind to this idiot here, disarm them and put them in compound number two. We have work for them to do. In the new society this is how we will treat criminals and those who refuse to try to contribute to their own welfare. The days of pandering and kow-towing to them and trying to understand what's upsetting them are over. That approach has failed. From now on they will pay their dues by doing menial and dangerous tasks for those of us who make an honest effort. The Slavebots are better than any ball and chain, even though the physical body is free, their mind is totally enslaved."

****

Steven Grace awoke from a dreamless sleep and took a moment to get his bearings in the unfamiliar surroundings he was in. He was still very weak, but he had recovered a little from his wounds. He slowly struggled to his feet and made his way to the lunch room, where he prepared a simple meal of canned food and water. This restored his strength a little more and he began to plan his next move. Rummaging around in his pockets he found his cell phone and checked it for damage. It seemed intact, although the battery was flat. Now he was cautiously searching the building for a compatible charger. The building had been vacated in a hurry, like all the others in that area, so he was hopeful of finding a charger he could use. He had to check and see how Erin was. He had been doing some thinking that morning over breakfast, trying to figure out what had happened to himself and to the rest of the world. He came across enough human remains to realise that people had turned on each other and torn each other apart, but he did not know yet what had caused it. He wondered if there had been a plague of some sort. From his work in chemistry he knew that it was possible that a deadly virus had spread throughout the world in a short period of time, creating mayhem as it went. Then the terrible realisation had hit him that he himself must have been one of the persons attacking others, though he knew not why. That explained why he had picked up his injuries. Something had definitely turned his mind off and turned him into some kind of primitive killer, a stranger to himself. He hoped he hadn't hurt people when he had been in that state, but a part of him knew that he must have. Something else had then brought him back to normal but he had no idea what that was either. From peering cautiously out the window he had seen several zombies prowling the streets and shuddered to realise that, up until a few hours ago, that had been him as well. He wondered what selective mechanism had restored him, and if it would turn out to be a blessing or a curse. A lot would depend on what happened when he found a phone charger. There did not seem to be one in the building he was in, and he realised that he would have to go further afield, although he did not want to. He thought about this for a while and wondered if it was worth the risk. No he had to know, regardless of the cost. Now where was the best place to look? There had been ordinary people in those buildings where that gun battle had taken place, there was a reasonable chance that there was a charger in one of those. It was close by, certainly close enough to chance going there. He was in no position to fight so he would be relying on pure luck, but he had nothing left to lose. He armed himself with a fire axe that he'd come across, checked for signs of activity, then went for it.

He slowly ventured out into the street, still dumfounded by the destruction of the world he had known. So this was what it looked like when God finally gave up on mankind. There didn't appear to be anyone around as he stoically made his way along so he used the axe as a walking stick. His leg was stiff and sore but luckily he had found a bottle of painkillers in an office at the warehouse, and swallowed enough to treat a horse. These deadened a lot of the pain and enabled him to make a gradual progress. If he came upon any hostiles now he wouldn't be able either to run or fight, so he needed his luck to hold for a while. It also dawned on him that he was still attired in clothes that were covered in dried blood. He hoped that some concealed sniper wouldn't mistake him for a zombie and shoot him. He finally came to where the gun battle had been and saw the bullet holes and empty cartridges everywhere. He wondered what those people had been fighting for? Probably killing each other over food or something, the last scraps of civilisation. There were bones strewn about too, picked clean by the zombies who had waited for the battle to yield its dead. In another place and time the abomination would have appalled him but he was now too tired to be shocked by this depravity anymore. He was living through his own horror and that was enough for him to contend with. He looked at the two buildings which had been involved in the gun battle, the one where the team from Eclipse Enterprises had hidden, and the one that had been Howal's lab. Which to choose? The red brick building that had been the lab looked more inviting for some reason and it was closer so he made his way wearily inside.

He hobbled past the shattered front doors and down the hall, looking for a place where someone would keep a charger. He walked straight into the laboratory and too late realised that there were four large zombies standing there silently watching him. Then another one came up behind him in the doorway. These were some of the zombies who had feasted on the bodies outside. When they had finished their gruesome meal they had wandered into the building, attracted by the smell of human occupation that still lingered like a perfume in the air. Like he himself had been until recently, they were bloodied and tattered from the various encounters they'd had with other people. They watched him through eyes that were bloodshot and blank, creatures of the night.

There was no escape, so he raised the axe in one arm and prepared to make his last stand, but all they did was to look briefly at him, then completely ignore him. Steven lowered the axe. Why did they not attack? Did they somehow recognise him as being one of themselves even though that was no longer the case? Had he gained some kind of immunity from the virus? He had no idea what the rules were in this strange living horror in which he had found himself, and he was getting too tired again to care. With the help of the axe and his one good arm he limped about until his eyes fell on a charger sticking out from under a sheaf of papers. Grabbing at it he plugged in his phone. It fitted! He found a socket and plugged in the other end. The light went on as the phone, like himself, slowly re-energised itself.

Wearily he sat down on a chair and waited. Soon there was enough power to use the phone and, leaving it plugged in, he called Leanne Turner, barely daring to breathe. After a few rings she answered; "Steven?" He hadn't realised she still kept his name on her caller id.

"Leanne!" he said, his voice a strangled croak. It was the first time in days he had used his voice and he sounded like a stranger to himself. The zombies turned at the sound of his voice, but they didn't show any increased interest in him. Two of them had wandered away by now but the presence of the rest of them was unnerving.

"Steven where are you, we were so worried? Are you still in the city, it said on the radio it's a no-go area?"

"Umm I'm not quite sure, in the middle of a warzone somewhere, yes in the city. Where are you, is Erin ok?"

"Yes she's fine, we're both fine, when the zombie apocalypse happened we were at my mother's place out in the country. You remember where it is, it's really isolated. Even the crows don't know where this place is. I meant for us all to get the cold vaccine before we travelled but I totally forgot, so none of us became zombies. I'm so glad you're ok. Do you want to speak to Erin?"

Steven groaned..........that damned vaccine! So that was what had made him go mad, oh well, it was too late now to go back and undo things.

"Yes put her on........Hi honey, how are you?"

"Daddy! How are you? I miss you! We were frightened that you had been eaten by the zombies! It said on the radio that they're eating everybody!"

"Don't worry about me honey. You guys stay put until all this is over and then I will come to see you, ok?" He did not tell her he was in a room full of zombies right now, or that he had been one himself until very recently. Some things she would never know, or at least for a long, long time.

After chatting for a while, Leanne came back on, and invited him to come stay with them until things returned to some semblance of normality. He paused only for a brief time. He'd not really thought what he was going to do next, strange as that seemed. He didn't know what condition his own house was in at the moment, and the city was clearly a dangerous place, so he accepted the offer. He needed to rest again, but hopefully he would be recovered enough to attempt the journey the next day. He told her he had been attacked by criminals who had robbed him of his car. Leanne was mortified by the revelation but that was his injuries explained away.

Following the phone call he suddenly felt overcome with relief. At least something in his life was safe and well. Now he had to hold it together long enough to get out of the city and reach the only thing he loved in this existence. He left his phone charging and the zombies guarding the place and lay down in a back room to rest. He had not planned on sleeping but sleep overcame him anyway and he forgot all. After a few hours he woke again and looked around for some food. He soon located the dining area and found the fridge, still pulled away from the hole in the wall. He wondered what had happened here. The fridge was still fairly full of food and drink, and he helped himself to all he could eat, gradually feeling a little better. He forced himself not to think about what he must have been eating during his time as a zombie. When that was done he slowly limped upstairs until he found a bedroom. He barely had time to barricade the door when he collapsed onto the bed. He lay awake briefly and suddenly a strange thought came to him; yesterday and today were the first days of his life that he had not dreamed any day dreams. Why was that, and why did that suddenly seem so important to him? He did not know. It must be because he was so busy trying to stay alive and figure out what to do with himself, he reasoned. Maybe his mind was too preoccupied with survival to go on auto-pilot right now? He could not figure out the answer, but suddenly it seemed to be something of momentous importance. Whatever it was, it would have to wait until later for the answer to reach him. For now he fell into another deep, deep slumber.

19 THE STANDOFF

Scott had come up with a plan for meeting Eddie Young. They would ask him to come meet them at a different building, one of their choosing. It was a large wholesale warehouse a few blocks down and diagonal from the factory where Eddie Young supposedly was. It must have been full of food and other goods at one time, but anything of use had been looted early on in the current crisis. There was a road running at the back of it where they had parked their vehicles; ideal if a quick getaway was needed. It also had extensive views of the surrounding area, perfect for observing if there was one man approaching their position, or a whole lot of them. If someone was intending to ambush them, then this plan was designed to throw their intentions into confusion and hopefully thwart their efforts. Not long after they had taken up positions, Tara's phone beeped, signalling that she had a new message. She quickly checked her inbox. It was a message from Eddie, asking when they were going to come to the factory. Tara texted back and said that there had been a change of plan and that he must come to them. She sent him the address of another building close to where they were. It was one they could observe from their hiding place but far enough away if they had to get out fast. Anyone coming from Eddie's location to the address she had sent him would have to go right past them and they would know if he had been lying. Now the game was on and the tension began to build. Scott and Brad were crouched up on the roof doing surveillance duty, using the scopes on their rifles to watch the place and see if a trap was being mounted. The area seemed quiet – too quiet in fact. There was a marked absence of zombies in the area, something that had alarm bells ringing in their heads. No zombies usually meant that something had driven them out. Was it just vigilantes or city employees or was it someone from the sinister Eclipse company? Down below Tara got another message from Eddie; there was a problem with the new plan. He had been exploring the attic part of the factory, looking for a better place to hide, when he had fallen from a ladder and sprained his ankle. They would have to come and meet him as he was unable to get around now.

"As if any further proof was needed!" Tom exclaimed. "This is a trap, there's no longer any doubt. They want us in that factory so they can ambush us, it's obvious!"

It was hard to disagree with this assessment, but what to do now? Beverley had been thinking; What was the point of dragging all their friends into a confrontation with danger, and perhaps getting them killed, or even worse? What had originally seemed like a good idea was now starting to look like they were walking headlong into a trap. Perhaps it was time to reassess the situation.

"I think we should call this whole thing off" she suddenly said. We can't risk the rest of us being hurt or turned into zombies. I had hoped that this Young guy might be genuine but I'm not convinced now."

Tara considered this for a moment, then she sighed with resignation; "I agree" she said sadly. "This has got the feel of a trap to it, but where does that leave us now?"

"Stall for time until we think of a plan" Doug suggested.

"Tell him we had a break down and you're looking for another vehicle. Say there's lots of zombies around, and you don't want to rush things and lead them to where he is. Then we'll get the hell out of here. Once we put some distance between ourselves and this place we can take another look at the situation and try to come up with a better plan."

"Yes" Brad agreed. Perhaps it's time to make contact with these people and straight out ask them what they want, and find out if they are willing to make a deal of some kind that would see your friends restored to their normal selves? There may be an easier solution to all this than we think."

This seemed like a good idea for now, so Tara sent Eddie the news that they were experiencing a delay but were working on getting mobile again. Then the friends prepared to leave the area.

****

Magee was in an armoured car, not far from the warehouse where the friends were, co-ordinating the operation. He was accompanied by three quarters of his entire security staff, leaving a skeleton crew to guard the complex, and also a few recent 'recruits'. When he got the latest message from Tara, he was smart enough to know that the plan had been rumbled and that the subjects had gotten the jitters. He also knew that there was more than one way to get a thing done, and he had one of his men contact the phone company whose network they were on. Like lots of other organisations, they were rebuilding and reorganising, and had a functional infrastructure going again. The phone company knew who they were dealing with and they were more than willing to ping the location of Mahoney's phone. As soon as he got it,

Magee ordered his men to close in. This business needed to be settled once and for all. If Mahoney was not going to come to him, he was going to have to go to Mahoney.

****

Steven Grace woke from the deepest sleep he had ever known. He was still at the laboratory. He got up and had a look around the other rooms to see what useful things he might find to take with him. To his joy he came upon some fresh men's clothes. He rummaged about until he found some his own size, then laboriously changed out of his tattered blood-soaked garments. Now he wouldn't arrive at Leanne's place looking like a zombie. Then he went downstairs, again using his axe as a walking stick. His leg was still stiff and sore but it was gradually getting better all the time. He took another of the painkillers, to help him with the task ahead. He hoped the bullet had passed right through rather than staying in his body. There was no sign of the resident zombies anywhere, and he guessed that they had wandered off somewhere looking for food. He raided the contents of the fridge again for breakfast, took some more of the painkillers, and then began packing the things he would need for the journey to Leanne's place. Whoever had been here had certainly been well prepared, and he hoped they would not mind him taking their stuff, assuming that any of them had survived the gun fight. Because of his injuries, progress was relatively slow but finally he had moved the bags of stuff over by the front doorway. Now to get a vehicle.........

He looked up and down the street, what looked promising? There were numerous vehicles on either side of the building. All the ones near the laboratory had been heavily damaged in the gun battles which had taken place, and he discounted them right away. He walked slowly down the block, first checking a car that appeared undamaged. It was locked, as were the next two vehicles. A pickup truck he liked the look of started but it was too low on fuel to be worth bothering with, so he went a bit further, limping slowly along. Finally, he spotted an SUV that had been abandoned at the side of the road. The keys were in it and it was automatic; perfect! He needed an automatic vehicle with his damaged limbs. It started first time and he noted with relief that it was full to the brim. The previous owner must have filled it shortly before the mayhem began. That would save him having to look for fuel. He drove back to the lab and slowly loaded the bags he had packed. A lone male zombie watched him with disinterest from across the street. He felt a pang of sympathy for the guy, but there was nothing he could do to help him. He marvelled at how quickly he had gotten used to having those things around. Now he had everything ready, and he set off, gingerly maneuvering his way around the various cars that were blocking the roads. He gradually made his way through the city, and noted that there were teams of uniformed people moving systematically along, area by area. They glanced at him, but did not accost him in any way. He did not know it but they were the restoration teams from the government who were searching for selected zombies, and bringing them back to normal. He also noted several ordinary people who were wandering around in a daze. They seemed bewildered by the mess they were in and the shattered city they had just woken up in. They were recently restored persons, who were wondering what the hell was going on, going through a similar experience as he had himself, two days ago. Whatever nightmare the nanobots had caused, it looked like everybody was waking up from it. He felt tempted to stop and advise them on what to do next, but he had somewhere to be, and he was feeling weak from all his earlier exertions. They would have to find their own path to healing, or at least they would for now, as an idea had begun to germinate in his mind.

Finally he was out of the city and heading east. He knew where Leanne's parents place was because it was near where he went skiing a few times. That seemed like another lifetime to him now. He had been a different person then. He wondered if he had dreamed it all. The thought occurred to him that, apart from a few brief moments, in that past existence he had always lived under a cloud of sadness. It had been existence without purpose or fulfillment. As he drove he suddenly realised that he wasn't daydreaming today either. He did not know why but this seemed to have a huge significance for him. His mind was no longer engaged in futile attempts to change his reality, attempts that would always end in failure. He wondered how much of his life he had spent lost in fantasies and illusions, probably years. He thought it was a pity he hadn't spent the time learning something, instead of wasting all that energy, but he could not change the past. He was somehow different now. Being a zombie had somehow cleaned out his mind of a lot of pointless clutter. He realised he had nothing to lose now except all his anger and frustration, all his fear, and the wanting to make himself something he was not. He realised that his life of quiet desperation would have to come to an end. He had nothing to lose but the chains of his own mind. He was a new man and as he drove he just let everything go. All the stupid dreams, his memories, all the anger, all his futile efforts at control. He just accepted things as they were. There seemed to be nothing else to do. Then something unexpected happened to him; the veil of illusion dropped from his mind and he saw everything as it really was. He became one with the universe, and each recognised itself in the other. When he finally rolled up to his destination and Erin ran to meet him, he was a changed man forever.

****

The warehouse they were in had a small shop at the front. Doug had been keeping watch on the street outside while some of the others gathered all their things in the back area. Just as they were ready to flee the place he spotted the armed men taking up position behind vehicles, walls and lampposts. Alarmed, he ran back in to warn the others. When they checked out back it was the same story, there were armed men everywhere. Scott and Brad had gone back up on the roof to check if the coast was clear when they too noticed that someone was closing in on them from all sides at once. They came back down in a hurry and confirmed that they had been rumbled. There was no getting out now. Hastily they locked the doors and pushed large items of furniture up against them. Then, grabbing their weapons, they spread out and took up various defensive positions around the premises, waiting for the assault to happen.

Some time passed and all remained quiet. No-one challenged them or fired on their position. Ten minutes passed, then twenty, then half an hour. The tension became almost unbearable. What the hell were these people waiting for? The friends did not know for sure but it looked like Magee was playing a psychological game, trying to wear them down. This was true. Magee knew from his own fighting days that the waiting was the hard part, and he knew the wearing effect it would be having on those inside the building. He did not want to risk killing valuable people assets, so he was adopting tactics which he hoped would dispense with the need to use force. Finally he calculated that the time was right to make a move so he activated stage two of the procedure. He ordered one of the slaves to advance on the front of the building. The man did not hesitate, walking forward toward the front door, brandishing a rifle in front of himself. When he got within thirty feet of the place, a bullet straight to the chest downed him. He fell without a murmur, struggled to his feet, and then fell again a few steps later. This time he did not rise again. Then there was the eerie silence again……and more tense waiting Ten minutes later another man walked forward, he was also waving a gun. He got to within the same distance as the first man had when he also was downed by a single shot. This pattern was repeated several more times. The men at the back of the building did not fire or attack, but simply remained in position, making sure there was no possibility of escape.

The friends knew something was badly wrong. Why were these men taking turns to advance alone in some completely futile form of attack? It was bizarre that they did not try to storm the place en masse, or even open fire on the building for that matter. They were not zombies but they were acting like they were in some kind of trance. Their pointless attacks resembled some kind of group suicide and it was starting to have a huge effect on the defenders of the building. How long would this go on for? What was puzzling as well was that the attackers were not the uniformed men of Eclipse Enterprises, but similar to the rag-tag members of the crime gang they had twice encountered in the last few days. Did Eclipse Enterprises have some kind of alliance with the criminal gang and had they been involved with them from the beginning? If so it was a highly unusual and one-sided relationship. Why were the gang engaging in a mindless demonstration of kamikaze attacks that was never going to succeed? So far they had not fired a single shot, what were they hoping to achieve? Were they all out of their heads on drugs?

Meanwhile, from his vantage position, Magee decided that he had made his point. It was time to make his introductions. He called the number of Tara's phone and waited. Inside the warehouse the friends crouched at their positions and waited for the massed attack that they felt must surely come. The phones ring startled them all in the tense silence that had pervaded while they were thus engaged. Mahoney was at a second floor window overlooking the front of the premises and armed with a 30.30 rifle. Scott was at the next window over. She looked enquiringly at him, waiting for a signal.

"Answer it," he called softly, "We may as well hear what they have to say. None of this is making sense to me."

Resting the rifle against the window ledge, Tara answered the phone and put it on speakerphone.

"Alright, who are you and what do you want?" she demanded. She was nearing the point where she had had enough. They were slaughtering people like animals down there.

"Hi Tara, my name is Billy Magee. I am the CEO of Eclipse Enterprises."

"I don't care who you are, why don't you just leave us alone? Stop hunting and harassing us, you have no right to do that!" Tara was getting near the end of her patience.

"It's not that simple Tara and please do not get upset. You see I am not your enemy, indeed I am your friend and ally, I want to help you, and I want you to help me."

"You're talking nonsense, you have armed men watching us and following us and spying on us, and you have kidnapped my friends and turned them into zombies, how dare you say you are my friend! Who are these people who are attacking us, and why are they behaving so strangely?"

"Tara, I have a lot to say to you, but it needs to be done

face to face. Will you meet me?"

Tara looked at Scott, with a questioning look on her face. What to do now? Scott was unsure. He had been in some tight spots but he had never faced an enemy that made no attempt to defend itself before. There did not seem to be any rational way of dealing with this predicament. While he hesitated, Magee spoke again; "Tara, I am going to send another man against you, and I will keep this up until you agree to meet me. All I ask is for a brief truce so I can explain my position, it's up to you."

The next man who approached was Eli, emerging from behind a parked truck. Mindlessly following orders he strode forward, waving a gun in each hand. He was getting nearer and nearer to the front door, but still he did not fire. The friends held their fire, wondering what to do. As the man got closer, Scott suddenly gasped. This was the first time he had seen Eli this close up. He now recognised the man who had killed his wife in a drunken car crash, then fled the scene, leaving her broken body to bleed to death at the side of the road in the rain. Scott felt the pain and anger burn him like a fire. His gun was still covering the gang leader. Then Scott's finger pulled the trigger. Later he would feel shame for this moment, but it was done hastily at a time of great stress. The bullet from the 30.06 struck Eli in the head, ripping through it and sending him sprawling in the dirt like a piece of garbage. Everyone gasped. It was the first time one of them had lost control. Then Mahoney knew what she had to do. This weird siege was turning the men she loved into animals. She could not let this madness go on, they would never be the same again when the dust had settled. She told Magee she would agree to arrange a truce. His fiendish plan had worked. She would meet him in the shop at the front, and he had to come alone. He agreed and after a while she saw a man approach on foot. Beverley looked out and confirmed that it was Billy Magee, she had met him briefly the day she had been at the complex. Magee reached the front door and Tom opened it, quickly frisking him when he stepped inside, while Brad locked the door after him. No-one else came near. All they found on him were two cell phones, his own and Howal's.

"I am unarmed. I have come to explain my position. All I ask is that you listen to what I have to say. It will not take very long." Magee was calm and confident. The means he had used to get here did not seem to trouble him in the slightest.

He was allowed inside, and shown to a chair. He looked casually around at them, taking note of their faces and appearance. He was still curious as to who the scientists had found to guard them all this time. His instincts told him they were worthy opponents although he was hoping that they would not be opponents for much longer. Tara put down her gun and sat opposite him while the rest waited in the background, watching with fascination.

Tara spoke first; "Alright what do you want with us?"

"What I want is not that important Tara. What our country needs is another matter. Right now I am working for the good of our country, for all our futures and for our children's future. You have seen the lengths I will go to, to achieve my objectives. That is my way of showing you that I mean business without having to risk hurting you in an all-out gun battle. Only one who has his eyes on a bigger picture will go as far as I will go."

"How does that involve us?" Tara asked.

"There is a new government in place in this country, and a new system of governance. Democracy has had its time, but it is unsuitable for the new challenges facing us as we move deeper into this century. Our company is an important partner with the new government, working together to promote all our interests and security in the world. Right now we are engaged in the greatest attempt to save a civilisation that has ever taken place on this planet, but to do that we need the brightest minds and the best talent available to us. We have lost so much of our manpower and knowledge in recent days and weeks and the only thing that will save us now is technological superiority and a determination to overcome. All the rules of the game have changed and we need something special to survive, nothing short of genius. You and Miss Shenton have been recognised as having the skills and abilities we need to give us that cutting edge, that is why we have been so eager to recruit you to our cause, and that is why we cannot allow you to work for anyone else but us. We know what you have been trying to do in your laboratory, but your work must only be for us and for our purposes. It must not fall into the hands of our enemies. Your government and your country are relying on you."

"Is that why you turned John and Alan into zombies, did they refuse to co-operate with you?"

Magee sighed; "They are not zombies Tara. I will admit that Hodson was one, briefly, but now two of the greatest scientific minds in the world are busy working in our laboratories, busy building the technology that will give us tomorrow. They have seen reason and have accepted that our cause is a just one, so must you and Beverley. There may not be anyone else who can take your places in the scheme of things. At the time you were fed that misinformation I believed that it was a ploy that would hasten your journey into our family. I did not want to risk a senseless gun battle with your friends here and wind up killing good people on both sides, so at the time it seemed like an idea. I realise now that it was not the wisest choice of action, and I apologise for any distress caused."

Mahoney was unsure now, was this another trick? "Why

didn't you just ask us if we wanted to join your organisation? This is a strange way to recruit people. Why sneak around watching us and trying to ambush us?"

"If I had simply sent someone up to your front door and asked you to work for me, would you have accepted any offer I made?"

Tara thought about this briefly; "No, probably not," she conceded wearily.

"I am used to being rejected by people who are largely the products of a failed society, failed educational system and cultural indoctrination. I know that Beverley Shenton refused a chance to join us before. That is why I have had to use other means to recruit people. One thing I can say is that most people quickly come around to our way of thinking when they do join us. We do not force or coerce that. It is the natural reaction to them finally seeing how they have been lied to and brain-washed in the past."

Tara needed to clear something up before going any further; "I want to speak with Hodson and Howal before I will believe you." This would test his sincerity.

Magee had anticipated this; "I can do better than that Tara. Look out the front window, over on your right hand side, by that white SUV.........."

Mahoney looked and saw Hodson and Howal waving encouragingly at her. Magee had known that he might need proof of his good intentions, so he had decided to bring them along at the last moment. They seemed normal enough so she waved back at them, though a little hesitantly. She turned back to Magee; "Bring them over here."

He made a brief call on his phone and shortly after the two

scientists walked across the street and a joyful, tearful reunion took place. Beverley and Tara had forgotten how these two were like family to them. Everything seemed better now that they were together again.

"Tara, listen to the man," they implored her. They had witnessed the terrible standoff, and were sick of the bloodshed. "Come join us, and work for a better world. It's the best option there is right now. We can worry about ideological matters when all this is settled, we don't have that luxury right now. The world is still in turmoil."

Tara was still undecided, still suspicious; "So what now, what if we don't want to join your little family?" she asked of Magee.

"Then that would place us in a difficult position. The new government tends to be of the mindset that anyone who is not with us is against us, and that is not a good situation to be in. I am your friend Tara, but the world we now live in has different rules than the world we were all used to, the old world which has passed and gone. In this new world I have to do what it takes to get things done and protect our interests, I can't pussyfoot around. I have great responsibility, our country is relying on me and people like me to defend it during a time of apocalyptic ruin. Do you realise that the old order is gone, swept away like autumn leaves after a storm? Our place in the world is vulnerable to those who would destroy us. We need to rebuild and do it fast, otherwise we will be overwhelmed. Our national intelligence services report that our enemies armies are mobilising, and we do not know what their intentions are. We do not know if we will be attacked and if so, how many will join against us. Our army has been decimated by the zombie apocalypse, and we would have to go straight to nuclear weapons in the event of an invasion. With nuclear weapons, even winning is losing. We have lost half of our population to zombification, with another quarter having being killed by zombies, accidents, criminals, suicide, you name it. Our company is working with the government to restore people from their zombie stupor. The process has been started, but we need to accelerate it. Time now is critical. As the zombies run out of food they will begin to die of starvation, unless dehydration gets them first. The next few days could save or damn us. That is why we need talented scientists, people like you Tara, and your friend Beverley, who can help us to develop the technology we need to regain our place in the world. Do you realise that some of our enemies have been largely unaffected by the zombies? They do not use our products, so they never took the vaccine, and they may see this as a once-in-a-lifetime opportunity to destroy us while we are on our knees?"

Beverley had a question; "I want to know about the men who we killed just now, why were they acting the way they were? I know they were not zombies, but they were behaving unlike anything I have ever seen."

"Those men were all infected by a new type of nanobots which we call 'Slavebots'. They were the same brigands that tried to kidnap you back at the District Hospital, worthless, disposable criminals who tried to bargain with your very own freedom for their greedy profit. When someone is infected by the Slavebots their mind is not their own, and they become easy to command, that is why I could use them in any way I wanted. As I explained before I could not engage in an all-out firefight and risk killing you two, so I just used them as cannon fodder to make a point. Don't worry about it, no-one will miss them except perhaps their defense Lawyers."

"So we could just have ordered them to put down their weapons and walk away?" Beverley asked, surprised.

"No, it's not that simple. When you first put them under the spell of the Slavebots, you give them a password and tell them that they must only obey whoever uses the password to command them. Since you don't know the password they would have ignored your orders. Their guns were empty anyway," he added, shocking them all further. "They didn't need bullets. As for the rest of them, well it is up to you to guess if their guns are empty as well, but I hope it won't come to that."

Tara had a final point to make; "Do you not realise that a few days ago Beverley and myself created new nanobots that can restore zombies? We know it works, we tried it out on dozens of zombies back at Howal's lab. It was part of the reason we were able to escape so easily. Just before we left the building we uploaded our work onto the internet, making it free to all. Every country in the world should have it by now, anyone could be making those things."

Magee shook his head, almost sadly; "No Tara, here I have a confession I have to make. While you were at Howal's laboratory busily creating your new nanobots, it occurred to me that you would indeed try to upload any advances you made onto the internet. That was a possibility I could not allow, the same way I could not risk you being taken by hostile forces and possibly used against us. The technology to restore zombies must remain in our hands, and ours alone. During the first night you were at that place, I had some of my technicians tap into your internet connection and sever it from the outside world. Then they put in place a connection to a server of our own, complete with fake websites we anticipated you would use. When you uploaded your data you sent it straight to us. We have had your technology all along. Allow me to say that your work is quite brilliant and that the nation is in your debt, and also in Beverley's debt. As we speak, we are using your technology to restore dozens of our citizens. Because it is liquid based, it is easy to use on large numbers of people in areas where the Ghost Hand is in short supply. You should be proud of what your work is achieving. You will both be rewarded and honoured by the new government for your contribution to society. Anything less than that would make thieves of us."

Tara and Beverley sat there speechless. The rest were all stunned as well. Whatever one thought of this guy, he knew his business. Had all their running been in vain?

Magee continued; "Now you know the full truth of where we all stand Tara. I am asking you again to please join our new order. You and Beverley will be valued members of our family, and you will never want for anything. Your male friends here are free to do as they choose, they may join us if they wish, we need good men for our security forces, or they may go their own way with no ill-feeling. I am going back to my men now. I will give you half an hour to decide what to do. Your friends Hodson and Howal may remain as you will want to consult further with them. I encourage you to ask them anything you feel necessary to clarify our goodwill or satisfy your curiosity."

He nodded politely and let himself out, leaving Howal and Hodson behind. He briefly glanced at Eli's lifeless body as he walked by. The big fool would never know the good he had finally done in this world. His greatest contribution to his fellow man was with the manner of his passing.

For a while the friends sat in silence and watched Magee walk back to where his command post was. There had been a lot to take in just now. No-one was sure what to say. Outside the remaining members of Crime Machine stood on silent guard, awaiting their turn to step forward if the order was issued. The security personnel of Eclipse Enterprises also waited, wondering if the Boss was going to win this one.

"I can't believe he stole our invention, he's got some nerve," Beverley said gloomily. "He's too clever by half, and there was us thinking it was freely available to all. I suppose at least it's helping some people, although admittedly the ones Magee authorises."

"What do you want to do Tara?" Doug asked, studying her face closely. "We need to make up our minds. We can't run forever. This guy has made his position clear, he will not allow us to just walk away."

"He'll keep sending those guys until we have killed them all, and then what, an all-out gunfight with the rest of his men?" Tom wondered aloud.

Tara knew what the answer was; "I have to go with him. If they are the government we cannot fight them and there really is no-where to run. What the rest of you decide is up to you, but I won't allow my friends to be hunted to the ends of the earth. He might be happy enough with me."

"A wise choice Tara!" Hodson enthused while Howal smiled and nodded approvingly.

"I will go with you Tara, I'm sure we can get used to the place," Beverley said loyally. The two friends had a kiss and a hug. Whatever happened they would still be together.

"That's even better!" Howal cried happily. He fully believed they were doing the right thing.

"I must go to my family. I've done my bit here," Brad said, and Tom echoed the sentiment; "Yes, me too. That is where I need to be right now."

All eyes were now on Scott and Doug.

"I want to go with Tara, but I don't know how much we can trust this man, Magee," Doug said. "I just don't feel that the time is right. What I propose is that we go with Tom and Brad for now. They may need our help anyway until this thing dies down. In the coming weeks and months we will keep in regular contact. If Magee double crosses you, then I will return and seek a vengeance he will never forget even if it costs me my life. However, if he proves to be a good employer, then perhaps we can take him up on his offer of employment. We will all need new jobs when the world returns to normal. The government we used to work for is no more, and we need to survive somehow."

"I agree, that's a good plan," Scott said. "I would dearly like to be with Beverley, but, as Doug said, there has been so much blood spilled recently that I am unsure who to trust. Maybe in time Magee will prove to be a man of his word, but right now it's too much of a leap of faith to join the ranks of the new order. I need time to weigh up the options. Parting will cause me pain after all we've been through, but when the time is right, we will be together again. Whatever happens from now on, there is a bond between our little group that will last forever."

And so it was decided. Tara called Magee and said the men would be leaving, possibly to return in the near future, but that she and Beverley would be going back with him. After kisses and goodbyes and tears, the four friends took their guns and left the building. When they walked to their vehicles out back, no attempt was made to hinder them, and they headed south. In a few hours they would finally reach the old farmhouse and have their own joyful reunion there. Then a short time later Tara and Beverley, along with Hodson and Howal, walked out to join Billy Magee and depart for Eclipse Enterprises.

EPILOGUE

In time the zombie apocalypse abated as the new government rolled out an extensive program of restoration, using the technology that had been developed by Eclipse Enterprises. Gradually life in the towns and cities returned to normal, and most people went back to their homes. The rebuilding project was aided immensely by the government's army of slaves who did most of the heavy lifting and got no pay beyond their immediate physical needs. This caused some disquiet in some circles, but anyone who voiced any dissent was branded unpatriotic and threatened with the same treatment themselves. Needless to say, critics of the program were few and far between after that. A lot of the early work involved clearing and burying any dead the zombies had missed, and all the bones that were left behind. Mass graves were used and in time a monument was built to remember them. They were the victims of man's brilliance, and of his folly.

Tara Mahoney and Beverley Shenton joined Hodson and Howal at the headquarters of Eclipse Enterprises, and began working on a number of important projects. As time went by they rose to very high positions in the organisation, and achieved a number of important scientific breakthroughs. Hodson and Howal continued to work in the area of nanobots and produced some amazing technology in the field of bio-weapons. In time they came to embrace the political ideology of their new friends, and they helped to create a new society where people had more freedom than ever before, not having to lock their doors at night, and being able to walk the streets day or night without being molested by some recidivist scumbag criminal. There was talk for a while that some people were going to launch a class action against John Hudson for the loss of loved-ones, property loss and for the general trauma of having been zombies, but the government quickly stepped in and said that it was the solar storm which had caused an unforeseeable catastrophe, and that it was an act of God, so the matter was quietly dropped.

Billy Magee eventually made it onto the Supreme Council, with a life-long membership, although he continued to play an important part in the activities of Eclipse Enterprises. Under the guidance of the council, the nation prospered, and the threat of foreign invasion disappeared. Indeed, the influence of the nation grew world-wide. The countries of its enemies suffered immense setbacks, as they would experience sporadic outbreaks of different variants of the zombie apocalypse. Every now and then an entire city would go demented and start tearing themselves to pieces for no apparent reason. People said it must be something in the water...........

The four friends remained for several weeks at the old farmhouse where their friends and families were hiding out. In time it became safe to leave and they knew their destinies lay elsewhere. With the exception of the Aunt and Uncle who decided that they liked the country life, everyone else came back to the city to live. Eventually the four friends took Magee's offer, and they joined the government security forces, operating as part of a zombie hunter patrol, tracking down zombies in remote places and restoring them. A lot of the zombies they located were on the verge of death, so they were just in time to save the lives of countless individuals. When that work was complete they would eventually take up positions as part of the security apparatus for the members of the Supreme Council. They made contact with their scientist friends and Eddie Young and had a reunion party. After a while there was a joint wedding when Scott and Beverley and Doug and Tara tied the knot.

One day in spring when the time seemed right, they met up with Josh and Ann's son and his family. Together they travelled to the lonely spot in the woods where their friends grave was. There they had a solemn ceremony as they paid tribute to the gallant last stand their friends had made, and laid flowers on their grave. A headstone was later erected to mark the place.

Steven Grace spent several weeks with his daughter Erin and during that time he made a full recovery from his injuries. A local doctor he attended told him that he had probably missed death by hours. He never went back to being a chemist. Given his new outlook on the world he knew that his calling was elsewhere. He returned to the city and set up a recovery and counselling centre for former zombies. There he would assist them in dealing with their experiences and helping them to find their true selves. As with his own self, he found that the ordeal of having been a zombie had a cleansing effect on the minds of those he counselled, and it made it easier for them to escape the clutches of conditioning and culture. Then they in turn would go out and help others. This was a phenomenon that was happening all over the world, and would have dramatic consequences for the whole of humanity in the age to come. In time he even counselled the man largely responsible for it all – John Hodson.

The End.

ABOUT THE AUTHOR

Nigel Martin is a well-known Irish Author who lives in Canada.

Printed in Great Britain
by Amazon.co.uk, Ltd.,
Marston Gate.